I am the one who figures ~~the movie half way through,~~ but I have to say this time you kept me guessing. Another great book!

— STACY PETERSEN STREET TEAM MEMBER

Carol's books are so wonderfully written! Her storylines are intricately woven as if she is using the high quality yarn she so often writes of. *The Inadvertent Princess* is another smashing success. A page turner from the beginning I was pulled into the story. I love how her books are just not romance but includes mystery, subterfuge, adventure and so many other genres.

— -BRANDY HATCHEL

.

— .

The Inadvertent Princess

Crowns & Courtships
Book 2: Royals of San Majoria

Carol Moncado

USA Today Bestselling Author

CANDID
Publications

Cover photos: Copyright:

Couple: lunamarina/depositphotos.com

Ocean: Copyright 2017, CANDID Publications

Author photo: Captivating by Keli, 2010

First edition, CANDID Publications, 2018

AUTHOR'S NOTE

The Inadvertent Princess begins in February 2017, which is in the middle of the timeline for *Winning the Queen's Heart*. It continues through the summer of 2017, therefore covering the timelines of *Protecting the Prince* and *Prince from her Past*. If you have not read those, there may be some spoilers contained in these pages.

I appreciate all of you!

— CAROL MONCADO

MARCH 2017

"My call you Kenny."

Kensington Wilhelm Edward Charles of San Majoria grinned. No one had ever called him Kenny. His very royal mother wouldn't stand for it.

"What's your name?" he asked the little girl.

"G'acie."

"Gracie? That's a lovely name."

The little girl's blond curls bounced as she nodded.

"Well, Gracie. Do you know where your mummy is?" He'd found the little girl wandering alone in the mall.

She shook her head. "Mummy gone."

"Gone?" Great. He didn't really want to contact the authorities. No one knew he was here, and Kensington wanted to keep it that way for another day or so until he met with Benjamin for the first time.

Gracie nodded.

"What about your papa?"

"Papa gone."

"Did your mummy and papa leave you at the mall?" he asked, confused.

She shook her head.

"Gracie!"

They both turned to see a brunette rushing toward them.

"Annie!" Gracie wrenched away from Kensington. She ran to the brunette who swept her up into her arms.

"Where'd you go?" Tears streamed down Annie's face. "You aren't ever supposed to leave my side."

"My sorry, Annie." Gracie's voice was muffled into Annie's shoulder.

Kensington nodded at the woman then turned. Gracie was clearly back where she belonged.

Rob glared at him, but Rob wasn't happy with any of this, despite the baseball hat pulled low over Kensington's forehead and the unnecessary glasses obscuring his eyes.

He started for the tchotchke shop across the walkway. His mother, for all her refined taste, loved the stupid knickknack type things. He hadn't said good-bye when he left, so he probably needed to bring her something she'd love back from Eyjania.

"Kenny?"

Kensington put the Eyjanian flag back on the shelf before turning to look at Annie. "Yes?"

"Gracie said you were helping her look for her parents. Thank you."

He smiled. "My pleasure."

Gracie held her arms up to Kensington. He lifted her up and gave her his stern uncle look. "You should never, ever sneak away from Annie."

"My not."

Kensington handed the little girl back to Annie.

"You're good with her."

He grinned. "I have a niece a little younger than her. She's a lot of fun." He leaned closer to whisper. "I'm her favorite uncle."

Annie laughed. "Are you her only uncle?"

Kensington shook his head. "Nope. I've got a younger brother, and her dad has a brother-in-law who's been his best friend since they were like born or something so basically a brother. Her Uncle Dare brought her ice skates, but I'm still her favorite." Kensington wasn't sure Sofia had an actual favorite, but he was claiming the title anyway. Rob glared at him again. Kensington took a step back. "It was nice to meet you, Gracie." He nodded to the brunette. "And you, Annie. I hope you have a more pleasant rest of the day." He turned back to the shelf of knickknacks before picking one up and starting for the register.

"Why did you call me Annie?" a voice behind him called.

He turned. "That's what Gracie called you."

She shook her head. "Gracie called me *auntie*. She just doesn't say it very well."

"Then what's your name?"

She wrinkled her nose. "Anabelle, but I've always hated being called Annie."

"Then I won't call you that anymore." She intrigued him. He gave her his best smile as the little girl's stomach growled. "Since Miss Gracie's stomach is grumbling, please allow me to take both of you to lunch."

Anabelle hesitated then nodded as Gracie whined, "My hungry, Annie."

Kensington walked next to them as they headed to the food court with Rob trailing behind. His bodyguard wore his usual grumpy face. He'd get over it. Neither Anabelle or Gracie presented a threat. If anything, food poisoning was the greatest threat.

Kensington paid for their lunch at the pizza place.

"You're not from here," Anabelle told him as they took a seat.

He shook his head. "No, I'm San Majorian."

"How long are you in Eyjania?"

"Indefinitely." He hesitated then went with his fairly standard answer when talking to the rare person who didn't know who he was. "Family business. For a few weeks anyway."

"What kind of business is your family in?"

That was a new one. He didn't get that question often. "Tourism," he finally said. True enough. It was part of the reason some people came to San Majoria, and being a part of the royal family meant he could persuade or dissuade people from visiting by their interactions with him.

"Trying to get people to stay at your family's resort for the Games of the Sargasso Sea?"

"Something like that."

The Games were held every other year and resembled the Summer Olympics. Since it was 2017, this would be kind of an off year. 2019 would be held in Islas del Sargasso and would be a preview of the Olympians for 2020. Islas del Sargasso would hold the Games in 2021 as well before they moved back to San Majoria in 2023 and 2025. A winter version alternated between Eyjania and Auvergnon in a similar fashion.

This year, he'd been put in charge of everything. Now that the winter games in Eyjania were over, he needed them to focus on their part of what needed doing for the summer games.

"So you could make sure Gracie and I have reservations? I'm not asking for a discount, but a reservation."

He grinned at her. "I'm sure something could be arranged." He'd make certain they had a place to stay even if he had to subsidize it himself.

Anabelle leaned forward to whisper to him. "I don't want to alarm you, but there's a guy staring at you. Has been the whole time we've been here."

He leaned closer to her. "Dark hair, blue suit, dark tie, perpetual frown?"

"Yeah."

"My family insists we all need security with us. The odds of anything happening are slim, but sometimes, you have to go along with what your mum tells you, even as a grown-up."

"Especially working for the family business."

"Exactly."

"So are they doing a background check on me yet?"

"Probably not." He winked at her. "I don't know your last name."

She grinned at him, a smile he quickly found himself loving. "Then maybe I won't tell you just yet. Not that there's anything awful to find," she quickly added.

"That's good."

"What about Gracie?" He could feel the twinkle in his own eyes. "Does she have something nefarious in her past?"

Anabelle hesitated longer than he would have expected. "Not really. She's my little sister. Midlife adoption. Then our parents died in a car accident." Anabelle smiled softly at her sister. "Now she's my responsibility. I want to take her to the Games this year. My parents had been saving for years so we could all go, because it's just not the same as going when it's here. But..." She ducked her head for a minute. When she looked back up, her eyes glistened with unshed tears but were backed by steely determination. "They won't be there, but we will."

Kensington reached over and took her hand in his. "Then I'll make sure you have a place to stay and tickets to any event you want to attend."

"Any event we want? Even the ones that have been sold out for months already?" Anabelle couldn't hide her skepticism.

He chuckled, a sound that warmed her through. It wasn't condescending or annoyed, just amused. "I have connections. I can get tickets to anything you want to attend, as long as you let me know. Promise."

"I'll need your contact information." He'd probably give her a generic email, not his personal information, but as long as it worked, she didn't care.

He pulled a card out of his wallet and wrote on the back of it. "The number on the front is my office. This is my personal number. Call or text anytime."

She took the card and wondered at the lack of information on it. In fact, it just had one line and a phone number.

Kensington

Was that his last name? His office location? A random palace in Great Britain?

"Thanks." Anabelle had never been so comfortable with someone she just met, but it was time to change the subject to something with far less potential for crying. "What's your favorite ice cream flavor?"

"You won't think I'm boring?" Kenny grimaced as he looked at her.

"Never." He was far too interesting to be boring. He'd traveled as part of his work for his family. And he had a card with a single word and an office number on it.

"Vanilla."

Okay. So he might have caught her off-guard with that. "Vanilla? Really?"

"Because you can make it into anything you want. Add whatever sauces you like. Sprinkles. Cherries. Syrup. Nuts. All those things. With something like Rocky Road, you're mostly stuck with what's in it."

He had a point. "But you can put syrup and whipped cream on any of them."

"Yes, but if you can only have one kind at home, vanilla is by far the most versatile."

She conceded the point with a nod.

Kenny leaned forward then pointed at another vendor. "Want some now? My treat."

Anabelle considered it, then nodded. She didn't need the calories - her grandfather made sure she knew that - but it sounded good, and Gracie would love it. "That would be great."

He asked what she and Gracie wanted then went to get it for them, but as he walked back, he glanced at his watch. Setting the tray down with one hand, he reached into his pocket with the other.

"Sorry. I've got to take this." He pulled his phone out and swiped across it. "Hey." Kenny walked a few feet away, and Anabelle couldn't hear what he was saying.

A minute later, he returned and sat at the table, though his demeanor seemed different. "My sister," he explained.

"How many siblings do you have?"

"Four. An older sister, two younger sisters, and a brother." He took a bite of his ice cream. "Question for you, though. If Gracie is your sister, why did you say she was calling you auntie?"

Anabelle poked her spoon at her ice cream. "I took her with me somewhere a year or so ago. When I said she wasn't my daughter, this new friend assumed she was my niece. It kind of stuck. It's easier than explaining she's my adopted sister."

"Even if you don't have any other siblings?"

She shrugged, not wanting to get into the particulars with a guy she barely knew, even if he did seem fantastic.

"So I know what kind of ice cream you picked out today, but what's your favorite?"

He would scoff at her after her reaction to his choice, but truth won out. "Chocolate."

Kenny grinned. "Vanilla may be my favorite, but that's a close second."

They continued talking, but something had changed. Anabelle didn't know what to make of the shift in conversation.

"Is your sister okay?" Something his sister said had to be responsible.

Kenny shrugged. "She's fine. She's on her way here from San Majoria."

"Is she bringing your niece?"

He shook his head. "Wrong sister. This is Esther, my youngest sister."

"The baby of the family then."

"My brother holds that position."

She tried to put his family together in her head. "Your brother is youngest. Your older sister is married and has a little girl. Then you. Then two other sisters."

"You got it." He took a deep breath. "What about you? Gracie is your only sibling, but what about aunts and uncles?"

"No. My parents were both only children. My mother's parents died before I was born. My father's father is living. He controls the trust fund money Gracie and I use to live on."

"Annie, my done."

Anabelle turned her attention to Gracie and dug a wet wipe out of her bag. "Come here, Miss Gracie." After wiping Gracie's hands and face, Anabelle took her bags and ice cream and motioned for Kenny to join her. They walked to the play area nearby.

"I'm afraid I have to go. My sister waited until the last minute to let me know she was on her way. Her flight lands in a few minutes. I need to meet her at the airport."

And there came the brush off. So much for those Games tickets. He talked a good game but... "It was nice to meet you. Thank you for lunch and the ice cream. Gracie and I appreciate it."

He turned on what had to be his best smile. "Can I have your number? I'd love to take you to dinner sometime soon."

"You don't need to spend the time with your sister?"

"Not all of it. Some," he admitted as he leaned down. "But I'd rather spend more time getting to know you."

Anabelle felt her face color. "I'd like that." She took his card out of her pocket and sent a text to the number on it. "There."

"Perfect."

They walked closer to the play area.

"I hope you have a great day." Kenny hesitated, then caught her off-guard.

He kissed her.

A brief fleeting touch of his lips to hers.

Then he was gone.

2

"Thank you for picking me up." Esther didn't look at him. "It wasn't necessary."

"You called out of nowhere. Of course I had to come pick you up. What's going on?" Kensington stared at his little sister.

"Nothing."

"I don't buy that."

"Well, it's the only answer you're going to get. Everything's fine."

He dropped it. She would tell him when she was ready. Maybe. He had a great relationship with Jacqueline Grace, but he'd never been as close to Esther. Astrid had always been something of a mystery - at least once her first husband came into her life. That seemed to be changing now that she had Jordan. His older sister was finally truly happy.

Jacqueline Grace seemed to be sort of floating through the moment. Harrison was finishing school and loved life. For the moment. As the youngest, very little of the family responsibility would ever fall on his shoulders.

But Esther... Something had seemed off with her for a while.

"So where were you today? You weren't at the house."

"I went to the mall to look for something for Mother." He didn't want to tell her about Anabelle or Gracie. His time with the two of them hadn't been anything special, but that, in and of itself, made it all the more so. The two of them had no idea of his real identity, and Kensington found he liked the anonymity.

If he saw her again, and this turned into something more than just a few dates, he'd have to tell her the truth and hope it didn't bother her that he'd withheld something so important from her.

Esther didn't answer but stared out the window. Okay then. Whatever was bothering her went deeper than he would have guessed.

"What would you like to do for dinner?"

She turned from the window. "What?"

"Dinner. Would you like to go out? Eat in? Order take out and send Rob for it?"

"I don't care. Take out is fine. Maybe there's a good Italian restaurant around."

"I'm sure Rob can find something." He pulled his phone out of his pocket. The text from Anabelle made him smile. He needed to call her later. He sent a message to Rob who replied that he'd take care of it.

The rest of the ride passed in complete silence. The driver pulled through the gates of Aberswythe Hall, the family's Eyjanian home. Once in the house, Esther disappeared upstairs, likely to the room she normally used while in the country.

He went to the office he and his siblings used when they were in town. Closing the door behind him, he sat behind the desk and called Astrid.

After a few pleasantries, he cut to the chase. "Do you know what's going on with Esther?"

Astrid's deep sigh came across the line. "No. No one does. Something happened last week, but she hasn't opened up to any of us about it. I went to Papa to see if he knew anything, but he didn't and wasn't quite ready to invade her privacy by checking her phone or anything yet, but she didn't meet with anyone as far as Papa knew."

"Is she seeing anyone?"

"If she is, none of us know about it."

Kensington pinched the bridge of his nose. "Okay. If you hear anything, let me know? I want to help, since we're both here, but I can't if she won't talk to me, and no one else knows anything."

"You'll know when I do."

"Thanks." He leaned back and propped his feet up on the desk. "And you're feeling better?"

"Some. The morning sickness isn't quite as bad as it was with Sofia, and it's better than it was a couple weeks ago. I think. Mostly."

"I'm glad. I haven't had a chance to talk to Jordan recently. How's he doing with it?"

"He's ecstatic. He's more worried about Sofia not taking it well, but we haven't told her yet."

Kensington grinned at the thought of his niece as a big sister. "I think she'll be as excited as both of you are. Have you decided when you're going to make the public announcement?"

"Probably not for a few more weeks. Finish the first trimester, at least. As long as I don't need to wear maternity clothes for a while yet, it should be all good."

"Stay home a lot then. Otherwise, you'll be on all the news sites asking 'burrito or baby'."

"I've been getting those since the week after I married Jordan. There may have been one before that, even, wondering if that's why we were getting married, but I was too upset to notice."

Kensington remembered barely seeing his sister during the three weeks between the announcement and the wedding. "I know, but Jordan is perfect for you. I think I'm going to spend some time at the ice rink while I'm here. Maybe I can give him a run for his money when I get back."

Astrid laughed. "Good luck with that. He's been skating since before he could walk. He's on the fake ice downstairs almost every day with Sofia. He won't let me out there right now, though. Says I don't fall well enough yet. After the baby's born, I'll be back to learning. Sofia, apparently, is on the late end for that. The baby will probably be on skates before he or she is six months old."

He chuckled. "So I won't give him a run for his money. Maybe I can at least give him someone remotely competent to skate with."

"His security team is learning."

Of course they were. The security personnel were just that wonderful. After another minute of conversation, they hung up.

Kensington pulled his cell phone back out of his pocket. He stared at the text from Anabelle before deciding to take the bull by the horns. A couple of taps later and ringing started on the other end.

"Hello?"

His smile came back. "Anabelle? It's Kenny. Can I take you out to dinner tomorrow night?"

"You are expected for dinner this evening."

Anabelle closed her eyes and prayed for patience. "I have plans, Grandfather. Gracie and I both do."

"And those plans are...?" He left the question hanging in the air.

"We have plans with a friend." A friend she hoped would kiss her again, but he didn't need to know that.

"They must be canceled. You will be having dinner here. Grace will not be required to attend."

Lovely. He didn't want to see his youngest granddaughter.

She'd long suspected he didn't really consider Gracie family because of her adoption. More implication it was true. "It would be quite rude for me to cancel at this late hour." Meaning anytime the day of the engagement. Her grandfather had ground that into her mother after the wedding, and her mother, in turn, impressed it upon her. It simply wouldn't do to leave someone in the lurch.

"Very well. Then lunch tomorrow."

"I'll be working. Gracie will be at school." Her grandfather insisted Gracie attend the most prestigious preschool in Akushla. Anabelle had managed to limit it to three days a week while she worked.

There was a noise on the other end of the phone. "My assistant will call you and make arrangements this week. I have something very important to tell you."

Before she could tell him not to hold his breath, he hung up. "Love you, too, Gramps." Sarcasm she normally tried to keep hidden seeped out.

Gracie had been dropped off at preschool first thing that morning, but Anabelle didn't have to go to work until nine. She finished getting ready, then walked to her car in the parking garage. The drive only took a few minutes. She parked behind the building and used her key to unlock the back door.

"Morning!" Rachel's voice came from the office. "You're late."

"Thirty seconds," Anabelle called back as she took her coat off. "You were probably later than that."

She could hear the chair rolling across the tile floor. Rachel's head poked out the office door. "Maybe. But I'm the owner."

Anabelle tried to give her best friend the witty banter that usually characterized their morning's together, but she just couldn't.

"Talk to your grandfather this morning?" Rachel asked.

"He tried to insist I come for dinner this evening and when I said no, lunch tomorrow." She pulled her gloves off and shoved

14

them in the pocket of her coat where it hung on the hook. "But Gracie didn't need to be there. Because of course she didn't."

"The guy's a loser, Annie." Rachel was the only one besides Gracie who got away with calling her that. "I know he's your grandfather and you love him, but he is."

"I know, but I have to keep him happy until I'm thirty." Then she could get control of the small inheritance left behind. It wasn't a lot, but enough that she wouldn't *have* to work, and Gracie would be able to attend university without worrying about money.

"Or you get married," Rachel pointed out. "He's supposed to give it to you then."

He wouldn't if he thought he could get away with keeping it.

"Think you could find a guy anytime soon?"

Anabelle studied the wall above Rachel's head, but knew her face was turning six shades of red.

Rachel gasped and jumped up, sending the chair careening into the wall behind her. "There already is one! Who?"

Anabelle reached for the apron hanging on the other wall. "His name is Kenny. He found Gracie when she wandered away yesterday. We had lunch. He asked me out. We're having dinner tonight."

"Do you need me to watch Gracie?" Rachel was practically vibrating with excitement. "She could even spend the night."

"He wants her to come to. He's already wrapped around her little finger. Claims he's the favorite uncle to his niece, too. I believe him."

Rachel calmed down a bit. "That's fantastic, Annie. I hope it goes well."

"I have no doubt it will. I think you'd like him."

"Bring him by."

Anabelle let out her first real laugh of the day. "I don't think Rachel's Raveling Repository is his kind of store." She started for the front. "I don't see him as the knitting type."

"You never know." Rachel went back to her office. "That shipment finally showed up this morning. Would you get it stocked before we open?"

"Of course." It was part of her job. The box waited for her on the counter. This particular yarn came from the States. Rachel had found the dyers online and loved their work. She'd just reached an agreement to carry some of it on consignment. "Is this the stuff from Kenzie's Kreations?" she hollered. "Or Show Me Yarn?"

"Both actually. It turns out they know each other and asked if they could ship together whenever possible."

She unpacked the different skeins and arranged them in the cubes set aside for these two vendors. If they sold well, and Anabelle was sure Rachel was right about them, they'd order more and expand their selection. Several of their other consignees hadn't been quite the same quality the last few months, and she expected Rachel to drop them if it didn't change soon.

As she finished organizing it, Anabelle glanced at the clock. "I'm opening the door."

"Okay. I'm doing stupid accounting. Holler if you need me." Rachel hated numbers, but couldn't quite afford to pay someone to do all of it for her just yet. Her brother, an accountant, helped, but since he worked for free, Rachel did as much as she could.

Anabelle turned the lock and flipped the sign to "open," smiling as she saw a woman walking up. She held the door wide. "Good morning, Mrs. T." The Icelandic woman had a last name Anabelle had never been able to master.

"Good morning, dear." She had lived in Eyjania most of her life, but still retained a moderate accent. "How are you this morning?"

"I'm fantastic. What can I help you find today? Surely you didn't finish everything you bought last week."

"No, but I did find out my grandson's wife is having a girl. I must get started on a blanket."

Anabelle smiled with her. "How wonderful!" Rachel's brother was married to the only girl out of Mrs. *Thorbjørnsdóttir's* fifteen or so descendants. A great-granddaughter would thrill them all. "We just got some wonderful yarn in from the States. The colors are gorgeous and may be just what you're looking for."

Mrs. *Thorbjørnsdóttir* stayed for half an hour, but mostly just to talk. Anabelle told her the same thing she always did. Bring her yarn with her next time and sit in one of the chairs to the side. Rachel had put them there for that very reason.

Every time, the elderly woman said she would consider it, but she never did. Another customer entered as Mrs. *Thorbjørnsdóttir* left and so the rest of the day went.

By the time her shift ended, Anabelle was more than ready for a hug from Gracie, a long shower, and dinner with the man who'd spent far too much time occupying her thoughts.

3

Kensington waited for the door to open. He shouldn't be this nervous. He was a prince, for crying out loud. He spoke in front of thousands on a regular basis, was on a first name basis with multiple Heads of State, spoke four languages fluently, and understood several others.

But a first date with a beautiful brunette and an adorable toddler?

That left him tongue tied and unsure of himself.

The door opened. Anabelle smiled at him, though she seemed tired. "Hi. Come on in. Gracie doesn't want to put her shoes on."

That made him smile. "Maybe she'll let me help her."

"It's worth a shot." Anabelle closed the door behind him. "Nothing else is working."

"Kenny!" Gracie ran to him, one sock on and one in her hand.

He swung her into his arms. "Hi, Gracie." She wrapped her arms around his neck.

"I miss you."

That made him chuckle. "I missed you, too, sweet girl. Do you want to go eat pizza?" She'd loved it at the mall, but he probably should have checked with Anabelle before suggesting it.

"Yes!"

"Then you need to put your shoes on." He sat on the sofa. "I bet you can do it yourself."

She nodded, very serious. "My can." After scrambling down from his knee, she ran toward the back of the apartment.

"Thanks." Anabelle leaned against the wall, her arms crossed loosely across her chest as she smiled at him. "I even told her you were coming, but it didn't matter."

"Nothing does when a toddler wants their way. Or at least that's my experience with my niece and her mom."

Anabelle moved to the chair near his seat. "I'm not even her mother."

"No," Kensington answered slowly. "But you are her primary caregiver. Have you thought about adopting her? I know it doesn't actually make you her mother, but it could give a certain weight to your relationship."

She shook her head. "No. Maybe someday, but not right now. There are other reasons why I can't for the time being."

When she didn't elaborate, he didn't push. Maybe she'd trust him someday, until then he wouldn't ask.

Gracie ran back out, wearing one snow boot on the wrong foot and a sandal on the other. At least that one was on the right side.

Anabelle sighed. "Gracie, you need to wear your black boots, sweetie."

Gracie glared at Anabelle then huffed back to her room.

"That girl..." She shook her head. "I love her, but sometimes..."

"I think that's a toddler's job. Frustrate you to the point you're ready to scream then give you a big hug and an 'I love you' that melts your heart."

"Sounds about right."

A minute later, Gracie clomped down the hall with one boot

on. She held a sock and her other boot in her hands. "He'p, p'ease?" she asked Kensington.

He picked her up and set her on his lap. "Of course."

In a minute, she was all set, and Anabelle helped Gracie with her coat. When they reached the street, Kensington held the door to the back seat for Anabelle to buckle Gracie into the car seat he'd made sure was installed properly.

He closed the door when she finished, inadvertently trapping Anabelle between himself and the car.

"Thank you," she whispered, her hand resting on his shirt.

"For what?"

"Thinking of a car seat for her. Most men wouldn't have invited her, much less made sure she was safe."

He wanted to kiss her. "Then most men are stupid." Why couldn't he? Just because it wasn't the end of the night?

Without debating it any longer, he lowered his head until he could brush his lips against hers.

Something about the electricity that crackled between them seemed right on a level he'd never experienced before.

"Then most men are stupid. I'm glad you're not."

"Me, too." He kissed her again then stepped back so he could open the passenger door for her. "You ready to get dinner?"

Rob had nearly thrown a fit about Kensington driving himself through Akushla with Anabelle and Gracie, but Kensington refused to use a driver. This was a date.

He hadn't always felt that way. In fact, he'd been more than willing to use his royal status and the perks that came with it to attract girls in high school and even the first year or two of university.

But the realization, again, that his last girlfriend was only attracted to him because of his last name, meant he wanted to keep that information to himself as long as possible. He liked Anabelle more than he'd liked any girl in the past, and he didn't want to find out she was the same way. If things didn't seem to be heading somewhere, he wouldn't tell her. Simple as that. If she seemed to like him without knowing he was third in line for the San Majorian throne, then maybe it would be time to tell her.

And tell her that he wouldn't be able to move permanently for a number of years.

The restaurant catered to families and so wasn't very busy on a Wednesday evening. The waiter took their order, made Gracie a balloon hat, and came back a minute later with their drinks.

Gracie colored on the brown paper table covering, jabbering about her day at school. She didn't like one girl but did another. Kensington took her offered crayon and began to draw an island, trying to get all three of them involved in something resembling a conversation.

After eating their pizza, they took Gracie to the indoor play area and let her run around.

Kensington and Anabelle sat on a bench where they could keep an eye on Gracie. He slid his arm along the back, but didn't actually wrap it around her. His thumb brushed against her upper arm from time to time as they talked about everything - and nothing.

Strange emotions swirled inside. He'd had girlfriends, several over the years, but never anything like this.

It was the rush of new, the pit of the stomach flipping over, the breathless anticipation of what comes next.

And when she looked up at him with a twinkle in those hazel eyes, he knew.

He was falling in love.

"I want details," Rachel yelled from the office as Anabelle walked in the back door.

"There's not much to tell." Not entirely accurate, but Anabelle wasn't ready to tell even her best friend yet. Not until she had a better idea where this was going, if anywhere.

"At least tell me it was better than that Phil guy." Rachel rolled her chair into the hallway.

"Anyone would be better than him." She'd gone on one date since her parents died. Phil seemed like a nice guy but could barely be bothered to look at Gracie and seemed more interested in finding out the details of Anabelle's trust fund than getting to know anything about her.

He'd called several more times, but finally got the hint when Anabelle washed her hair five days in a row.

"You took Gracie with you?"

Anabelle couldn't hide her smile as she tied her apron on. "It was his idea. He even had a car seat in his car so I didn't have to insist we take mine."

"Impressive."

"Gracie ran around the play area for over an hour. She slept well last night." Superficial information would hopefully keep Rachel satisfied.

"That's not what I really want to know." Or maybe not. "Did he kiss you?"

Anabelle brushed past her friend, knowing her face was turning eighteen shades of red.

"He did!"

Yes. He'd kissed her after she'd put a sleeping Gracie to bed. Intense and overwhelming, it sent her into an emotional tidal wave she wasn't sure how to cope with.

"I'm not ready to talk about it, Rach." She leaned against the wall, facing the front of the store rather than Rachel. "Not after what my grandfather did."

"Your grandfather has nothing to do with this," Rachel reminded her. "He can't keep you from making a future with any man you want."

"But he can try. You and I both know he will. At least I know

Kenny has money. That would help some. Grandfather is just that shallow." She dropped her chin to her chest. "I keep waiting for him to use his connections to try to set me up with Prince Darius."

"He's a little young for you."

"Like Grandfather would care."

She could hear Rachel moving toward her. "Why not shoot for the stars and at least think he'd try to set you up with the king?"

Anabelle snorted. "I feel sorry for whoever ends up in that spider web. King Benjamin has the personality of an rock."

Rachel wrapped an arm around "You never know. He might not be that bad."

"He's that bad, and you know it."

"Probably, but your Grandfather wouldn't go there anyway. Prince Isaiah probably has some princess from another country all picked out already. I bet he wanted Benji to marry Princess Astrid."

"She's already a Crown Princess. That would never work."

"Unless Isaiah is trying to annex San Majoria. I wouldn't put it past the guy. He's slimy."

Everyone knew that. No one knew why the king and Queen Mother put up with Prince Isaiah. "You shouldn't call him Benji," Anabelle pointed out. "You wouldn't call Queen Elizabeth 'Liz', and even if you're not crazy about him, the position he holds deserves your respect."

"It irritates me that he's probably the only real monarch I'll ever have. Why couldn't we have someone classy like Queen Elizabeth, or I'd even take King Alfred I over him."

"King Alfred was an actual honest-to-goodness knight who did the honorable thing against great opposition." Anabelle headed for the door where Mrs. T was waiting. "I don't think any modern king is quite the same."

"Probably not. I just hope they actually display his dagger next year for the millennial." Rachel turned around. "I'm headed back to work."

Anabelle unlocked the door and let Mrs. T in. "Good morning. Surely you're not done with that yarn yet."

"Oh, no, dear. But another grandson's wife told us yesterday she's expecting a baby as well. There's been some complications. They said the baby is fine, but they had some testing done already and know she's having a boy."

"So you need some blue."

"Perhaps. Maybe some green instead. There was a lovely green in the basket you showed me yesterday."

Anabelle knew exactly the one she was talking about. "Right this way." Rachel had rearranged some during the evening shift the night before.

While Mrs. T weighed her decision, the bell over the door jangled. Anabelle turned to see a young woman walk in.

"Good morning," she called. "I'll be with you in a moment."

"Take your time."

Anabelle turned her attention back to Mrs. T, but kept an eye on the other woman as she wandered around the store. She didn't seem to be looking for anything in particular, just picking up this skein or that pattern and putting it back.

"I think this will be all, dear." Mrs. T set her choices down on the counter. "Thank you again for your time."

"It is truly my pleasure, ma'am." Anabelle gave her most genuine smile.

"How many times have I told you not to call me that. I'm Mrs. T or even Amma like everyone else does."

"But you aren't my grandmother," she gently reminded Mrs. T. She leaned forward and lowered her voice. "I never knew my mother's family. I do like to think my gran would have been much like you."

Mrs. T's wistful smile tugged at Anabelle's heartstrings. "And if I had another granddaughter, I would want her to be just like you."

"And if none of your family lived nearby, I would be happy to fill that role." Anabelle patted the wrinkled hand gently. "But I happen to know you have two dozen people over for lunch every Sunday, and you're related to every one of them. The last thing I would want to do is make them feel like I was trying to usurp their spot in your life. I'll settle for being your favorite yarn lady."

Tears shimmered in Mrs. T's eyes. "Ah, my dear, you will always be more than just my favorite yarn lady."

4

Kensington looked around the street and didn't see Esther. Where could she have gone? He walked down the sidewalk, peering in stores. Until he found what he was looking for.

The bell jangled as he walked in. Cubes filled with yarn covered one wall. A cozy sitting area on one side was home to a table filled with tea bags and a variety of cups on saucers. Another wall held assorted accessories. Kensington thought they were knitting needles, and crochet hooks, and other things he didn't know what he'd do with.

"Kenny?"

He turned to see Anabelle coming out of the hallway. "Hey! I didn't know you worked at a yarn store."

"Yep. It's owned by my best friend. I work here a few days a week to help her out."

"I don't actually need you, you know." A blonde woman walked into the front.

"Sure you do."

"Because I love having you around. I could do most of this by myself or with someone more part time than you are." The woman held out a hand. "I'm Rachel. You must be Kenny."

He grinned. "I must be. It's a pleasure to meet you."

Rachel glanced at Anabelle. "I wish I could say I'd heard all about you, but someone is being incredibly tight lipped about your date last night."

"You had a date last night, *Kenny?*" The person he'd been looking for chimed in.

"Ladies, this is my sister, Esther. Esther, this is Anabelle and Rachel."

Anabelle took a step around him and held out her hand. "It's nice to meet you."

Esther covered her shock well, shaking Anabelle's hand. "Likewise." She shot Kensington a look that asked why his friend wasn't addressing her the way most people did. Your Royal Highness. Princess. A bit of a curtsy.

Kensington gave a slight shake of his head. She'd understand. They all did. Sometimes it was nice being anonymous.

They chatted about yarn. Esther had somehow learned to crochet and knit but hadn't in a while. She wanted to make a baby blanket for a friend. Kensington suspected it was for Astrid's baby, but didn't ask.

She eventually decided on blues and greens that matched the ocean back home. Something still seemed off about her, but Kensington hadn't been able to put his finger on what it was, and Esther wasn't talking.

His sister finished shopping and went with Rachel to the counter to pay. Kensington took a step closer to Anabelle. "How did Gracie sleep last night?"

"Like a log. She's usually awake before me, but not this morning. I need to find a way to let her run off her energy more often."

"It'll be warm enough to play outside before long."

"She will love that, and so will I if it means she'll sleep longer on a regular basis."

"I'm leaving now, darling."

Kensington and Anabelle both turned. How had he not noticed the elderly woman before?

Anabelle gave the woman a hug. "Have a wonderful day, Mrs. T. Pass along my congratulations to your grandchildren, okay?"

"Of course. I'll be back soon."

"I'll be looking forward to it. I want to see the hats you knit for your daughters-in-law. You never did show me."

Mrs. T hesitated. "I will bring pictures. I already gave them their hats."

Anabelle put her arm around Mrs. T as they walked to the door. "I don't think I've ever seen any of your work. Sometimes you bring pictures, but you've never brought it in."

"My memory isn't what it used to be, dear. Perhaps one day I will bring them in before I give them away."

"What I really want to see is that quilt. You talked about it for months."

Mrs. T's expression fell. "I still have that one, but it is packed away. Perhaps one day I will be able to get it out and give it to its intended recipient."

Anabelle glanced back at Kensington, clearly troubled by the elderly woman's sudden melancholy.

A car pulled up outside. "There is my ride," Mrs. T announced, suddenly back to her cheerful self. "Have a wonderful day, dears." She hurried out the door and into the car. A young man, perhaps a year or two older than Kensington held her door then drove her off.

"She seems lovely," Kensington told Anabelle.

"She is. It's weird. She has this huge family, but she always seems kind of lonely, like she comes in just so she can talk with us."

"Not us," Rachel chimed in from the counter. "You. She's nice to me and all, but she's here to see you."

"Maybe you remind her of someone?" Kensington guessed.

"Maybe. She's very sweet, and I hate that her family might not be taking good care of her."

"You know they are," Rachel called over her shoulder as she rearranged some of the yarn. "My brother is married to her granddaughter. But she still comes in to see you."

"Whatever the reason, I'm glad she has you." Kensington put his hand on her shoulder. "If you're really worried about her, we can try to talk to her family. Let them know your concerns."

Anabelle shook her head. "No. I think you're right. Maybe I just remind her of her best friend when she was my age, or something like that. I know her whole family comes over every Sunday, and they have a big dinner. She adores them, and it really does sound like they adore her."

"Good." Kensington made a mental note to see what he could find out, just to be sure. He glanced around to make sure his sister was occupied elsewhere. "Now, the most important question. Can I take you to dinner again?"

Anabelle looked up at him. "I would like that." She hesitated.

"What is it?"

"Do you think we could go just the two of us? No Gracie?"

He smiled at her. "I would like that, too. I don't think Gracie will, though. Could we hang out with her for a little bit, then leave a sitter when she's asleep?"

"She would like that better, but what if we want to go to a nice restaurant where I need to wear heels and sparkles and you need to wear a suit?"

She had a point. "You're right. That wouldn't work very well. What if we took her ice skating Saturday, then I take you home, then come back and pick you up a little while later?"

Her smile widened. "That sounds like a great plan."

"What sounds like a great plan?" Esther walked up to them. "I really would like to hear about it, but I need to get going, and we're in the same car, Kenny."

"Then I guess it's time for me to go." Kensington reached for Anabelle's hand and squeezed gently. "See you soon."

If Anabelle were in a HEA TV movie, the three weeks after meeting Kenny would have been a montage with a violin music overlay. They spent part of everyday together, mostly with Gracie, but not always. At least she had enough money coming in to pay a babysitter a few hours a week.

As long as her grandfather didn't cut her off.

But she didn't want to focus on that. Instead, she wanted to daydream about Kenny and the way he kissed her so sweetly as they watched the sun go down.

So what if it went down in the middle of the afternoon and was never fully up in the sky. Such was life in the northern Atlantic.

And he was fantastic with Gracie. She easily believed his favorite uncle claim.

Sitting with her back to his chest and his arms around her was her new happy place. Where she was now. Where she wanted to stay. "Tell me about your meeting."

"It was at the palace, trying to get a contract signed for the Games."

She glanced over her shoulder at him, impressed. "Did you meet with the king?"

"He hasn't been handling these meetings. His uncle was involved with some of the negotiations, though I didn't see him today either." It sounded like that irritated him. Why? Yes, the Games were a major event, involving a ton of tourism for the host country, but to expect the king or his second in command to be involved with a resort?

"Are you trying to get a contract for the athletes to stay at your place?" If the teams were involved, that could be why.

"Nothing like that, but my father is incredibly important in San Majoria, and for Isaiah to snub me as my family's representative won't sit well with Papa." His thumb rubbed up and down her forearm. "I'd rather talk about something else, though. What did you and Gracie do while I was at my meeting?"

"We went to the ice rink and skated for a little bit."

"Gracie can skate?" He sounded impressed.

"Not well yet, but I think she's pretty good for her age."

"My brother-in-law is Canadian. He grew up in a rink, and loves to skate. He's got my niece skating, too."

"How old is she?"

"Just turned two. He's only been her dad since last summer, but you'd never know it to watch them together."

Anabelle wasn't sure what she was supposed to say to that.

"He and my sister met and got married in less than three months, but they're so happy together. The three of them are basically the perfect little family, except they're adding a fourth one to the mix later this year."

Something inside Anabelle twisted. Men like that really did exist? When her parents died, she was left with full custody of Gracie. She wondered if she'd ever find a man who would love both of them. Though she and Kenny weren't quite at the love stage, she could tell he and Gracie were falling hard for each other. When this ended, it was going to be hard on them all.

Because it would end. Kenny's business in Eyjania would be completed, he'd return to San Majoria, and whatever this was would be nothing but a painful memory.

"Can I take you to dinner tomorrow?" he asked. "Just the two of us, like a proper date?"

"Maybe. I have a meeting in the afternoon. I have no idea how long it will last."

"Why don't I make dinner at my place, then? You can let me know when you're done and come over."

That surprised Anabelle, and she twisted until she could look up at him. "What?" Of all the time they'd spent together, none of it had been at his home. She didn't even know what part of town he lived in while he was here. Did his family have a rental? A resort here? Several resort companies had properties in both Eyjania and San Majoria, as well as Islas del Sargasso and Auverignon.

Or did they have a home? One he often stayed at.

He kissed her softly. "Come to my place. I'll cook us dinner. We'll have a fire going. Maybe a little dancing. Just the two of us."

"That sounds fantastic." She leaned her head against his shoulder. "Rob won't mind?" His bodyguard was with him constantly, but she rarely saw him.

"He'll be fine with it."

"He did a background check?"

"Yes," Kensington admitted. "But I told him I didn't want to know any of it, not unless there was a security issue, and I didn't figure there would be. He told me there wasn't. End of discussion."

For the next hour, they talked about everything - and nothing.

The next day, her stomach churned. Things were going fabulously well, so why was she so nervous about this meeting with her grandfather?

His lawyer had called telling her that a car would pick her up, and there would be no acceptable excuse for missing the appointment.

The car drove through Akushla, but not toward her grandfather's palatial home near the shoreline. She didn't know where it was going until it pulled up to the outer gates of the palace.

Many years earlier, her grandmother had been friendly with the late king's mother, though Anabelle had only been to the palace a couple of times for the current Queen Mother's garden party. She'd barely seen a member of the royal family, much less spoken with one of them.

So who were they here to see? No answers were forthcoming while she followed an unsmiling assistant through the halls and up a wide set of stairs to some offices. She sat outside one of them for a long time until finally a different assistant told her she could go in.

She sat down in the leather chair next to her grandfather and across the desk from Prince Isaiah, King Benjamin's uncle.

The smug look on their faces told her she was not going to like whatever it was they had to say.

5

F rantic pounding on the door caught Kensington's
attention. He flipped the kitchen towel over his shoulder
and headed for the door. Rob didn't stop him, so whoever
it was must have clearance. They had to in order to get all the way
to the front door. After the attack on Queen Christiana in Ravenzario a couple days earlier, security had been tightened, even
though they knew her uncle was the one doing the attacking, and
it wasn't a widespread concern.

He opened the door without looking, stumbling backwards
when Anabelle pushed her way inside.

"Kenny?"

"I'm right here, love."

He caught a glimpse of a tear-stained face as she launched
herself into his arms.

"Hey." He held her close. "What is it?"

Her muffled sobs contained words, but he couldn't make out
what they were. They stood there for long minutes as her shoulders shook. He wanted to ask questions, to try to find out what

was going on, but he waited. Was she okay? Sick? Had something happened to Gracie?

Finally, the sobs slowed to hiccups. Kensington led her into the nearby living area and settled on the couch with her tucked into his side. "I couldn't understand a word you said, love. Are you all right? Is Gracie?"

Anabelle sniffled. "She's fine. I'm fine, physically."

He pulled her closer. "Whenever you're ready."

She turned her head into his chest. "It's my grandfather."

Anabelle hadn't really talked about her grandparents, just to say her grandmother was deceased, and her grandfather controlled the life insurance money her parents had left for her and Gracie. "Is he okay? Is that who your meeting was with?"

She nodded. "I didn't know until I got there, but the meeting was at the palace with Prince Isaiah. They made all the arrangements without even asking me about it. Or the king either."

Dread filled Kensington. Isaiah wasn't to be trusted. "What arrangements?"

She tried to pull away, but gentle pressure kept her next to him. "They want me to marry King Benjamin. Told me I was going to if I didn't want to be completely cut off from the inheritance money."

His heart sank. "Are you going to? Is he even willing?" Kensington's father had long feared Isaiah was manipulating Benjamin, but did it extend even to personal relationships? To marriage?

"I don't know. I guess so. I met him briefly a little while ago. He looked me up and down, shrugged, and said 'I guess she'll do.'"

"Lovely." Kensington ran a hand up and down her arm. "What can I do?"

"I don't know that there's anything anyone can do. I can refuse to marry him, but then Gracie and I will have to move. She'll have to go to preschool, and I'll have to get a job that makes enough to support both of us. It won't be easy, but I'll find a way."

Emotions and something else Kensington couldn't define flooded through him. "You can't marry Benjamin if you're already married," he whispered into her hair before kissing the top of her head.

"But I'm not."

"You could be."

She sat up and turned to look at him. "I could?"

Kensington felt his heart in his throat as he slid off the couch and onto one knee. "Marry me."

"What?" Anabelle whispered. "Marry you? You can't be serious."

"I am completely serious. I don't have a ring handy, but as soon as I can get home, I'll get you a fantastic one."

And tell her the truth about who he really was.

Anabelle swiped at the tears on her cheeks. "I don't care about a ring, but I can't ask you to do this. You don't want to be on their bad side, believe me. Making the royal family mad at you can't end well. They could keep people from ever staying with your family again."

"I'm not worried about them." He took a deep breath. Time to come clean.

"What are you doing?" A new voice entered the conversation.

Kensington got to his feet, Anabelle's hand still in his. "Esther, I didn't realize you were home." He tugged on Anabelle's hand until she stood next to him.

"Did I interrupt something?" Esther arched an eyebrow at Kensington.

"Nope. Not a thing." He squeezed Anabelle's hand.

Kensington's mind raced forming a plan.

He would tell Anabelle about it later. For now he needed to give her space to pull herself together then have dinner.

Just like they planned.

Then they would pack up Gracie, head to the airport, and fly off to Athmetis where he knew a preacher who wouldn't ask too many questions.

Somewhere in there he would have to find the time to tell her who he really was. It wouldn't be fair to her to go through with the ceremony without telling her she was about to be a princess.

"Would you like to join us for dinner?" he asked his little sister.

Esther shook her head. "No thanks. I already ate." Just as he'd hoped.

Kensington turned to Anabelle. "Why don't you go freshen up, and I'll put the finishing touches on our dinner? Then we can continue our discussion from earlier."

Annabelle nodded. "That sounds great."

He pointed her towards the downstairs washroom. Or at least the closest one. He didn't know how many washrooms this place actually had.

When she was gone, Esther raised an eyebrow at him. "It looked an awful lot like a proposal, brother."

Kensington shrugged. "Think what you will."

Esther smirked at him and turned to walk away.

Time to make dinner and plan a better proposal.

First class. Anabelle had never splurged this much, even with the modestly significant funds her parents had left. She'd flown business class to Europe a couple of times, but that was it. This time Gracie had enough room to curl up in the seat and rest her head on Anabelle's leg.

But Kensington was three rows away. Apparently, his family's plane was unavailable, and they couldn't get three seats together on this flight. Of course, the fact that his family had their own plane would take some getting used to. Come to think of it, she still had no idea what kind of work his family did. He'd never actually confirmed her resort theory.

She didn't quite understand why, but their flights were booked under separate reservations. Maybe to help make sure no one from the palace had any idea where she was going and who she was with?

But would Prince Isaiah or King Benjamin, or even her grandfather, be watching for her to run away with another man or run away at all?

The flight would land in Athmetis late in the morning. She didn't know what the plan was after that, but by the end of the day she'd be Mrs. Kenneth... What was his last name?

Of all the things she needed to know about him, was that really the most important?

No. Of course not, but it still struck her as a bit odd.

She knew the important things. He was kind, generous, a gentleman, and he cared so much about her and Gracie.

Did he love her? Did she love him?

No. She didn't. Not yet, but she could.

Could she really marry him without loving him? It was better than her alternatives - being broke and homeless or marrying King Benjamin who had a reputation for being cold and unfeeling, and she'd met exactly once .

"Annie?" Gracie's sleepy voice.

"I'm right here, sweetie."

Gracie didn't say anything else, but snuggled in a bit deeper and went back to sleep. Anabelle rested her head against the airplane pillow. Her eyes closed and she drifted off, but woke when an announcement came over the intercom about their arrival in about twenty minutes. Kenny turned around and winked at her.

Anabelle ducked her head and felt her face color then busied herself getting Gracie ready to land. Before long, the wheels thumped onto the runway in Athmetica.

Kenny tried to make his way back to them, but they got separated by the other travelers. Anabelle grabbed Gracie's backpack and helped her put it on before pulling her own bag out from under the seat. With Gracie on her hip, she maneuvered her way out of the plane and onto the jetway. Kenny wasn't waiting for them there.

She set Gracie on the ground with one little hand tucked tightly in hers and pulled her phone out of her pocket with the other. Once turned back on, it began to vibrate with missed calls and messages.

Grandfather.

It buzzed again before she could read any of them. She sighed and swiped across to answer the call. It would be better if she did. "Hello?"

"Where are you?" His voice crackled across the line.

"Gracie and I are on a day trip. We'll be back later." She thought Kenny had said they'd fly back this evening.

"When? We have a meeting with Prince Isaiah to discuss specifics for the wedding."

"I never agreed to marry King Benjamin, Grandfather." She saw Kenny waiting for them as they emerged from the jetway. Gracie tugged on her hand until Anabelle let go so she could run to him. "I'll talk to you later."

"This isn't over, young lady. You *will* marry the king." He didn't say "or else," but Anabelle heard the implication in his voice.

"We'll talk later." She wouldn't commit to it, even just to get him off the phone. Before he could reply, she hung up.

Kenny held Gracie in one arm and took her hand with the other before giving her a soft kiss. "Who was that?"

"My grandfather. He wanted to discuss the same thing we did yesterday. I told him we were on a day trip." She bit her bottom lip. "We are flying back to Eyjania today, aren't we?"

"We can, or we can stay here a few days. It's up to you."

Anabelle hesitated. "I think we better go back." Besides, they didn't have any clothes or anything packed for an overnight trip.

Kenny looked around and led her to a semi-private corner. "There's something I need to tell you," he started.

"Annie," Gracie interrupted. "I need to *go*."

Kenny blew out a deep breath as Anabelle reached for Gracie. When they returned a few minutes later, Kenny stood next to a man in a black and white suit. Kenny took Gracie from her, and they followed the man to a limo parked out front.

"What's the plan?" she asked as they pulled into traffic, but she didn't look at Kenny. She stared at her hands where they gripped the straps of her bag.

"You're going shopping for a dress for you and something for Gracie. The driver knows where to go, and they know to put it on my account."

Anabelle blinked and looked over at him. "You have an account at a store that caters to women who are eloping?"

He chuckled. "No, but my sisters probably do. It's taken care of. The staff will help you get ready. If you don't find anything you like, they'll point you somewhere else and make the arrangements. They've got someone lined up to do your hair and make-up. Nothing too fancy, probably, but you won't have to figure it out yourself. Then the driver will bring both of you to my family's home." He pulled his phone out of his pocket. "There's the confirmation I was looking for. A preacher friend of mine will meet us there. I've already talked to him, and he's made the arrangements for the license."

A weight lifted off Anabelle's shoulders. "You've taken care of all of it?"

Kenny winked at her. "I think so."

No more mention of what he'd wanted to tell her. It couldn't be bad, or he wouldn't go through with the wedding. She'd find out later.

Right now the only thing that really mattered was finding a way out of marrying King Benjamin.

6

Kensington needed to find Anabelle and talk to her before this ceremony actually commenced. He'd been told the car had arrived on the property, but hadn't seen her or Gracie yet. He and an old friend of his, a preacher who'd listened to him when he'd needed a shoulder and a man of God to point him in the right direction after his last breakup with someone only interested in his titles, stood next to him.

"Are you sure about this, Your Royal Highness? You don't think your family would want to be here? That the country doesn't want their own chance to watch their favorite oldest prince get married?"

Kensington shook his head. "No. It has to be this way. Maybe we'll have a wedding later, but this needs to happen now."

The preacher frowned. "She isn't pregnant, is she?"

He couldn't contain his chuckle. "Nothing like that. There hasn't been any contact of that kind, not outside of a few not-quite-chaste kisses."

"Good."

"But can you leave the titles and everything out of this?" The wedding wasn't the time to find out she was about to be a princess. "Kensington is marrying Anabelle. Not Prince Kensington, Duke of This, Earl of That, and Baron of the Other Thing."

As the other man laughed and nodded, he also glanced at his watch. "I'm about out of time, though. I hate to rush you, but I have a meeting I can't miss in about forty-five minutes, and it's at least half an hour away."

Kensington started to reach for his phone to text Anabelle, but before he could, movement at the top of the stairs caught his eye. The housekeeper, a woman who'd worked for his family for decades but moved here when her husband retired, hurried down to the beach.

"I've got the music on my phone," she called as she reached the sand. "And we'll have a photographer in a minute, too."

That's right. Her husband had dabbled, much like Astrid's husband, Jordan, did. She tapped a few times on her phone before music sort of filled the air. The phone's speaker wasn't top notch. Why hadn't he thought to grab his bluetooth speaker to use?

But his thoughts stopped in their tracks when Anabelle appeared at the top of the stairs, Gracie's hand in one of hers and a bouquet in the other. Her smile would have lit up the whole of outside if the sun wasn't already shining bright.

A minute later, Gracie stood by the preacher and held the bouquet as Kensington took Anabelle's hands in his.

"Dearly beloved..."

Kensington tried to focus on the words, but found himself unable to tear his attention away from Anabelle. Her simple dress and hairstyle were perfect for the woman he'd been falling in love with.

"Kensington?" the man at his side prodded. "Do you take Anabelle to be your lawfully wedded wife?"

His smile widened. "I do."

"And do you Anabelle, take Kensington to be your lawfully wedded husband?" He continued through the list of things they would be to each other, ending with, "keeping yourself only unto him until death do you part?"

Anabelle's smile grew. "I do."

"Then by the power vested in me by the king of Athmetis, I now pronounce you husband and wife. Kensington, you may kiss your bride."

Kensington's foot shifted in the sand as he leaned toward Anabelle. "My pleasure." He framed her face with his hands and touched his lips to hers. As much as he wanted to deepen the kiss beyond what they'd previously shared, he didn't let himself. Judging by the way she gripped his shirt, Anabelle wished for more, too.

After posing for a few pictures with just the two of them and some with Gracie, he held her hand as they walked back up the stairs.

"There's a meal waiting for you, sir," the housekeeper called from a few steps below where she helped Gracie.

"Thank you. We're going to eat, but then we need to get back to the airport for our flight back to Eyjania."

"Already?" He heard the disappointment in her voice.

"I'm afraid so, but we'll come back for a visit soon." He winked at Anabelle who turned the most becoming shade of red. "Maybe when we have time for a real honeymoon."

"We'll be here waiting for you, sir. Bring your sisters, and that niece of yours."

Kensington stifled a chuckle. "I'll see what I can do."

On the patio, past the luxurious pool and under an awning, sat a table with food. He held a chair for Anabelle then took his own seat as Gracie scrambled onto the third chair. After he said the blessing, Anabelle dished up a serving for herself and Gracie while Kensington helped himself. He would need to learn how to do the father thing, even if he was really Gracie's brother-in-law.

There was a weird thought.

"So, I learned something about you," Anabelle said as she situated a napkin in her lap.

"What's that?"

"Your name isn't Kenneth, and the single word on your business card wasn't just the name of a random palace in Great Britain."

Rather than the smile her smirk said she expected, Kensington sobered. "No. It's not Kenneth. It's Kensington. It never occurred to me you might think that. Usually when I hand out a business card, the person already knows my name, so I never even thought about someone who might not know Kensington isn't just a British palace, but also my name." With a bunch of middle names and more titles than most people ever held for cars. How was he going to tell her about that? "Honestly, my mother would likely be appalled to know you've been calling me Kenny." She was wonderful, but had a thing about nicknames. He leaned closer and kissed Anabelle softly. "But I kind of like it."

She groaned. "I probably need to start calling you Kensington all the time though. Otherwise I'm sure to slip in front of your family."

"My father would think it's hilarious. So would my grandmother. We all have these kind of pretentious family names, and no one dares shorten them for us because of the family connection and all, plus my mother has a thing about nicknames. They're mostly fantastic when you get to know them, but they can be kind of stick-in-the-mud until then."

"Okay, so you're Kensington. What about the rest of your family? Who are they?"

He hesitated, but only for a second. Would she recognize the names of the San Majorian royal family? "My older sister is Astrid. After me is Jacqueline Grace, then Esther, and my brother is Harrison. My parents are Edward and Miriam. My grandmother is Grace, but I doubt anyone ever called her Gracie."

Anabelle seemed to be thinking.

Had she finally figured it out? And how would she feel?

He held his breath waiting to find out, breathing a sigh of relief - for now - when she changed the subject.

Anabelle wondered if it was too much to wish she could sit by her new husband on the way back to Eyjania. Unfortunately, the flight was almost full. Kenny - no, Kensington - being the gentleman he was, gave the two first class seats to Anabelle and Gracie and took a seat in business class for himself.

She realized he'd managed to make the trip without Rob. Because they were going to his family's property on the other end? And it was a direct flight both ways?

Or had he snuck off without telling Rob and how mad would his security team be?

Did that mean she and Gracie would have security before long? She wasn't sure how she felt about that. Maybe she should have asked before marrying Kensington.

Too late now. Even if they were off to a very unconventional start, she knew deep down that marrying him was the right thing to do. Almost anything would be better than marrying King Benjamin.

Gracie stayed awake for most of this flight, but played quietly with her toys and stared out the window, pointing out mountains and other things she saw below.

It was nearly Gracie's bedtime when they landed, long after dark this far north.

Rob met them as they emerged into the baggage claim area. He looked annoyed but not mad. That was something. He didn't mention the wedding and neither did Kensington. One thing they didn't have were rings.

Kensington apologized for that while they ate. He said there was a family heirloom ring designated for his use but he obviously hadn't had time to get it. She hadn't even thought about a wedding band for him. Everything else had freaked her out too much.

"Anabelle and Gracie will be staying at the house with us," Kensington told Rob. "We will need to hire someone to pack up their apartment and move their things."

Anabelle stopped in her tracks. "Hold up there, Kenny." She used the nickname on purpose. "What if I want to do the packing myself? And why can't you move in with us?" She knew that wasn't an option, but they hadn't discussed any of this.

"No one will be moving in with anyone." Rob glared at Kensington.

"Sorry, Rob." Kensington started walking, leaving the rest of them to follow. "Not an option. There are reasons to be concerned for the safety of both Anabelle and Gracie. They're coming to the house with us." He turned to look at her.

Anabelle had to admit she saw nothing but compassion and concern in his eyes.

"Our house is gated and secure. Your apartment isn't. That's why you should move in with me. If you want to pack everything up yourself, that's fine. I just wanted to make things easier."

She felt her shoulders relax. "I know you did. Maybe we can go over tomorrow to pack the things I wouldn't want to leave to anyone else then hire someone to do the rest?"

He moved to her side and slid an arm around her waist. "I think that sounds perfect. I have a meeting first thing in the morning, but after that we can go over, and I'll help however I can."

"Thanks."

A car waited for them outside. Rob opened the back door for the three of them to climb in. He then sat in the front next to the driver.

The drive to Kensington's home was quiet. Gracie started to

nod off. Kensington carried her inside when they arrived and put her in the room across from his. He'd basically dismissed Rob as soon as they arrived.

Once Gracie was snuggled under the blanket, Anabelle turned to find Kensington right there.

He rested his hand on her hips and pulled her close. "I know this isn't exactly the wedding or wedding night every girl dreams of," he told her softly. "But it's what we've got. I'm not going to pressure you or ask for more than you're willing to give. If you want to stay here with Gracie tonight, I understand." A self-assured grin crossed his face. "But if you would rather join me across the hall, that would be all right with me, too."

Anabelle rested her hands on his chest, but didn't look him in the eyes. "I'd be lying if I said I wasn't intrigued by your offer."

"But?" he prompted when she didn't go on.

"I'm not sure I want to leave Gracie alone in a new place, not when she wasn't awake to know where she is and where I'll be."

His hands slid around her waist. "I can understand that."

Her fingers fiddled with the button at about her eye level. "But if you had some sort of baby monitor or something so I could hear her if she woke up scared, that might be okay, too."

As soon as the last word left her mouth, Kensington's lips covered hers in a kiss so intense it left her breathless. When he moved away, long minutes later, she whispered, "So you have something like that?"

He rested his forehead on hers. "If we don't, we will in the next twenty minutes." With one arm around her waist to anchor her to him, he pulled his phone out with the other hand. He tapped on the screen a few times then waited for a reply.

"Yes. We do have one. My sister stays here with her daughter sometimes." He gave her another intense kiss. "I'll be right back."

Anabelle clutched her stomach as he walked out.

They were married.

Kensington was her *husband*.

She hadn't given this enough thought.

She knew what was expected, but wasn't prepared. There had been no time to go shopping for something cute or sexy or somewhere in between. Kensington probably wouldn't care, but it bothered Anabelle a little bit. Her wedding dress was long gone, left behind in Athmetis to be preserved and shipped later, though Kensington hadn't changed out of the very beachy shirt and slacks he'd been wearing.

Rather than waiting for him in Gracie's room, she went across the hall to the one she knew to be his. Maybe she'd find some inspiration that wouldn't be completely embarrassing.

The wooden valet held a suit, likely meant for a meeting he'd missed due to their trip or for the next day.

But it gave her an idea.

A smile played at her lips. If only he didn't hurry back too fast.

7

Kensington sat in the outer office waiting for Isaiah to decide he was worth the other man's time. He knew Isaiah thought making Kensington wait gave him the upper hand, but Kensington was on to him. Simply by knowing what game Isaiah was playing gave Kensington the upper hand. Sure he was kept waiting, but Isaiah couldn't complain he'd been late, and he'd brought work to do knowing this would happen.

Not that he could concentrate on any of it.

Every time he closed his eyes, even just to blink, he saw Anabelle.

Waiting for him when he returned with the baby monitor.

Wearing one of his dress shirts.

Nervously biting her lip as he walked toward her.

Kissing him.

Curled around a pillow with the sheet over her bare shoulders as he left before she woke up.

"Kensington?" Isaiah's assistant spoke for the first time in nearly an hour.

Kensington looked up with a raised eyebrow.

"His Royal Highness Prince Isaiah will see you now."

Kensington was a little surprised the man didn't include all of Isaiah's other titles in an additional effort to emphasize his importance. He might do more of the day to day running of the nation, but Kensington outranked him in the scope of things. For now, Kensington was third in line for the San Majorian throne after Astrid and Sofia. Isaiah came behind all nine of King Benjamin's siblings, his own older sister, and all of her children and grandchildren.

All the reminders did was serve to amuse Kensington.

When he entered the office, Isaiah still looked annoyed at being interrupted, despite this meeting being on the schedule for weeks.

"Everything all right?" Kensington asked. "I trust there's no major emergency going on that caused the delay."

Isaiah shook his head. "No. In fact, it's good news. My nephew will be announcing his engagement later today."

It took all of Kensington's acting skills to control his response. "Benjamin is getting married?"

"Yes. He is marrying a local woman in a couple of months. Anabelle is quite honored to have been chosen."

Kensington took a seat without waiting for Isaiah to invite him to. He leaned back trying to project an ease, a comfort, he didn't really feel. "Anabelle Gregorson? I'm kind of surprised Ben is willing to marry a woman with custody of her little sister."

"You know her?"

"We've met." Kensington did his best to remain nonchalant.

"The child will be taken care of. Ms. Gregorson does not want to subject her to the rigors of palace life, so an appropriate caregiver will be found for her."

Like any of this had been discussed with, must less agreed to by, Anabelle.

The statements also meant they had no idea about his wedding to Anabelle the day before.

He should probably make sure his father knew before Isaiah found out.

The meeting was predictably short with Isaiah sticking to his position despite its irrationality, and Kensington not giving in. Ten minutes after walking into the office, he walked out. In the back seat of his car, Kensington pulled out his phone and called his father's direct line.

After telling him about the meeting, Kensington hesitated.

"What is it?" his father asked. "Something else is going on."

"You're not going to like it," Kensington told him. "But it's too late now, and you wouldn't have been able to talk me out of it anyway."

"Does it have something to do with your quick trip to Athmetis yesterday?"

Of course he knew about that. "Yes. While I was there..." Time to rip off the bandage. "I got married."

Silence greeted him from the other end of the line. "Married?"

"Yes. To a wonderful woman. She's already been checked out by security. Her name is Anabelle Gregorson, and I fell in love with her at first sight. The feeling was mutual. She's raising her younger sister who is a little older than Sofia."

"So you're essentially a father as well."

"Basically." No explosion from the other end of the line. That was good.

"Why did you decide to elope instead of introducing her to us and having an actual wedding?"

Here came the more delicate part of this conversation. "Her grandfather controls their inheritance. He was going to force her to marry a man of his choosing or she would lose everything. I couldn't let that happen. Not when I could make a difference. It had to happen quickly before her grandfather made her."

"I see." Kensington could almost see the wheels turning in his father's head. "Was this other man so awful? Or she just wasn't in love with him and fancies herself in love with you and your titles?"

Kensington pinched the bridge of his nose. "That's just it. She doesn't know about my titles. She thinks we run resorts in both countries. I tried to tell her yesterday, but Gracie had to go to the bathroom, and I never had another chance."

"Gracie?"

"Her sister."

"Your grandmother will like that." His father's amusement came clearly over the line.

"I know she will."

"So the other man was awful then?"

How to put it? "He's not awful, but he's not known for being warm and fuzzy either. She met him once, and he was indifferent at best. Really, condescending would be a better word."

"So you know him?"

"We've met." Kensington tried to remain noncommittal. His father hand taken the news of the wedding better than expected. He likely wouldn't take the news that Kensington had "stolen" Benjamin's bride quite so well.

"Do I know him?"

"Better than I do."

"What aren't you telling me?"

Kensington stared out the window. "This is the part you're really not going to like."

He could almost see the wheels turning in his father's head. "A member of the royal family? Who? Darius?"

"No."

"Isaiah wanted her to marry Benjamin?" The incredulity matched Kensington's own two days before.

"Yes. She met him the other day. He looked her up and down, said she'll do, and walked off."

"So you married her instead?"

He needed his father to understand. "I was already falling in love with her. I've known her longer than Astrid knew Jordan before their engagement was announced."

"But she doesn't know who you are, everything that goes along with becoming your wife."

"It's not like I'm the heir," he pointed out. "And with the baby coming, it's even less likely that I ever will be."

Kensington heard his father's office door open and then the voice of his father's assistant. "I have to go. I'll see you soon." The vague threat hung in the air between them. "I do love you, Kensington, but I'm afraid this decision is going to end up costing us. I wish you'd come to me first. I'll talk to you later today."

He hung up as the car pulled to a stop in front of Anabelle's apartment building. Time to put his father's disapproval out of his mind and help his wife pack.

Anabelle opened the door without looking through the peephole first, something she regretted as soon as she did.

Prince Isaiah pushed past her and into the living area. "The announcement will be made this afternoon."

She blinked. "What announcement?"

"Your engagement to my nephew."

"There is no engagement."

The prince held out a box. "Your engagement ring. The wedding will be in March."

Anabelle pushed the door closed, though she wasn't sure it latched. "I am not marrying your nephew. Not in March. Not ever."

"You will if you want to keep your *sister* with you." Something sinister lurked in his eyes and in his tone of voice.

"I will not take my sister to live in the palace." She would never see Gracie. Somehow Anabelle knew Gracie would be kept from

53

her - if not officially, it would be the reality. "I will not be marrying King Benjamin."

"Of course you won't."

Anabelle turned to see Kensington walk in.

"Hi, Isaiah. How'd you beat me here?" Without waiting for an answer, Kensington slid an arm around her waist. "Honey, I'm home." The light tone of his voice couldn't hide the seriousness underpinning it. After a quick kiss, he kept his arm where it was and turned to Isaiah. "Did you tell her your plan to leave Gracie with 'an appropriate caregiver'?"

Anabelle moved away from him, putting herself between Isaiah and the hallway to Gracie's room. "What?"

"We didn't think Ms. Gregorson would want to be burdened with raising a child while settling into a new marriage. It would be temporary until things were more comfortable."

Kensington crossed his arms over his chest, "You mean until Ben has his heir, you whisk the baby away to be raised as you see fit, and Anabelle is superfluous? Or do they need to have two kids first? Twins would certainly save time."

Anabelle gasped at Kensington's attitude toward King Benjamin's right hand man, his use of such a familiar nickname, and the accusation that Prince Isaiah had yet to deny.

"The decision has already been made. Her grandfather signed the contract."

Another gasp ripped from Anabelle as she grasped her abdomen.

"You don't have marriage contracts." Kensington shut the door and went to sit on the couch, propping his feet up on the coffee table and crossing them at the ankles. "This isn't Mevendia. Besides, if Anabelle didn't sign it, it can't make her do anything. Her grandfather could threaten to take away her inheritance, but he can't force her to do anything." He winked at her. "Besides, I'll see they're taken care of."

Isaiah pulled himself up to his full height. "On the contrary.

Her grandfather has power of attorney. He can sign documents on her behalf, and he did."

Kensington looked at her. "Is that true?"

Anabelle could only nod through her tears.

"When was it signed?" Kensington asked Isaiah.

"Last night."

Kensington chuckled. "Too bad. Because she was already married by the time it was signed. It's invalid."

The blood drained from Isaiah's face before it turned red. "Married? To who?"

With his fingers linked behind his head, a smug look appeared on Kensington's face. "Me."

"You?"

"Yep. We eloped yesterday."

Anabelle couldn't keep up with the volleys of conversation between the two men. Why hadn't they stayed away after all? If she wasn't in town, this couldn't be happening.

"Do your parents know?"

"I haven't talked to Mother, but Father is ecstatic. My grandmother is going to be thrilled with Gracie. So will Sofia. Technically, they won't be cousins, but close enough. She'll have a little girl to play with after we move to San Majoria permanently."

What? Anabelle's head spun, but she wasn't about to confront Kensington about announcing his plans to return to San Majoria without talking to her. Not now. Not when it was infuriating Isaiah.

"Consider this your expulsion from Eyjania." Isaiah glared at both of them. "You have twenty-four hours to leave the country or face arrest and public deportation."

Anabelle's knees buckled, the wall behind her the only thing that kept her from ending up on the floor.

Kensington actually laughed. "Oh please. That's an empty threat and you know it. Only the king can do that without following all sorts of proper procedures that you know will never fly. Even though you've got Ben wrapped around your little finger, he wouldn't approve that. He knows how my father would react." He turned his head to look at Anabelle, an apology for something written all over his face before he looked back at Isaiah. "And Ben would never risk alienating the king of such an important trading partner."

The apartment began to swim before her eyes as she tried to wrap her mind around what Kensington had said. The king wouldn't deport them because of how Kensington's father would react. Benjamin wouldn't want to alienate the king of Kensington's country.

Kensington's father was king of San Majoria.

That meant...

She couldn't say it. Not in front of Isaiah. The prince couldn't know she hadn't known.

Kensington stood. "Now, I suggest you remove yourself from my wife's home. We won't cause any trouble for you or Benjamin, but neither will you cause any for Anabelle. She has the full support of the Majorian family behind her. You would do well to remember that."

"This isn't over." The threat in Isaiah's voice wasn't even veiled. "In fact, I suggest you leave the country, whether you think I can force you to or not. There will be no more discussions about Games with you or anyone else in your family or on behalf of San Majoria. You may be right that King Benjamin won't have you publicly deported, but he has put me in charge of the Games, and I guarantee it won't end well."

Kensington didn't stand up, but just stared at Isaiah from his seat. "You don't scare me, and I'm quite certain you don't scare my father."

"I'll be in touch." Isaiah turned and walked out, slamming the door behind him.

Before Anabelle realized he'd moved Kensington was in front

of her, gathering her in his arms. "I've got you, love. I'm sorry you had to live through that."

She wouldn't let him pull her too close. "Your father is the king of San Majoria?" Until he told her, she could have misinterpreted what he said.

"Yes, he is. Technically, my name is His Royal Highness Prince Kensington Wilhelm Edward Charles, Duke of Pennington, Earl of Caromache, and Baron of Navarricia."

This time when her knees gave out completely, Kensington caught her, swept her into his arms, and held her close.

8

N ot exactly how he'd planned for her to find out, but she had. Kensington held Anabelle in his arms as he lowered himself carefully into the obviously well-loved arm chair.

"Why didn't you tell me?" she whispered, settling her head against his shoulder. He took that as a good sign.

"I wanted to, but it was kind of nice having someone special in my life who didn't know, and therefore didn't care, about all the titles and tiaras that go with eventually becoming my wife. I wanted to tell you yesterday, but I couldn't find the time before the wedding. The minister had to leave right after, remember? If I took the time to find you, we would have had to wait until today, and I was really hoping it wouldn't matter."

He felt her take a deep, shuddering breath. "Do I know the real you?"

"Except for the fact that my family is royal and not simply wealthy, yes."

"Then the only thing that bothers me, at least at this point, is that you weren't completely honest and didn't let me choose if I wanted to live the rest of my life in the limelight that comes with marrying a prince. It's one of many reasons I didn't want to marry the king. I don't want my life, my parenting choices, my clothes, scrutinized by people I've never met and media types who care far more about getting their picture than they do about safety."

He tightened his hold. "We have paparazzi in San Majoria, but they aren't allowed to get close enough to cause harm. The penalties are stiff if they do, but as a general rule, we have a good relationship with the media."

"I saw the pictures of your sister and the man she married. I don't know why I didn't realize that's who it was when you told me her name. You can't say that went very well."

"They weren't putting Astrid or Jordan in any danger, were they? They were far away, though I think a couple of them were charged with trespassing. My sister and Jordan are extremely happy and, this isn't public news yet, are expecting a child. He didn't know who she was until the news came out. He thought she was just from a wealthy family until his sister called from Canada and told him."

"But he had a choice. He didn't have to marry her once he knew he'd someday be prince consort."

"Yes and no, but that's a discussion for another time."

"Annie?" Gracie's voice caused both of them to turn their heads toward the little girl, who clearly just woke up.

"What is it, sweetheart?"

Gracie climbed up next to them in the chair as Anabelle resituated herself.

"Somethin' scare me," Gracie told them.

"The door slamming?"

The little girl nodded.

"It won't happen again."

Gracie snuggled close to Kensington, her eyelids already starting to droop again. "'Kay." In just a minute, she was asleep.

"We have to live in San Majoria?" Anabelle asked him once

Gracie's soft snore filled the air.

"For now, probably. I'm in charge of the Games of the Sargasso Sea. But, once I'm a little further down the list, it won't matter as much."

"The list?"

"The line of succession. Right now, it's Astrid, Sofia, then me. Soon they'll add another baby to the mix. It wouldn't surprise me if they have more than two kids. The more kids they have, the less likely I'll ever be asked to take the throne. Until they're done, though, when Astrid is pregnant or has infants, the rest of us are asked to take over some of her official engagements, which means spending most, but not necessarily all, of our time in San Majoria."

"I guess I can understand that."

"We don't have to live in the main palace, either. There's plenty of room in my apartment there if we want to, but we don't have to. My family has several other homes we can choose from or find one of our own whenever we want. And we don't have to go public with our relationship until you're ready. At least, not until we see how this whole thing with your grandfather, Isaiah, and Benjamin is going to play out."

"Is that why you didn't show a whole lot of respect to Prince Isaiah?"

"That's because he doesn't deserve it. If he was female, he'd be a manipulative shrew. I don't know what the male equivalent is, but he is one."

"I think it's a boar, but that doesn't quite fit."

Kensington smiled. "Well, then, he's a manipulative boar. He's been trying to run the country through Benjamin for years. Besides, if we were at the same event, and they were lining up royalty in order of rank, I outrank him because I'm much higher in my line of succession than he is."

"That's also why you call the king by his name or even a nickname." He could hear it dawning on her. "Because you actually know him."

"Not really. I called him Ben to irritate Isaiah, but we've only met a few times at official functions. We're not friends. My father and his were close. Not as much with Benjamin, probably because of the age difference but also Isaiah limiting his outside influences. I know my father is concerned about how much Isaiah has managed to isolate Benjamin." He probably shouldn't be so open about his father's feelings on the matter with someone his father had never met, but Kensington thought it would be okay.

"That explains why he would let his uncle choose a wife for him."

"Yes, it would." He kissed the side of her head. "Now, why don't we pack what you want to take with you on the family plane and let someone else take care of the rest? I do think we should probably head to San Majoria as soon as we can. I'll call my father and ask him to send the plane for us tonight. We can spend a few days vacationing before settling in."

Anabelle sat up and turned to look at him. "Does this mean I'm a princess?"

Kensington winced. "Kind of? You'll probably be referred to as Princess Anabelle from the beginning, but I'm not sure if you'll actually hold the title. Everyone calls Catherine, Duchess of Cambridge Princess Kate, but she's not. I don't think princess is even part of her titles until her husband becomes Prince of Wales after Queen Elizabeth passes and Prince Charles is no longer Prince of Wales but King of England. But when Prince Carl Philip of Sweden got married, his wife became Princess Sofia, even though he's not the heir apparent, his sister is. I'm pretty sure Prince Richard of Montevaro's wife is also officially a princess, though he was first in line for the throne when they got married. His sister was already queen, but didn't have any children." He sighed. "It's all very complicated in what titles go where and when."

She just blinked at him. "Long answer short?"

"Every country is different. I'm not sure if princess automatically follows our marriage or not, but most titles will have to be conferred by my father regardless. It's normally done immediately prior to a wedding with a statement included that it takes effect when the marriage becomes official. You will likely be referred to as Princess anyway. Once my father does make it official, you will also be Duchess of Pennington, Countess of Caromache, and Lady Navarricia."

"I guess I can live with that." She kissed him. "I understand why you didn't want to tell me. I wish you had, but we'll find a way to make it work."

A weight lifted off Kensington's shoulders until his phone buzzed quickly three times. His father's text tone. When he read the short note, he groaned.

"What is it?"

"My father is on his way, and he's not happy."

Anabelle smoothed her hand over her abdomen and down the sides of her hips. She'd met one king already this week and was about to meet another. Her father-in-law would be arriving any minute. Rob told Kensington the plane had landed half an hour earlier.

Kensington slid his arm around her waist and pulled her to his side before turning her to face him. "It's going to be okay. You know that, right? My father is annoyed at the circumstances with the Eyjanians, not with you or even us getting married per se."

"I know, but I've never had a conversation with an actual king before. Meeting King Benjamin earlier this week doesn't count."

"My family is going to love you." He winked at her. "Honestly, I think you should be more nervous about meeting your father-in-law than meeting the King of San Majoria, but I don't think you should be nervous about that either. Jordan gave him a black eye one time, and he still loves Jordan, so don't worry about it."

Before she could respond, Kensington kissed her. It didn't get out of hand, but Anabelle still felt her face color when a throat cleared behind them.

Kensington let her go. "Father!" The two men exchanged a hug.

The king almost pushed Kensington away. "Forget you. I've known you your whole life. I want to meet my new daughter-in-law."

From the grin on Kensington's face, Anabelle knew he knew his father didn't mean anything by the comment.

She dropped into a small curtsy and bowed her head.

"You must be Anabelle." He held his arms open. "My dear, it is a pleasure to meet you."

Anabelle straightened and found herself wrapped in a big hug. When he released her, she bowed her head again. "King Edward. It's a pleasure to meet you, too, Your Majesty."

"Please, call me Edward, unless we're in public." He kissed her cheek. "Now, where is Miss Gracie? I'm told I have a new grand-daughter, more or less."

"She's already in bed, I'm afraid." Anabelle stepped back toward the stairs. "I can get her."

"Nonsense. Never wake a sleeping child unless you absolutely have to." He turned back to Kensington. "You and I need to have a word, son. Then the three of us will discuss the near future as a family."

Kensington and his father walked toward a section of the house she'd not explored yet. She followed a bit behind, hoping she'd find a chair in a room near wherever they stopped. They went through an outer office to an inner one and closed the door behind them. Anabelle took a seat on a chair against the wood paneled wall. Were all royal offices about the same? Rich woods, expensive paintings, plush furnishings? Prince Isaiah's had looked much the same, though the decorating style of his office made it seem less welcoming.

She sat there for at least fifteen minutes while the two of them talked. Every possible scenario from being exiled together to being imprisoned for marrying without permission from the monarch went through her mind. None of them were likely, but it didn't stop her fear.

Anabelle jumped when the door opened.

The king smiled at her. "Come in, my dear."

With a deep breath, she stood and brushed past him as he held the door. Kensington was on his feet next to a wingback chair in a sitting area. She went to the seat next to him, though she didn't sit down until her father-in-law motioned for her to.

"Your mother and I had a long discussion while I was on my way here," the king started. "We think it would be best to see how my meeting with Benjamin goes before making an official decision on an announcement or where you'll live after the Games, and so on."

"You think Benjamin will actually meet with you?" Anabelle asked, surprised by her own boldness. "I don't think he particularly cares about any of this, except that he needs an heir eventually. As long as the woman didn't have any glaring faults, I don't think it matters who Isaiah tells him to marry."

"I would imagine Isaiah will try to have the meeting on his own, but he wouldn't dare stand up to me too much. There's too much at stake for him to make me mad." He crossed his legs and looked much more at ease than Anabelle could ever imagine being. "Have you talked to your grandfather since all of this happened?"

"Not yet." She dreaded it. "He's going to cut off all of our inheritance. I don't care so much for myself, but it's the only thing

Gracie would have of our parents. In the world of royalty, it's not much, I'm sure, but it's all we have."

"I understand that. From a purely financial standpoint, neither of you will ever want for anything again, but from the emotional side of things, it's a very different story."

He understood. "Exactly."

"While we're waiting to see how the meeting goes, we do think it's best if the three of you leave the country. My meeting isn't until first thing in the morning. Part of me says stay here just to show Isaiah he doesn't control us. Part of me says for you to go - either to San Majoria or Auverignon tonight. The plane can be back for me by afternoon if you go home, and I can be home before bed tomorrow night. Or you can go to Auverignon, pick me up, and we'll fly back to San Majoria together."

Kensington looked at her. "What do you think?"

"I don't particularly want to wake Gracie up to get her on a plane tonight, but I also don't really want a confrontation with any of the royal family either. I just want all of it to go away." She caught the look on Kensington's face before he masked it. "Except the part where we got married. I really like that part. I detest the rest of it."

"Understandable. Would you prefer to go to Auverignon in the morning then return with the plane to pick me up in the afternoon?"

The weight of it all settled over Anabelle like a winter coat. "No. I think, given the options, it would probably be best to just go to San Majoria tonight, if that's all right with you. It does seem sort of silly to waste the fuel when the plane will be leaving here tomorrow. Could the three of us go somewhere else for the night? Somewhere Prince Isaiah and King Benjamin wouldn't know where we were, then leave with you tomorrow?"

King Edward thought that over. "There's a cottage on the property. Why don't you go there until it's time to leave? If anyone asks, we can honestly say you're not at the house, but it's still secure."

Anabelle looked at Kensington who nodded.

"That sounds like a good compromise. Thank you."

The king smiled, a smile Prince Isaiah and King Benjamin were unlikely to ever master. "It is my pleasure."

9

Less than twenty-four hours after his father's arrival in Eyjania, the four of them were on a plane back to San Majoria. Esther hadn't left with them. Kensington hadn't seen her since she interrupted his proposal to Anabelle three days earlier.

His father refused to talk about his meeting with Benjamin and Isaiah, saying only that everything was taken care of and there would be no long term repercussions for San Majoria or the Games. He then went to the other portion of the plane, shut the door, and didn't reappear until after the pilot told them they would be landing in about twenty minutes.

He sat in a chair across from the couch where Kensington sat with Anabelle and a sleeping Gracie.

"I spoke with your mother again. We had discussed a possible plan last night and think it's for the best. For now, we think you should lay low. No announcement. Explain to the people later why there wasn't one and ask their forgiveness. We think you should go to the Lowery House on the coast of San Mediano. Go about your day-to-day life, but don't draw attention to yourselves. How does that sound?"

Kensington knew the question was just to be polite. The plan had already been set in motion. Anabelle had told him she trusted his judgment about whatever his parents came up with as far as this decision went. He nodded. "That will work, but we're allowed to *be* married, right? This isn't some courtship thing where we're pretending the wedding didn't happen until we're ready to tell everyone, is it?"

His father shook his head. "No. Nothing like that."

Kensington had been afraid they would say something along those lines so it was a relief they didn't.

Ten minutes later, the plane landed. Twenty minutes after that, they had disembarked in a closed hanger, departed in a darkened vehicle, and arrived in the palace garrison rather than the portico. Anyone watching might think something unusual was happening, but would have no idea what it could be.

They went straight to his parents' apartment on the top floor of the residential wing. He hoped the rest of his family wouldn't be there, but no such luck. Everyone but Esther and Sofia were waiting for them.

Amid the mayhem, hugs, and congratulations, Kensington found himself separated from Anabelle, his face framed by his mother's hands.

"Congratulations," she said, tears in her eyes. "I am so happy you've found her."

"Me, too, Mama." He kissed her cheek. "Thank you for understanding."

"Of course. Your father told me everything." A wave of sadness crossed over her face before it disappeared. "I can't wait to get to know your wife and her sister."

Kensington looked around. "Where is Grandmother?"

"She's not here. She had a very early morning today and has

another one tomorrow on San Minoria, so she's already there. She'll be back tomorrow for lunch."

"I've missed her."

"And I know she's missed her lunches with you." Kensington and his grandmother usually ate lunch together at least once a week when they didn't have other engagements. "I think she'd like it to be just the four of you tomorrow afternoon so we will have to spend the morning getting to know your wife and Gracie. I would imagine your father will give her a title when he officially confers yours on your wife."

Kensington put his arm around his mother's shoulders as they watched the rest of his family surround and accept Anabelle and Gracie as two of their own.

"Will she have the title of princess? Since I'm not the heir apparent and all. I know that varies depending on the country, but Father and Grandfather both had sisters."

"I think so, but we'll have to double check. I would assume so, but now that I think about it, you're right. It's not always the case. Regardless, she's your princess, isn't she? The one you've prayed you'd find."

"Yes, she is. I don't think either of us would have chosen to marry so quickly, but I'm falling hard for her. I have been since the first moment I saw her. That reminds me. I was buying you a souvenir when I first met them."

"You will need to visit the Jewel Vault soon. There's a ring there waiting for you."

"We will." Kensington wondered about the wisdom of Anabelle wearing an engagement ring in public before the official announcement was made. If they were ever together, there was always the chance pictures would be taken, even if there was no official announcement about his location. If the pictures showed her wearing a family heirloom...

Well, that was part of what got Astrid and Jordan in trouble. She'd been wearing a family ring simply because she missed her first husband. The tabloids ran with it. He'd talk to Anabelle about it. Maybe she could wear it at home.

Finally, his family moved away from his wife, allowing his mother to move toward Annabelle. Harrison and Jacqueline Grace came to stand by him. Jacqueline Grace gave him a big hug.

"I'm happy for you, big brother."

"Thanks."

"They seem great," Harrison added. "And you've managed to find a parentally approved way to get out of most public functions for a while."

That made Kensington laugh. "I doubt I'll get out of all of them, but it will probably be a while before I have a full plate of appearances again. I've got too much going on getting ready for the Games."

His father called for everyone's attention, telling Anabelle to stand next to Kensington. His mother's assistant came in with a tray full of champagne glasses. Two were a bit off to the side. One was given to Astrid, likely non-alcoholic out of deference for her unborn child. The other went to Gracie who'd managed to find a way to his arms.

Once the rest of the family had their glasses, his father raised his own. "To Kensington and his bride, Anabelle. May the years ahead be full of joy, perseverance, love, and peace. To the newlyweds."

"To the newlyweds," the rest of the family echoed.

Kensington took a sip of his drink then, at the urging of his brothers and sisters, kissed his wife.

Their first night in San Majoria had been spent in Kensington's quarters in the main palace. The three-bedroom apartment had plenty of room and everything they needed to live on their own, except a full kitchen. He'd explained there was a shared one as well as a shared living area down the hall.

After all the excitement, they'd all slept in, except Gracie who spent time with Sofia and her nanny. Now they were on a boat headed for San Mediano, the medium-sized island of the main trio in San Majoria.

"Tell me about the Lowery House?" Anabelle asked from her spot in a chair near a window.

"It's the smallest house we own in San Majoria. Though," Kensington admitted, "that's a relative term. It's not far from the beach and has a private cove. That's where Astrid and Jordan met. I'm not sure what you want to know, really. We'll have a suite of rooms that are ours. For the most part, we each have our own rooms that we prefer in each of the houses we own."

"And we'll be in yours?"

"Maybe but probably not. My father, as monarch, gets the best suite, then it's usually chosen by oldest to youngest, but since we're actually going to be living here, we get to choose out of all of them. The rest of the house is sort of joint, but there won't be any of the family visiting very often."

Before he could tell her anything else, or she could ask any more questions, the sounds of the motor changed, and they seemed to slow down. A minute later, they were at the dock.

Gracie had spent the whole trip with her nose pressed against the glass, but when it was time to disembark, she wanted Kensington to carry her. As relieved as Anabelle was not to have to carry the little girl's weight as often, she hoped she wasn't being completely replaced.

Once on the dock, Kensington set Gracie down and knelt next to her. "See the bench over there?" he asked, pointing to one about ten feet onto dry land.

Gracie nodded.

"Why don't you see how fast you can get there?"

Without answering, Gracie took off at a run.

"Why...?" Anabelle started.

"Something I remembered I needed to mention to you. We need to consider a nanny for her. Even though I won't be doing many appearances for a while because of the Games, and you won't be doing any, it would be good to have someone she can get to know and is always our go-to when we do need to leave her for an engagement or an overnight trip. That way she can sleep in her own bed and be taken care of by someone she's comfortable with."

Anabelle had never seriously considered getting a nanny, though her grandfather had tried to insist she needed one. That was more so he could hire the nanny then control Gracie. He'd tried to play it off as concern for Anabelle and the crimp having a little girl would put in Anabelle's social life, but she would have none of it.

But what Kensington said made sense. "Then we should find one. I presume there's some sort of agency or somewhere we can get one who will keep her mouth closed about what's really going on?"

"My mother said she already had some ideas. Our nanny growing up is retired near here. She would likely be happy to come work for us at least until we get settled and figure out our long-term plans. Spend some time here every day and then more when we need her."

That sounded like a good plan. "Can I meet her before deciding?"

"Of course. I'll have my mother set it up."

They reached the bench where Gracie waited. She grabbed one of their hands in each of hers and started pulling. "Let's go!"

Laughing, she and Kensington allowed Gracie to pull them along. A few minutes later, the house came into view.

If this was the smallest house they owned, Anabelle wondered if she'd ever learn her way around the palace which was surely the biggest.

Four stories tall, though Anabelle wondered if they weren't

extra tall stories, it was covered with windows and surrounded by landscaping native to the islands.

Inside, she found her suspicions were correct. The ceiling had to be nearly twenty feet tall on the main floor. In the main room, a small group of men and women waited for them.

A man in a butler's uniform stepped forward and bowed at the waist. "Your Royal Highnesses, welcome to Lowery House."

"Thank you, George," Kensington answered for both of them. "We're happy to be here. I do believe I see a face or two that's new to me, and they're all new to my wife. Would you introduce us?"

The concept of royalty caring about the names of those who worked for them seemed odd to Anabelle, though it didn't surprise her that *Kensington* would ask.

George introduced everyone, though one man seemed to hang back a bit further. When she glanced at Kensington, his face was an unreadable mask.

Odd.

She'd have to ask him about it later.

"Thank you all for greeting us today," Kensington said after the introductions ended. "I know you all know the value of discretion, and have signed agreements to that effect. I would like to thank you in advance for keeping the status of my relationship with the princess and young Lady to yourself."

Did he know something she didn't? Or was he using the titles for ease of communication?

"I know the king sent a reminder this morning of your non-disclosure clauses. All we ask is that you remember them."

There were calls of "yes, sir," and nods all around, with a look or two of indignation to go with them. A couple of people were clearly offended that the reminder was given.

"If you will excuse us, the last couple of days have been quite long. My wife and I would like to freshen up. Thank you."

Kensington took her hand as Anabelle took Gracie's. The three of them walked down a hallway to a wide, sweeping set of stairs.

The second floor still had tall ceilings, though not as tall as the first floor.

"Why don't we go to my regular quarters? Later, we can look around and you can choose which one you'd like."

"Right now, Gracie needs her nap. Can she lay down in your room?"

Kensington hesitated. "How about across the hall?"

"That's fine." After showing Gracie where she'd be and tucking her sister in, Anabelle went back to Kensington's room.

"I'm glad we're here," he whispered as he pulled her close. "I'm glad you're with me. But I've wanted to do this for a couple of days, and the timing never seemed right."

And he kissed her.

Kensington leaned back in his desk chair and considered the man across from him. "My understanding is that you weren't supposed to be working when the family was here."

Bertrand didn't flinch. "That was when the family would only be here for a few days at a time. After forty years of exemplary service, broken up only by my time in military service, I made one grievous error. Your father asked that I serve as your assistant, at least temporarily, so I am not out of work indefinitely."

He did need a new assistant. "My father gave me the authority to make the final decision." Which Kensington wasn't sure he knew how to make. "Why don't you tell me what happened that day?"

"I was taking things outside for the dinner you were going to have for the Duke's birthday as well as Canadian Thanksgiving. I knew my hands would be overly full on the next trip, so I propped the door open. That Princess Sofia could find her way out was the furthest thing from my mind. I planned to close it as I went out. I offered my resignation as soon as the king told me what happened. After further discussion, and in light of my decades of otherwise exemplary service, this compromise was reached."

Kensington considered the older man. If his father trusted that what happened was a grievous, one-time, nearly-tragic error and Bertrand could be trusted, then Kensington would go with his father's judgment. "Very well. You will act as my assistant, but you aren't to be in the residential portion of the building without an escort and aren't to have any contact with my wife and sister-in-law."

"Of course, sir."

"In that case, we need to discuss plans for my arrivals and departures to be as clandestine as possible. I will be working almost exclusively on the Games which will require some travel, but I won't have many official appearances for a while, so I shouldn't need to come and go very often otherwise."

"Understood."

After a few more minutes of conversation, Bertrand brought up something Kensington hadn't thought about.

"Easter is in ten days. Will you be attending services here or in Cabo Juan-Eduardo?"

He didn't have a good answer for that question. "I don't know. I'll talk to my wife and see what she wants to do. I'd like to spend it with my family, but I doubt we'll be ready for the world to know about our marriage just yet. Is there a local church we could slip in and out of then go to the palace?"

Bertrand nodded. "There are a number where you could remain unnoticed in a balcony, back row, or alcove. I can make the arrangements, but it may be best if Miss Gracie stays here."

He made a good point. "I'll discuss it with Anabelle. We also need to set up interviews for nannies, though it would be better if we could find the best option from the beginning."

"Perhaps have Princess Astrid help with the process? If it becomes known that they are looking for a second nanny so that their current nanny can focus on Sofia when the new prince or princess arrives, you could be doing the initial interviews on her behalf. When you've found one you believe will be a good fit, have her meet with..." Bertrand hesitated. "My apologies, sir. I'm not certain of your wife's title."

Kensington sighed. "Neither am I. For now, until we know what titles my father will bestow on her, why don't we go with Duchess?" It seemed like a safe bet. If anything, Anabelle would later get an "upgrade" to princess. Better than starting with "princess" and finding out her title would be downgraded later. "Call Astrid's assistant to discuss a nanny search?"

"Except Princess Astrid and Duke Jordan haven't announced that they're expecting yet, so they can't publicly look for a new nanny. Perhaps there is someone already familiar with the family you can call on temporarily? A former nanny perhaps?"

"That's a good plan." He'd wondered if the other man would come up with the same plan. "Thank you." Another thought occurred to him. "I would like to attend a Palm Sunday and Good Friday service if possible."

"I'll see what I can find, but I believe it can be arranged."

Kensington dismissed Bertrand and turned to look out the window. This house, as close as it was to the water, didn't have many ocean views. This would be more complicated than he thought. From hiring a nanny to being able to attend church services, he hadn't considered those things. All he'd thought about was official appearances at fundraisers or events.

Bertrand surprised him. Kensington hadn't expected to want to keep the man on staff, but in their first real interaction, he was proving competent.

His phone buzzed. A smile crossed his face as he read the text from Anabelle. Enough work for the day.

Technically, they were on their honeymoon.

Three days later, they sat together in a small alcove in the balcony of a nearby church found by Bertrand and watched the service.

Back at Lowery House, they had lunch with Gracie who had loved exploring her new home.

Once she was asleep, Kensington stood on the balcony with Anabelle, looking out at the ocean in the distance.

"Thank you for making sure I could go today." She slid her hand through his elbow as he leaned against the railing and rested her head on his shoulder. "I know it's only been a few days and there's a good reason for it, but I'm kind of going a little stir crazy. Even with the grounds to wander around on, it's not the same as going out with people."

"I know, and today wasn't what you were hoping for, but it's the best we can do for right now. Next Sunday, we'll spend part of the day with my family. That's a crowd right there. We'll go to church here then go to the palace on San Minoria where my sister and Jordan live. We'll have lunch there. Once we get a nanny for Gracie, we can go out a bit more. Maybe have lunch or shop a little."

"That's something." Anabelle sighed. "I guess I never knew how much I liked being among people until I can't. I get why, but that doesn't mean I like it."

Kensington turned his head until he could kiss her. "I know, love. Soon. Once we figure out everything with Benjamin, Isaiah and your grandfather, then we can tell the world and do as we please."

She kissed him again, and he forgot all about the view.

Anabelle took a deep breath. The brief meeting earlier wasn't enough to calm her nerves. They were shot.

She hadn't even enjoyed Easter service as much as she normally did.

"They're going to love you." Kensington's breath was warm on her ear.

"I hope so." The boat pulled up to the dock Kensington told her was newly constructed, the last one having washed away in a storm several years earlier when no one had used the property on a regular basis for some time.

He held Gracie in his arms and took Anabelle's hand as they stepped onto the dock. With his fingers linked securely through hers, she felt a little more confident.

Kensington let go of her hand as they climbed the stairs to the door. She followed him through the hallway and up some more stairs. Voices and laughter came from one of the rooms.

A minute later, she wished she could hide behind Kensington a little longer.

"Good afternoon, dear." The king held out his hands and kissed her cheek. At least she'd actually talked with him before. "I know you met them briefly, but allow me to introduce the rest of my family again. My wife, Miriam."

Anabelle smiled and curtsied.

And then. "My other son, Harrison, and second daughter, Jacqueline Grace."

She nodded at them.

The king pointed to a family group a bit further to the side. "And my oldest daughter, Astrid, her husband, Jordan, and my granddaughter, Sofia."

"It's so nice to meet you again," the crown princess said with a smile. "Sofia will be so happy to have someone near enough her own age to play with."

"I'm sure Gracie will enjoy it as well."

The queen clapped her hands together. "Oh good! After lunch, we'll have an egg hunt on the beach."

"That sounds wonderful," Anabelle admitted. Gracie hadn't been part of one the year before.

The king looked to the side. "I believe lunch is ready."

Anabelle followed at the back of the group, trailing slightly behind Kensington. Fortunately, he showed her where to sit without making it obvious that she had no clue what the protocol actually was.

She found herself in a situation that was fairly unusual for her. One where she didn't immediately make friends with several people in the room. Normally, Anabelle defined extroverted. Seldom had she met a stranger.

But surrounded by the royal family something changed. Was it even that they were royalty? Or that they were royalty who were her in-laws?

"Anabelle, can you tell us a little more about yourself?" the queen asked.

She set her fork on her plate. "What would you like to know?"

As best she could tell, those present were seated in order of importance, with Astrid being near the king on one end, with her husband and daughter next to her, followed by the other sister. Kensington also sat next to his father, then Gracie and Anabelle, with his younger brother on her other side next to the queen at the foot.

"We know you're raising your sister, but I believe Kensington said you had a job as well? What do you do?"

Easy enough. "I didn't really need to work. My grandfather gave me enough of an allowance from my inheritance to live on, but I liked it." It was enough to live comfortably on, but she'd never be wealthy like her grandfather was.

"She works for her best friend," Kensington interjected.

"Worked," Anabelle corrected. "She owns a yarn store in Akushla. I worked for her three days a week. She needed someone who would work cheap to let her get some other work done. Otherwise, she'd be out front all day. Business generally was just busy enough she couldn't get any paperwork done, which is good, but meant she had to do a lot of it at night. Her brother helped with the books, but he's a newlywed and just finished university, so is establishing himself."

So much more than they needed to know.

"Do you knit? Or crochet?" Astrid asked. "I know Esther does, but I've always wanted to learn."

"You have?" Kensington asked. "You know you can buy sweaters, right? And that we basically live in the Caribbean. How often do you need a hat or scarf or gloves?"

"Never. But that's not the point." The Crown Princess turned back to Anabelle, dashing her hopes that they'd forget about her. "Could you teach me?"

"I actually met Princess Esther at the shop one day, but I'm afraid I won't be able to teach you. I can do something simple, but that's about it. I know enough about the yarns and weights and things to help others, but not to do much with or teach anyone else. If Rachel ever comes to visit, I'm sure she'd be more than happy to teach you, though."

"That's what YouTube is for," Harrison said from Anabelle's right. "You can learn how to do almost anything there."

From there the banter did move on, leaving Anabelle to her meal and helping Gracie.

"Where's Grandmother?" Kensington asked. "I thought she was joining us."

"She will be later," his father told them. "She had something else on her schedule for lunch."

Part of Anabelle looked forward to meeting the Queen Mother. Kensington spoke so highly of her and from everything she'd heard, Anabelle thought she'd like the woman - and the woman would love Gracie. That was important to Anabelle. That they all love her sister.

"Can you tell us what life is like in Eyjania?" the king asked. "What do the people think of Benjamin and his family?"

"Edward." The queen's sharp reprimand caught Anabelle by surprise. "I know you're concerned about Isaiah's influence on Benjamin, but this is not the time or place for that conversation."

The king's face remained impassive in light of his wife's

rebuke. "You're right, my dear. Anabelle, perhaps we can talk another time. I would love to get the insight of a modern Eyjanian on some of these things."

Anabelle didn't eat anything else. The roiling in her stomach wouldn't allow her to.

Eventually, the king pushed back from the table. "I think it would be an excellent time for that egg hunt, before these two young ladies need to take a nap."

Anabelle stood, along with everyone else and turned to pick up Gracie, only to find she was already situated in Kensington's arms.

Unneeded, Anabelle trailed the group and wondered when this day would end.

11

Two days after Easter, Kensington stood in his father's office. "I'm glad you decided to keep Bertrand on," his father told him as they gazed over the ocean.

"I'm still not convinced it was the right decision. He seems perfectly capable at his job, but is it really safe?"

His father gave him a sideways glare. "Do you think I would recommend it if I believed there was any sort of danger to you or your family?"

Kensington lifted one shoulder in acquiescence.

"It was a grievous error, nothing more. I believe, had the worst happened, he would have offered to plead guilty with the death penalty on the line. He's served the family since he was a teenager, starting part time in the kitchen as a dishwasher and working his way up, taking time off only for military service."

"And now he's my temporary secretary."

"It may be more permanent than you plan."

"How so?"

"The Games are coming up soon. You will be working on them extensively. You need someone who is up to speed on everything and stays that way. Changing assistants mid-stream wouldn't be wise."

"I already did by moving to Bertrand."

"True." His father made a rare concession. "However, you know why that was necessary."

Kensington didn't respond. His last assistant had been caught talking repeatedly with a reporter. As far as anyone knew, no information had been exchanged, but the contact hadn't been reported properly either. The man had been dismissed immediately prior to Kensington's trip to Eyjania. Until his return, he'd been sharing Harrison's assistant, albeit long distance.

"You think Bertrand is more trustworthy than he was?"

"Infinitely."

It took everything in Kensington to stifle a sigh. "Very well. If you trust him with my family's life, then I suppose there's no reason why I shouldn't."

"Very good." His father reached for something on a side table and held up an envelope. "This is an invitation to Princess Yvette of Mevendia's wedding in June."

Kensington blinked. "Is she even eighteen yet? I thought she was Harrison's age."

"She is. Mevendia still has marriage contracts. Your mother and I attended Prince Malachi's wedding last January. King Antonio of Mevendia and King Richard of Ravenzario signed a contract when Yvette and Prince Nicklaus of Ravenzario were quite young. It's still in effect."

He tried to remember the story behind those families. "Richard, his wife, and Nicklaus were all killed in a car accident years ago, weren't they? Christiana has been queen as long as I can remember."

"Correct, but the wedding is apparently still being planned. Perhaps they're going to have a celebration of life or something instead. I don't know the details. I just know 'representatives of the San Majorian royal family' were invited."

"So they don't particularly care who goes?"

He sat in one of the leather armchairs facing the window. "That's my read on it. I may give Antonio a call. If it's a celebration of life for the three of them and the nanny who was also in the car, then it would be best if your mother and I went since we actually knew them. If it's something else, I may send Jacqueline Grace and Harrison."

"That might be the better option."

"With Astrid's pregnancy, I think she'd rather stay home by then. You'll be in the middle of the Games, so you and Anabelle are out."

"Jacqueline Grace and Harrison it is. When are Astrid and Jordan making their announcement?"

"Next week, I believe. The papers are already speculating."

"They've been speculating for months, haven't they?"

"Since before the wedding," his father confirmed. "The picture of the two of them kissing in the surf didn't help."

"Anabelle and I won't be doing any of that where it could get caught on camera."

"Invitations to Harrison's graduation party were sent out today."

"I'll have Bertrand watch for it. Maybe we can make it."

His father glared at him. "You'll be there. It's already on your calendar, as is the graduation itself."

Kensington smirked as much as he dared. "I know. I'll be there. Anabelle's attendance depends on what we've found about her grandfather and any potential threats against the two of them. If we're not sure, they stay home."

"Agreed. So far there's nothing."

He couldn't read his father's tone of voice. "Is that good?"

"I'm not sure. It could be. I'd feel a lot better if we found a little bit of evidence of *something* so that we'd feel more confident that we found all of the evidence rather than her grandfather being that good at hiding everything. I'd have expected to find something about how he's keeping an eye on them or having someone in San Majoria do it for him. But nothing? That seems odd."

When he put it that way... "I would appreciate it if you'd keep me updated if you do find anything."

"Of course."

Kensington stood. "I need to get back to San Mediano. Grandmother is meeting me and Anabelle for lunch. I really don't want to miss it because it's likely the last one until after the Games. I've just got too much to do, unfortunately. I'll be having business lunches many days and want to spend as much of my time as I can with Anabelle and Gracie outside of work hours. I'm hoping Grandmother will be able to make it to San Mediano for dinner, but the weekly lunches will have to wait."

"I'll walk you out." His father pushed to his feet. "I quite enjoyed my time with Anabelle and Gracie on Easter. I know your mother did as well."

Speaking of Easter... "We missed Esther. I know you're not telling us what's going on with her, but is she okay?"

His father sighed. Kensington took that to mean things could be a lot better. "She has challenges to work through right now, ones best handled far from the media spotlight. She'll be fine."

Which meant she wasn't right now. He wondered if Harrison knew what was going on. "You don't need to walk me out, but thanks for the offer."

His father gave him a big hug and held on for several seconds.

"Come see us on San Mediano. Gracie hasn't stopped talking about the egg hunt and the whole family."

"Perhaps." The phone on his father's desk rang. "Have a safe trip back," he said as he reached for the receiver. "I'll see you soon."

Kensington let himself out of his father's office and nodded to the assistants in the outer portion before heading to the portico. From there, it was a short drive to the docks and then a boat ride home.

He wondered if Anabelle was nervous about lunch with Grandmother. They'd only met in passing on Sunday so this would be their first real interaction. Kensington knew they would love each other if Anabelle could calm down enough to be herself.

He sent her a text to tell her he was thinking of her, then opened his tablet case to get to work.

Why was she so nervous? At this rate, Anabelle's stomach wouldn't be settled enough to eat anything at lunch with the Queen Mother. Everyone in Kensington's family had been very nice and accepting of her, but this woman was the matriarch. Sure, the king was... well, the king, but even he wouldn't dare cross his mother. Most good kings probably wouldn't.

"Ma'am?"

Anabelle looked up from the picture she was coloring with Gracie. The picture she was trying to concentrate on coloring anyway. "Yes, George?"

"The Queen Mother's car will be arriving in a few minutes. I thought you would like to greet her."

It was a suggestion, but not at the same time. "Is Elise available to watch Gracie?" The nanny had worked for the royal family when the children were young and had retired, but was helping out for the time being.

"I'm certain Her Majesty would welcome the young lady as well."

Also not really a suggestion. Anabelle put her crayon back in the box. "It's time to go, Gracie. Remember Kensington's grandmother? You met her Sunday."

Gracie shrugged and kept coloring.

"Her name is Grace, just like yours."

"I 'member."

"She's going to be here in a few minutes, and we need to go say hello to her."

Gracie gave a dramatic sigh, but put her crayon away. Anabelle took her by the hand and followed George. She'd learned her way around most of the house, but there were a few areas she still wasn't sure about. Getting to the front entrance was one of those things since she hadn't used it yet.

All of her comings and goings had been via a side entrance, and there had been precious few of those.

George didn't actually say anything, but still managed to indicate where Anabelle and Gracie should stand.

Anabelle crouched near Gracie and straightened her clothes. "Remember your curtsy?"

Gracie nodded and scratched the stork bite on the back of her neck. Anabelle needed to check it again later. The red spot/birthmark had been a bit dry lately.

"When the Queen Mother gets here, we both curtsy, all right?"

She nodded again as Anabelle finger combed her fine blond hair off her face. Anabelle licked her thumb and used it to clean Gracie's cheek before standing at the sound of a car pulling up outside.

"Where's Kensington?" she asked George.

"On his way back from San Majoria after a meeting with the king. He should arrive shortly."

The tall wooden door was pulled open by a staff member who stood hidden behind it as Queen Grace walked in.

Anabelle squeezed Gracie's hand and curtsied, bowing her head as she did. Out of the corner of her eye, she saw Gracie's attempt. Not bad for someone who hadn't had much practice.

"Oh, bother."

Anabelle looked up at the queen's words. "Pardon?"

"I am not the queen, and even when I was, I was the Queen Consort, not the monarch." She pointed at Anabelle. "No more curtsies, understand?"

Anabelle managed a weak smile. "Yes, ma'am."

The queen raised an eyebrow. "How about Grandmother? All of my grandchildren call me that."

Anabelle swallowed her sigh of relief. "Of course, Grandmother."

Grandmother turned to Gracie. "Now, we met the other day, but just for a moment. I do believe we share the same name."

"Uh huh. G'acie."

With a chuckle, Grandmother reached for Gracie's hand. "I don't think anyone ever called me Gracie, but it certainly suits you." She looked to the side. "Good afternoon, George. Where are we having lunch today?"

"The east balcony, ma'am."

"Oh good. It has a lovely view. One of my favorites."

Anabelle had no idea which balcony that was, so she let the former queen lead the way. She tried to stay only a half-step or so behind, that way it wouldn't look like she was lost.

"You probably need a map, don't you?" Grandmother glanced back over her shoulder. "I remember what that was like."

"I'm learning."

"Of course you are. You won't have to think twice about where you want to go before long." Grandmother looked down at Gracie. "I bet you know your way around some, don't you?"

Gracie smiled. "I does, G'anmama G'acie."

The queen stopped dead in her tracks and threw back her head for a full-throated laugh. "Oh, my dear! I love that! Grandmama Gracie has a ring to it, doesn't it? G and G. The alliteration is wonderful."

"Gigi," Gracie pronounced. "I call you Gigi?"

"It is a bit less of a mouthful than Grandmama Gracie." The queen nodded decisively. "Gigi it is."

They resumed their walk toward the east balcony.

"Do you know what we're having for lunch?" Grandmother asked.

"I'm afraid not. Kensington spoke with Cook this morning, I do know that, but not what was decided."

"No matter. Cook always does a wonderful job. I'm certain it will be delicious."

"I'm an okay cook," Anabelle admitted. "But it still seems odd to me to have someone cook for us so I try to do it myself whenever I have time." Which was always. "I'm kind of surprised Kensington hasn't insisted on Cook making our meals, or at least tutoring me."

They reached the balcony. "I'm certain Kensington appreciates your efforts."

Anabelle let loose with a full-fledged grin. "That sounds like a polite way of saying he chokes down my efforts because he doesn't want to offend me."

Grandmother just shrugged as Gracie ran to look over the railing at the edge of the balcony. She turned to look at Anabelle. "I am glad for this chance to get to know both of you. You are always welcome at my weekly lunches with Kensington, though he's already warned me they will be coming to a temporary end until the Games are over. Perhaps you and I can try to have lunch together instead." She bowed her head slightly. "If that fits in your schedule."

As if there was anything else on her schedule. "I would love that."

By the time he made it to the east balcony, Kensington was much later than he'd hoped to be. He needn't have worried, though. Anabelle and Gracie were laughing with his grandmother like they'd been family all along.

"There you are!" Grandmother looked up from her lunch as he

walked out. "We didn't wait for you when they told us they weren't sure how long you'd be."

"I'm glad you didn't." His kissed his grandmother on the cheek then turned to do the same to Anabelle.

"Do you think I don't know you kiss your wife? It's all right."

Anabelle gave him a smirk but turned her face for a quick peck.

"Kenny! Where mine?" Gracie reached for him.

"Kenny?" Amusement filled his grandmother's voice. "I like it almost as much as Gigi."

Kensington hugged Gracie and kissed her cheek before setting her back down. "Who's Gigi?"

"I am. It's what Gracie calls me now."

A smiled crossed his face. "Do I get to call you Gigi now too?"

"No, you don't, young man. Only Gracie. And perhaps Sofia. And the new baby." Grandmother arched an eyebrow his direction. "And any other great-grandchildren who come along."

He took his seat as a member of the staff brought him his food. "I'll be sure to let Astrid know."

As he ate, Kensington learned his grandmother and Anabelle planned to get together without him for the next several months. He was happy to hear it. It would be good for Anabelle to have time with other people.

That gave him an idea. But it had to be in just a couple hours. When Grandmother left, they put Gracie down for her nap. Elise stayed with her, but Kensington led Anabelle to the side entrance where the car waited.

"We're driving ourselves," he told her and handed her a floppy beach hat. "But this way no one should know who we are."

With a baseball hat tugged low over his eyes and sunglasses waiting for him when he parked the car, Kensington left the palace. Security would make sure they weren't followed by any reporters. Fortunately, his presence on the island had gone mostly unnoticed.

"Where are we going?"

"Just to a market not too far away. It won't be anything exciting, but it's out of the house at least." Maybe he could find a trinket for her. His mother had loved the figurine he'd picked up in Eyjania. He needed to remember to get something for her from one of the souvenir shops after the Games started.

He parked in the only empty spot he could find, far from the entrance, because he wasn't using his clout to do this.

By the time he emerged from the vehicle, Anabelle waited for him by the rear. He took her hand and decided to simply enjoy doing something as trivial as walking hand-in-hand.

As they wandered through the market, Kensington noticed a couple of sideways glances at him, but no one said anything and none of them lingered. As far as he could tell, no cell phone pictures were taken either.

The market was near a dock for cruise ships, and, as such, was filled with tourists. Though not run by the cruise industry like in some countries, many of the shops would appeal to the foreigners. That was one reason he chose this location. Fewer locals who might recognize him.

"Where do you want to go first?" he asked as they stopped to look around.

"It doesn't matter."

Three sides of the marketplace square held buildings filled with shops and restaurants. The fourth, toward the dock, held a building where passengers would check back into their ships.

"Maybe we can find something for Gracie," she suggested. "A toy or puzzle that she'd like."

"We can certainly look." That sort of thing was more likely found in the middle of the marketplace. The center was filled with vendors like a street fair, though more permanent.

Some of the booths held goods clearly made by the artists who manned them. A few contained food local to the islands, and San Mediano in particular.

"What is that?" Anabelle asked pointing at one of the food booths. "It looks delicious."

"I think it's kind of like a fish taco, but it's not something I'm familiar with," he told her, his voice quiet. If he was recognized, it wouldn't do for him to be on record admitting he wasn't sure what a local dish was.

They watched as the woman shredded a bit of fish, plopped some sauce on it, and wrapped it in something that looked kind of like a tortilla but wasn't.

"Try one?" she asked Kensington as she handed a plate of four to an American family from one of the ships.

"Sure. Just one please. We already had a big lunch, but a snack would hit the spot." If they liked it, they could always get another one.

She made it the same way as the previous one, but this time she tossed some shredded cheese on top. The other family must have asked for it without.

Kensington handed over a couple of bills to a teenager working with the woman then took the plate from her.

Anabelle pointed to a small table being vacated by a couple whose shirts proclaimed them to be newlyweds. Once seated, Anabelle bowed her head and closed her eyes for a moment, then reached for the taco.

She took a bite and handed it to him as she chewed. He watched the reactions cross her face. Finally, she swallowed and shrugged at the same time. "Not bad. Probably not something I'd eat daily or even weekly though."

Kensington took a bite and let the flavors roll around on his tongue. Definitely a local fish, though he wasn't certain which one. The tart flavor of the sauce prevented that, but complemented it at the same time. He agreed with her assessment and took another bite before handing it back to her.

"I wonder if the cook could take the basic recipe and make a few tweaks," Anabelle wondered before she took another bite. "It's a bit too spicy or something for my taste, but just a little less, and I think I'd like it more."

"I'm sure she could." He opened the little bit left and took a picture of the inside. "She probably even knows what it is."

He took one more bite then let her have the rest. Finished, they started back toward the artisanal section of the market to find something for Gracie.

12

With her hand snug in Kensington's as they wandered around the market, Anabelle felt more normal than she had in a long time. Quite a feat given she was wearing a giant hat so no one would get a picture of her if they recognized Kensington.

The fish thing had been all right, but she wasn't sure it would sit too well in her stomach. She generally didn't do anything too spicy or tart or whatever that was.

They walked down the walk between the vendors in the middle and the shops on the other side. Nothing stood out to her. Kensington didn't seem to notice anything either.

Next they went down the center aisle, with vendors on either side.

"What about that?" she asked, pointing at a wooden puzzle set. "She loves dogs, though we've never had one."

Kensington picked it up. It wouldn't be too hard, but would hold up through whatever she could dish out - and probably a few other kids, too.

Grandmother's insinuation about more great-grandchildren

came to mind and caused Anabelle's face to heat. They hadn't talked about children, not really. Just that they both wanted more someday. That discussion shouldn't really take place until their relationship had gone public.

"Are you all right?" Kensington asked, a bag dangling from his hand. He must have bought the puzzle when she wasn't paying enough attention.

She turned on her brightest smile. "I'm fine. Did you see anything else she might like."

"Not at that booth."

They continued wandering slowly, taking it all in until Kensington pointed at some homemade dolls. "What about one of those?"

Anabelle let go of his hand and picked one up. "Maybe." Did Gracie have a real doll? She thought through all of the toys back at Lowery House. "I don't think she has anything similar."

They poked through the dolls until they found one that at least sort of resembled Gracie. With yellow strips of fabric for hair and bright blue stitching for her eyes, it nearly matched Gracie.

Kensington paid for it, then for two others that resembled each of them.

"That one has too much hair." Anabelle ran her fingers over the boy doll's head. "You've got far less." She bit her lip to hide her smile.

Kensington clutched his chest. "You wound me, love."

She let the grin out. "Truth hurts." Anabelle didn't mind Kensington's thinning hair, but wasn't completely sure how he felt about it. His reaction told her what she needed to know.

As they walked away from the booth, his arm wrapped around her waist and pulled her close to his side.

"Just wait," he whispered. "Your sons, or maybe your grandsons or both, are going to have a hairline that resembles mine."

She could feel her face color again at the implications.

"Maybe," was all she could manage to squeak out. "Or maybe they'll get the hair genes from my side of the family."

He kissed the side of her head before loosening his hold on her. "I'd be okay with that."

Before she could suggest a dessert or drink of some kind, Kensington's phone buzzed in his pocket. She knew he'd told Bertrand to hold as many of his calls as possible, so it was either someone who had his personal number or something that couldn't wait.

He pulled it out of his pocket and sighed as he read it. "I guess that's it. I've got to get back."

Anabelle didn't say anything. Grateful as she was to get out from behind palace walls as it were, she wished for more time. More interaction with other people.

She understood, even agreed with the caution, but still chafed under the restrictions.

By the time they returned to Lowery House, Kensington was on the phone with a vendor or venue or someone who, for the moment, had a more important hold on his time.

How long until the Games were over, and they could settle into a regular routine, whatever that looked like? They wouldn't start for at least ten or eleven weeks, at the beginning of July. Meantime, she knew she'd see less and less of Kensington until it was over.

Upstairs, Gracie still slept. Suddenly weary, Anabelle stretched out on the bed she usually shared with Kensington and let herself take a nap, something she rarely did.

She woke feeling somewhat better. Gracie loved the puzzle and the set of dolls resembling their family.

"Where Kenny?" the girl asked as they started coloring again.

"He's in a meeting." Or on a phone call. Or doing something important regarding the Games. "Remember? He has to work a lot for the next few weeks then we'll get to see him a lot more."

Gracie nodded. "'Kay. Where Gigi?"

"Gigi went back to her house. Remember the first castle we went to when we got here? When we very first met Astrid and Sofia and Jordan and everyone else?"

Another nod, though Anabelle wasn't srue she really remembered. "That's where Gigi lives. She's going to come see us whenever she can, though."

"My go see her," Gracie pronounced. "My go 'morrow."

Anabelle didn't verbally approve or disapprove of the plan, but knew it wouldn't happen. Gracie would likely forget about the whole thing by then.

Instead, she changed the subject to the ocean scene they were coloring. She had Gracie identify the sea life as best she could. There were several Gracie didn't know, but she did know quite a few.

"We go beach?" Gracie asked.

"Sure." Anabelle used the turquoise to color the water. "Tomorrow we'll go down to the cove." The spot where Princess Astrid met Jordan.

"Kenny come," Gracie pronounced.

"No, sweetheart. Kensington won't be able to come. He has to work, remember?"

Those four words were likely going to define her relationship with her husband until the Games ended. If only she had something she could do to help, or fundraising events she could attend, or pretty much anything she could do besides spend her days with a little girl. Though she adored Gracie, this was going to drive Anabelle crazy.

Kensington fastened his cuff link and tried to ignore the glare from Anabelle. "No. You're not going. Neither is Gracie."

"Of course Gracie isn't. She wouldn't sit still through a graduation. I'm not going to ask her to, but why can't I go?"

"Because the investigation into your grandfather isn't finished."

She threw her hands in the air. "It's been nearly two months, Kensington. I'm sick of sitting around here. I want out of the house. I want to see people. Streaming church on my computer doesn't count."

He sighed. "I'm sorry, Anabelle. It's not my choice to make. Security has said the two of you need to stay put a bit longer."

"Then why didn't you tell me?"

The hurt in her voice caught his attention and he looked up to notice she was wearing a nice outfit, much nicer than she usually wore around the house.

He blew out a breath. "I'm sorry, Annie. I didn't know you even knew about it, much less thought you'd be able to go. Even if we were sure about your grandfather, my brother's graduation isn't the time or place to show up together. It would only take away from his day, and I don't think either of us want that."

Her shoulders slumped. "I guess not, but it was on the calendar with just a date and time, nothing about who it was for like there usually is for your appointments."

Kensington moved to stand in front of her and rested his hands on her hips, tugging her closer. "I'm sorry, love. I don't know who added it to the calendar or why it didn't specify who would be attending."

She snaked her arms around his waist and rested her cheek against his chest. "I know it's not your fault, but would you do me favor?"

"If I can." He'd learned long ago not to promise something so open-ended, not until he actually heard the request.

"Until this house arrest is over, if there's anything on the calendar that I would be at under other circumstances, would you let me know for sure whether I'll be in attendance or not?"

"It's not really house arrest, love. I know you know that. I know it feels like that. I'll do my best to make sure you know about things ahead of time." He held her in his arms for several minutes before he had to let her go. With a soft kiss, he took his leave.

Thanks to a couple of meetings he couldn't postpone, there wasn't time for him to take one of the boats to San Majoria. Instead, a helicopter flew him straight to the palace in Cabo Juan-Eduardo. From there, he joined the rest of his family, except Harrison, for the trip to a nearby stadium for the ceremony.

Rather than sitting in the stands with the rest of the families, this time, his family remained separate for security reasons.

Though everyone coming in was subjected to a metal detector and cursory search of their bags, having his family away from the rest of the crowd would make security easier not only on the security team, but on the rest of the crowd as well.

"Why couldn't Anabelle come?" he asked his father as they stood behind the glass looking down into the venue that would hold a gymnastics meet in a few weeks.

"Because this glass isn't tinted or bullet-proof." His father glanced over at him. "And, to be quite frank, I don't trust the two of you to stay away from each other in this kind of situation. It's far too easy to forget that there are eyes on you constantly here because there's a barrier. The revelation that there's a special woman in your life, even without the marriage part, would take over your brother's day. I refuse to let that happen."

Kensington stifled a sigh. He'd suspected something similar, but at least it wasn't that Anabelle could have come, and he'd misinterpreted something.

Promptly at noon, the procession of students began. It took several minutes for Kensington to find his brother.

On stage.

"Is Harrison giving a speech?" he asked his father.

"Not that I'm aware of, but it certainly seems he's being singled out for one reason or another."

Kensington knew both of his parents, as well as Harrison, would want the recognition to be for something worthy, not because of genetics.

"There's nothing in the program." His father handed a copy over. "Unless he's one of the unnamed award recipients or presenters."

The graduating class finished filing in and the rest of the ceremony began.

Kensington sat with his family, though his father stood when they recognized him as a special guest. About halfway through the pre-diploma portion of the ceremony, Harrison stood.

"It is my honor to present the award for most inspirational student. Every year, the graduating class, with input from the other classes, chooses a student who has inspired all of us to work harder, try longer, and be better people." He launched into a story about overcoming and persevering.

Halfway through, Kensington recognized who the recipient was, though he didn't know her name. Injured in a car accident two years earlier, and left paralyzed, the young woman had worked hard to graduate with her peers. She'd also taken the lead in one of the Special Olympics-type teams, though Kensington couldn't remember which one. Harrison's speech had been drowned out by cheers and hollering from the graduating class as the girl, in her wheelchair, made her way to the stage.

Wearing one of the biggest smiles Kensington had ever seen on him, Harrison gave her the rolled-up parchment and a pin she could display or wear. Harrison shook her hand and leaned closer to whisper something that made her smile widen.

They both returned to their spots and the presentations went on.

After graduation ended, the whole family gathered for photos in the same area the rest of the students seemed to gravitate to.

Harrison took pictures with his friends and seemed reluctant to leave.

Kensington understood. He'd felt the same way. University out of the country would offer Harrison more anonymity than any of the other siblings had achieved locally. However, with the new phase of life would come new, different responsibilities, including a more active role in the "family business" when he wasn't away at school.

Wrapping his brother in a bear hug, Kensington told him how proud they all were, but all he really wanted to do was return to San Mediano, a certain brunette, and his favorite blond little girl.

13

"Kensington, except for church around Easter and the shopping trip, we haven't left the grounds in over a month. I haven't even seen your grandmother." The former queen had events she couldn't reschedule that interfered with their plan to have lunch together.

Anabelle crossed her arms over her chest and glared at him. "I'm not asking to go to some giant festival or street market, I just want to take Gracie to the park. It's a three-minute drive and that includes getting off the grounds. We could walk in under ten minutes. She just wants to play with some other kids, even for a little while. Send a whole team of security with us. Send every off-duty cop you can find. I don't care, but I need out of this house before I go completely stir crazy."

Kensington stared at her from across his desk. Not exactly how she'd envisioned this conversation going when she first planned it in her head, but oh well.

"I'll talk to Rob and see what he can work out." He leaned forward and rested his arms on the desk. "I know you don't like being confined to the house, but I also know you're still worried about what your grandfather might do."

"I know, but you said last night your security teams hadn't found anything and said they don't think there's any reason to be concerned."

"They also said they wanted to wait a couple more weeks to see if anything turned up. Benjamin and Isaiah aren't happy still. I have no idea what deal my father worked out with them, but so far, it's not enough to make security chill out. None of us can imagine Benjamin being behind anything, but no one's sure just how far Isaiah will go after someone makes him mad."

"But your family? Wouldn't his own people be livid if he went after the royal family of San Majoria?"

"Probably, but who knows if that matters to him? He's not king." His eyes were full of compassion. "I will try to get a few hours for you."

"Then I won't whine about the next couple of weeks," she conceded. Honestly, she'd expected a "no." She took a step toward him and smiled. "Thank you."

"I just want you both to be safe."

"I know. I do, too. But no one knows we're here with you."

Kensington stood and walked around his desk, pulling her into his arms. "I still don't think we can be too careful at this point." He kissed her softly. "I kind of like both of you, and until we're sure..." Another kiss. "I'll talk to Rob right now, though. I know it's important to you."

"Thank you." She stood in his arms for another minute. "I'll let you get back to work."

"Thanks, love. Why don't we have lunch together today? Just the three of us. Maybe take a picnic to the gazebo."

"That sounds wonderful."

He kissed her again then moved back. "I'll talk to Rob," he promised again, "and see you in a couple hours."

His phone rang, and she left, not wanting to bother him any

further. Gracie and Elise, former nanny for Kensington and his siblings, were in the garden. They spent an hour out there, with Gracie running around playing tag with an imaginary friend.

Of all the things Anabelle regretted, it was a lack of friends for Gracie. She wanted the little girl to have a friend or two she could count on, who she could grow up with. Anabelle still had contact with several of her childhood friends. She'd been in touch with Rachel often, the only one who knew everything about her parents, and grandparents, and Gracie, and even Kensington.

Anabelle wished she and Rachel could get together, but knew how unlikely that was to happen anytime soon. Maybe, after the park went well, she could talk to Kensington about flying Rachel and her family to San Majoria for a few days.

Two days later, she finally got her first wish.

"Are you ready to go, ma'am?"

"We are." Anabelle held Gracie's hand as they walked to a car with dark tinted windows. A minute later, Gracie was buckled into a car seat, and they pulled out of the garage.

In an effort to keep from attracting attention, only one other car would go with them. A total of four guards would be there, though it wouldn't surprise Anabelle if there were more she didn't know about.

The short drive took several times longer than it should have because the drivers decided to take a circuitous route. It should have taken three minutes, but took almost fifteen instead.

Finally, she helped Gracie out of the seat, and they took off for the playground under the watchful eye of Rob and his men. For half an hour, she watched as Gracie played on the jungle gym and caught her when she went down the slide.

For whatever reason, the playground was devoid of any other children, but Anabelle was okay with that this time. If this went well, maybe they would let the two of them go out more often.

And that's what happened.

Over the next week, she and Gracie ventured out again and

again. Each time they went to one of the parks on the island, choosing a different one each time. A week after the first outing, they were at a playground on the other side of the island.

"Annie, look!" Gracie pointed to another little girl coming down the slide.

"Go on," Anabelle encouraged her. Gracie ran across the grass until she reached the jungle gym. By the time Anabelle reached the bench to the side of the play area, Gracie and the other girl were running around playing tag.

"She's adorable. Are you new to the area?" The woman sitting on the next bench over smiled at Anabelle.

"We haven't lived here long. Gracie hasn't had a chance to make any friends yet. She's going to be ecstatic and talk about this for days."

"I understand. It's only been six months since we moved. I found a neighborhood playgroup finally, though, and that's helped."

"That sounds wonderful," Anabelle admitted, though she knew Rob would never go for such a thing. But for now, she was going to enjoy her time with a grownup who wasn't also an employee or Kensington.

If only it could happen more often.

The change in Anabelle over the last two weeks since the park visits started was remarkable. Kensington sat in a chair in their room, and she curled up next to him, sipping her morning coffee as they talked about their plans for the day.

"There is something I'd like to do tomorrow," she told him. The hesitance in her voice set him on edge.

"What's that?"

"You know that first lady I met?"

He nodded.

"We saw her and her daughter again yesterday, along with one of her friends. They invited me to a Mommy and Me Play Date at the Turtle Sanctuary tomorrow. They know Gracie isn't my daughter, but they want us to come. I'd really like to."

"What does Rob say?"

"I don't know. I wanted to talk to you first."

Kensington shrugged. "It's up to him. I'm okay if you go, if he says it's okay." He pulled her closer. "It won't always be like this, love. You'll always have security, but the idea that you actually need permission will lessen with time."

She kissed his chin. "I know."

They still hadn't found *anything*, and that made Kensington, his father, and the security teams nervous, but he wouldn't tell Anabelle that. Not until there was actually something to tell.

Anabelle sat up then kissed him. "I'm going to find Rob." She turned when she reached the door. "They're having a family potluck dinner thing this weekend."

She didn't ask if he wanted to go or if they should, just told him it existed. Going would run the risk of outing Anabelle and Gracie as his new family. Staying home would run the risk of alienating his wife. "Mention it to Rob, and I'll talk to him about it later."

The smile made it worthwhile. "Thanks." She turned again and left.

That afternoon, Rob approved the turtle sanctuary, but hadn't decided about the family event yet. The next day came quickly, but Kensington had obligations of his own, which took him to San Majoria.

"Are you ready, sir?" Bertrand poked his head in the office. "Your meeting is in ninety minutes." And most of those would be spent traveling across the water.

They'd become more lax about coming and going in secret, but Kensington hadn't spent as much of his time with Anabelle and

Gracie as he would have liked anyway. He made it home most evenings, but most of his days were spent on San Majoria or San Minoria dealing with other Games related issues. They were only a couple months away, and his time would be more in demand as they got closer.

Something uneasy settled inside him as the boat sped across the water. He needed to see them, but wasn't sure if that was a good idea for several reasons. "Will we drive by the turtle sanctuary?" he asked as they transferred to the car. If they wouldn't, it didn't matter.

"It's on the way."

"I'd like to stop for a few minutes if we have time."

"Yes, sir."

Kensington looked over some papers while they drove. Slamming brakes and screeching tires sent his seat belt into locked mode and his papers flying to the floor.

"What was that?" he asked.

"Crazy driver, sir." The man pressed a finger to his ear. Kensington could see his demeanor change. "To the palace," he barked. "Now!"

The driver squealed the tires again as they went back into motion.

"Get down!" the security guard yelled. "In the floor."

"What happened?" Kensington didn't follow the instructions but looked toward the sanctuary. "Anabelle! Gracie!"

The two men exchanged a look. The guard said something Kensington couldn't hear, then said, "The sanctuary."

They reached the front Kensington could see Rob out front, mouth moving - likely barking orders at others through his ear piece.

"What. Happened?" Kensington demanded as the car came to a stop.

He didn't get an answer.

Sirens screamed in the distance, coming closer with every second.

They drove straight onto the concrete, stopping by the door and foregoing social niceties that said to avoid such a thing. A small knot of security personnel walked toward them. Kensington knew he should wait, but didn't. He bolted out of the car and toward the people he prayed would be protected within.

"Anabelle! Gracie!" he called as he got closer.

The team parted enough for him to see Anabelle and another woman being held up and helped by two other women.

"Kensington!" Anabelle tore free and flung her arms around him. "They took her."

Dread filled his core. "Who?"

"They took Gracie," she sobbed. "And another girl."

His mind shifted to overdrive. If they took two girls, maybe it was random. Maybe the threat of more dire consequences that came with the abduction of a member of the royal family would lead to their release. If they'd been abducted for ransom from a well-to-do looking group of moms and children, they'd be all right. It happened other places.

It rarely happened in San Majoria.

"It's my grandfather."

Kensington tightened his hold on her. "What makes you say that?"

"I just know it was."

"We have to go, sir."

Hands grabbed at them, rushing them back to the car he'd come from. Before they were even buckled in, the car accelerated.

His mind couldn't process what Anabelle had said.

Someone had taken Gracie?

With sirens wailing in front and behind them, the trip to the palace was blessedly short.

The car didn't stop under the portico, but went straight to the garrison. From there, they were ushered to a nearby sitting room.

Most of Kensington's family descended on them. They'd met Anabelle exactly twice, but his sisters surrounded her like she'd always been one of them.

His father, younger brother, and Jordan wrapped their arms around Kensington.

"We're going to figure this out," his father promised. "We don't know what happened, but we'll figure it out."

"What about Jenny?" Anabelle's panicked voice caught their attention. "Where's her mother?"

"On her way," Father promised. "We'll search for both of the girls like they were our own."

"Sir?" A member of the public relations staff came into the room. "The press is asking for a statement."

The king sighed. "Then I'll give them one."

ensington's arm around her waist, holding her tightly to his side, was the only thing keeping Anabelle upright. Her arms were wrapped around her waist, hugging herself in hopes that she wouldn't lose her lunch all over the reporters.

"I have a statement to make. I will not be taking any questions." The king's tone would brook no arguments. "A short time ago, two little girls were taken from the San Majoria Turtle Sanctuary. One of the girls, Lady Grace Gregorson, is the sister-in-law of my son, Prince Kensington, and is being raised by Kensington and his wife, Anabelle, Duchess of Pennington, after the death of their parents over a year ago. Kensington and Anabelle eloped on Athmetis six weeks ago. We will not discuss that decision or the decision to keep it private at this time. Also at this time, it is not known if Lady Grace and the other little girl were targeted or simply victims of opportunity. All branches of law enforcement are working together to find them. Photos will be released momentarily. If you have any information, please call the number provided. A reward is being offered for information leading to the whereabouts of the girls. We ask for your prayers during this difficult time. More information will be provided as it is available."

Pressure from Kensington's arm turned Anabelle back toward the door. They followed his father and ignored the questions called after them. Once back in the security conference room where they'd been before walking to the press conference she saw her new friend's tear-streaked face.

"Where is she? Where is my daughter?" Caitlin looked about like Anabelle felt.

"We're doing everything we can." King Edward stood in front of Caitlin and rested his hands on her shoulders. "We won't stop looking until we find them safe and sound."

Caitlin looked at Anabelle, anguish in her eyes. "Who are you?"

Kensington answered before Anabelle could. "She's my wife. Gracie is my sister-in-law, but no one outside of my family and trusted staff, three people in Athmetis, and a few people in Eyjania know that we're married."

"They don't even look alike. If someone wanted Gracie, why would they take Jenny?"

A man Anabelle recognized from Caitlin's pictures was ushered through the door. With a small cry, Caitlin launched herself into his arms.

"Ladies, I do need both of you to go with security and tell them everything you remember." The king looked apologetic, but Anabelle knew it needed to be done.

Not that it would do any good. She hadn't seen anything. It all happened so fast. One minute, she was talking to Caitlin and two of the other women while six kids splashed in the water. Gracie and Jenny had started up the beach area when a group of older boys ran by along with several men playing Frisbee. By the time the small crowd cleared out, the girls were gone.

She told the investigators what she did remember - one of the kids wore swim trunks that looked Canadian, another wore green, the men wore tank tops. They went across the beach area from right to left.

"Anything else at all?"

Anabelle shook her head. "That's all I remember."

"Had you seen any of the men earlier?"

"They were all in our tour group. A couple of our security team were clearly security, but I know a couple of them were dressed down and mingling with the crowd. Those other men didn't stand out at all. They weren't overly interactive or overly reclusive. I would have noticed. Your men would have, too."

The two men exchanged glances but didn't say anything. They both scribbled down some notes then pushed back from the table. "Thank you for your time, Your Royal Highness. We'll be in touch if we need anything else. If you remember anything else, please let us know immediately."

She managed to stand on wobbly legs. "I will."

Something niggled at the back of her mind. "I don't think they went out the front."

"What's that?" one of them asked.

"I think they ducked into the brush nearby. There are some large bushes or brush that you can walk through, then it's more dense near the fence. I think they might have gone that way." Anabelle wasn't completely sure why she felt that way, but she did.

"Thank you, ma'am."

Rather than returning to the conference room, she was ushered up the wide staircase to the Green Reception Room. Queen Miriam was at her side by the time she made it through the entry. Caitlin and her husband were already there.

The next few hours were a blur, but by nightfall, there was still no sign of anything. Caitlin and several members of her family were offered accommodations for the night, though Anabelle doubted any of them would get any sleep.

She hadn't seen Kensington in hours as he spent his time with his father and the security teams while she stayed surrounded by his family.

When her phone buzzed, Anabelle lifted her head just enough to look at the message.

Rachel asking how she was. She'd talked to her best friend for a few minutes an hour or so earlier, but hadn't wanted to worry Rachel.

Unable to think of anything else to do, Anabelle started to walk. First, she walked up and down the hallway, then she found a door to a balcony with stairs leading to the garden below.

Time stood still as she walked the garden trails. Her heart tried to pray, but her mind couldn't form the words.

He knew.

Anabelle knew God understood the incoherent cries of her heart. That's what mattered.

Her feet carried her back to the staircase leading to the balcony. Kensington emerged from the building as she reached the top.

Weariness and frustration rolled off of him. "There's still no sign."

Anabelle just nodded. If, as she suspected, her grandfather was behind it, there wouldn't be.

"What about the van that nearly ran us over?"

Kensington's father had braced himself against the conference room table as he studied a map, but that made his head snap up. "What?"

"It's being looked into," Rob told the king. "We don't know if it's connected or not yet, but it seems likely. The time and location are right."

"So is the crazy driving part." He looked over at his father. "All of the papers I was looking at went flying when they slammed on the brakes. I may end up with a bruise on my chest from the seatbelt."

"Did you get a plate number?" the king asked. "Make and model?"

"They're pulling it off the street cameras, but I don't have it yet. As soon as we do, we'll likely put it out to the news crews as someone we want to talk to."

"Whatever we do, it can't be anything that puts the girls in jeopardy." The king finally took a seat.

"Of course not."

Kensington's father looked at him. "What does Anabelle think?"

"That her grandfather was behind it. She might be right, but then again, she might not." He shook his head. "I can't imagine Isaiah doing something like this for revenge, but can't shake that thought either."

His father leaned back. "Isaiah? You think that's a possibility?"

Kensington stared at the map of Cabo Juan-Eduardo, not sure what he was supposed to be looking at. "Not really, but he was livid about our marriage. I don't know why he'd arrange a kidnapping though. Keep some of the athletes from coming to the Games maybe, but not kidnapping a little girl and her friend." He shook his head. "He seemed inordinately interested in Gracie moving into the palace, but kidnapping?"

"What's the deal with her grandfather? I know she doesn't like him, and he's controlled her through threats of cutting off her inheritance, but is he evil or just not a very nice man?"

"I don't know. I'm not sure Anabelle does. She doesn't want to talk about it, though I guess she'll have to now. I get the impression she doesn't particularly like him and that he's controlling and manipulative, but she's never indicated that he's truly evil or anything criminal."

"We'll look into him, sir." Rob put his phone down. "It looks like the van is where the girls were, but there aren't actually any cameras where they left the park. Anabelle was right about where she thought they went. A fence had been cut, allowing them out the side and not one of the gates or main entrance. They had to have known who Gracie is to your family, otherwise, they likely would have tried to sneak out the front gate."

"Agreed."

Kensington walked to the windowed wall looking into the security office. "So what do we do?"

"You go find your wife." His father put a hand on Kensington's shoulder. "You've told us everything you know, which is exactly nothing. She needs you, and I get the feeling you need her, too."

With a nod, Kensington left the conference room, and pulled out his phone. A thought came to him and he scrolled through his contacts until he found the right one.

"Rachel's Ravelry Repository."

Kensington breathed a sigh of relief. With the slight time difference, he hadn't been sure she'd still be at the store. "Rachel?"

"Yes?"

"This is Kensington. Have you talked to Anabelle today?"

"Briefly. She seemed upset but said she just wanted to check in." He could hear the irritation in her voice. Anabelle had told her everything after they arrived in San Majoria, and Rachel had been mad. Mad she'd missed the wedding. Mad she hadn't been able to say goodbye, but hopefully not so mad she wouldn't talk to him.

"Is there any way you could come down here for a few days?"

"Why? What's going on?" Fear had entered her voice.

Kensington slumped back against a wall. "Gracie's been kidnapped. We're not sure..."

"What?" Rachel's yell stopped him in his tracks. "What happened?"

"We're not sure yet, but I'm positive Anabelle could use you here if it's possible."

"I'm headed home as soon as we hang up. I'll be on the next flight."

"Let me know the details, and I'll make sure someone picks you up from the airport."

"Just a minute. Mrs. T, are you all right?" He could hear her talking to the elderly woman he'd met briefly. "Kensington, is the number that popped up on my caller ID the right one for you?"

He rattled his number off.

"That's it. I'll call you from my cell phone as soon as I have my plans confirmed."

"Check the flight schedules first. If you need to go straight to the airport do it. Anything you need can be purchased here, on me, if you need to."

"Thanks." She hesitated. "Take care of Anabelle, Kensington. If Gracie isn't found soon, it's going to destroy her. That little girl is her heart."

"I know. Gracie is my heart, too. We're doing everything we can."

"I know you are. I'll call or text you soon." She hung up before he could say anything else.

Before he could go find Anabelle, Jordan found him. "Any news?" Kensington's brother-in-law asked.

"Not yet. I just talked to Anabelle's best friend. She's on her way as soon as she can."

"Good."

Kensington pinched the bridge of his nose. "I don't know Anabelle well enough yet. Not to help her through something like this if it's not resolved positively and fast."

"Whatever it is these guys want, they want Gracie alive," Jordan reassured him. "They knew who she was and took her on purpose."

"I know." Even if it wasn't confirmed, deep down Kensington knew that much.

"And that's good. They'll go out of their way not to hurt her and keep her happy."

"I know that, too." He let go of his nose and looked at Jordan. "But that doesn't stop me from feeling incredibly helpless in more ways than one. I don't know where the little girl who is becoming like a daughter to me has been taken, and I don't know how to comfort my wife."

Jordan rested his hands on both of Kensington's shoulders. "Just be there for her. Hold her close, be a shoulder for her to cry on, and let her express what she needs to when she needs to. Pray as hard as you can. That's all you can do."

Pray.

Kensington had been, though not coherently. Maybe it was time to fix that.

15

Unable to keep her eyes open any longer, Anabelle finally dozed off on a couch that cost more than her first and second cars combined.

Sleep came, but fitfully at best. Disjointed dreams, nightmares, filled her mind. Upon waking, Anabelle knew she hadn't slept long enough.

Gracie was still missing. If she'd been found they would have woken her up. Her mother-in-law, Princess Astrid, and Princess Jacqueline Grace sat at a table on the other side of the room. Anabelle started toward them, only to have Queen Miriam rush to her side.

"You shouldn't be up, dear. You need your rest."

"It wasn't very restful," Anabelle admitted.

"Of course it wasn't." The queen guided her to a sofa. "Let's get you some tea."

Anabelle wanted to argue with her, but didn't have the willpower to do so. "Has there been any news?" She still had to ask.

"None that I'm aware of, dear." The queen set a steaming cup of tea in front of Anabelle. If nothing else, it would give her something warm to hold. She felt abnormally cold, her fingers nearly deadened.

Her mind barely registered the needle prick sensations as they began to wake back up. She must have slept on them wrong. "They'd tell you, wouldn't they? Even if it was bad news?"

The queen hesitated, then nodded. "I believe so, though I believe, good or bad, they would wait until it was confirmed. They wouldn't want to either get our hopes up too high only to have them dashed when there's still no news or watch bad news crush us when it's not certain."

"You barely know her." Anabelle shook with a single sob. "She wanted to get to know all of you better. She talked about Easter constantly until we started talking about the trip to the Turtle Sanctuary."

"And we'll have that chance as soon as she's found." The queen offered her a snack.

Anabelle shook her head. "I don't think I can keep anything down. I'm nauseated." A sip of tea was all she could handle.

Princess Astrid's husband walked into the room. "Kensington went over to the chapel."

She took some solace in that. At least one of them was formally asking for help from the Almighty.

"Would you like to join him?" the queen asked. "I am certain that you're praying just as hard as the rest of us without going to the chapel, but there's solace in being there as well."

Anabelle shook her head. If she tried to move, she'd likely fall. The only thing that could make her try was news that Gracie had been found.

"The Lord knows our hearts, even if we can't quite formulate the words." The queen patted her hand. "We had a bit of a scare with Sofia last fall. She made it to the beach unattended, a wave hit her, and by the time we made it down there, she wasn't breathing."

Jordan took a sip from Astrid's water glass. "I gave the king a black eye trying to get down there when I saw her from the balcony."

"You gave the king a black eye?" Anabelle thought Kensington had told her something about it.

Jordan shrugged. "He was in my way, and my daughter was unsupervised on the beach."

They all started telling stories about Sofia and the rest of the family as children. Anabelle didn't quite laugh, but she did find herself smiling and her mind focused a little less on Gracie's still-missing status.

The stories flowed around her, with the others laughing about a time a four-year-old Kensington got away from his nanny only to be found sound asleep on his father's throne. That one made Anabelle grin.

"I do love these stories," she told the queen in a quiet moment. "I don't know enough about Kensington when he was little."

"He told me you called him Kenny until after your wedding." Her smile told Anabelle she wasn't upset by it.

"That's what he told me his name was. What else was I supposed to call him?"

Jacqueline Grace laughed, a delicate, nearly graceful, laugh Anabelle could never hope to imitate. "I love it. No one would dream of calling me Jacquie."

"Do you want to be called Jacquie?" Harrison poked Jacqueline Grace's shoulder. "I can totally do that next time I've got cameras in my face."

"No. Thank you. I've got this two-name thing going on, and I'll keep it that way. If you go out there and call me Jacquie, I'll never hear the end of it."

Anabelle finally felt steady enough to stand. When she did, she just walked to the window and stared out at the ocean a little ways away.

An arm slid around her shoulders. "Are you all right, dear?"

"As much as I can be. I won't fall over, I don't think."

"We'll know something soon."

"I hope so." Anabelle wiped under her eyes. She'd started crying without realizing it. "I need to know she's okay, that she's being taken care of."

"If it's someone who knows who she is, as we suspect, you can be certain they are taking good care of Gracie and her friend. They know the full wrath of the country will come down on them if they don't. It'll be bad enough when they're caught, but if they've mistreated the young Lady, it'll be even worse."

"More likely they want to take her somewhere far away."

"Our men and women, and those of all the law enforcement agencies around are doing everything they can." The queen smiled. "I know you wish it could be under other circumstances, but I was told a couple of minutes ago, that a surprise had arrived for you." She nodded behind Anabelle.

Anabelle turned, her mind barely registering what her eyes were telling it. "Rachel? Mrs. T? What are you doing here?"

Mrs. T stepped forward and curtsied to the room in general. "I'm here because I have something very important to tell you."

Could anything that didn't involve getting the girls home safely be important enough right now? "What's that?"

Mrs. T took a deep breath. "I'm your grandmother."

Kensington sat on the front pew. His head hung down as he rested his forearms on his knees and clasped his hands together. His prayers had coalesced into something a bit more coherent, but not much.

His mind ran through a slide show of his time with Gracie, from the first time he saw her in that shopping mall to earlier in the day when she'd given him a hug goodbye and a kiss on the cheek. The feel of her arms around his neck wouldn't leave him for a long time.

Not for the first time, he found himself wishing he and Anabelle could adopt her, though he knew that was unlikely for many reasons. At least it was probably legal in San Majoria for him to adopt her without it affecting his spot in the line of succession, though that didn't really matter too much.

A noise behind him caught his attention, though he didn't turn to see who it was.

"Sir?"

"Yes?" It was a member of the security team. He knew that without looking.

"You need to come with me."

That made Kensington's head snap up. "What is it?"

"I'm not sure, but your mother has summoned everyone. She said it's important."

Kensington looked up at the guard. "Is there news?"

The man shook his head. "No, sir."

Kensington hurried through the palace halls to the sitting room where he'd been told everyone gathered. "Rachel." He greeted Anabelle's friend with a kiss on the cheek then saw who stood behind her. "Mrs. T? I didn't realize you were coming."

"Mrs. *Thorbjørnsdóttir* has something to tell all of us that she thinks might be relevant," Rachel told them. "She only wants to tell the story once, so we waited for you to get here."

Kensington sat next to Anabelle, his arm wrapped around her shoulders and his other hand holding hers. He wondered what the elderly Icelandic woman could possibly have to say.

"It started over twenty years ago," she began. "My only daughter met a young man, fell in love, and eloped. Two years later, their car drove off a switchback on the way home from Lake Akushla. The doors were open, but they weren't in the car. No bodies were ever found, so they were presumed dead."

"Why were they presumed dead? Why wouldn't they have stayed with the car?" his father asked.

"Accidents at that switchback are common," Mrs. T explained. "Depending on traffic, they're not always seen right away so, if they're ambulatory, people will sometimes leave to find help or a way to the nearby village. Occasionally people survive the accident, but wander off in the woods and aren't found for days or their bodies aren't found for years. When they didn't show up after a couple weeks, they were presumed dead." She stared at her hands. "Not long after that, things happened that made me wonder if they had survived but couldn't tell us for some reason."

The woman dabbed at her eyes with a handkerchief. "Eighteen months ago, Clari, my granddaughter, started dating Rachel's brother. Right around that time, Anabelle, your parents were killed in a car accident on the same switchback. I'd already been shopping for yarn at Rachel's store, but I took notice because of the connection."

Anabelle gripped Kensington's hand. "And you think my mother is your daughter?"

Mrs. *Thorbjørnsdóttir* nodded. "I know she was."

"How can you be so certain?" Anabelle asked.

"A mother knows." Kensington's own mother spoke softly.

"Did she have a birthmark on her right shoulder blade? Sort of heart shaped?" Mrs. T asked.

Kensington watched as Anabelle nodded.

"In the eighteen months since your parents were in the car accident that killed them, my husband and I have done some research and looked more closely at our last communications with your mother." She took a deep breath. "We believe your other grandfather is actually a criminal mastermind. Your parents wanted out of the life, but he threatened to kill all of them, including you, because she was pregnant at the time, though barely."

Anabelle had turned white as a ghost.

"Your grandfather has the power and connections to do just about anything he wants. For some reason, he wants Gracie." Mrs. T started to reach for Anabelle but stopped, likely afraid of the response.

"I believe I can explain that."

Everyone turned to see Esmeralda, Crown Princess of Islas del Sargasso walking in.

"Esme!" Most of those assembled stood at her entrance. The queen gathered the younger woman in for a hug. "What are you doing here?"

"As soon as I heard, I knew I needed to come." Esme took a seat on the other side of Anabelle as everyone else sat back down. "I'm so sorry. I had no idea there was still any danger, or I would have said something a long time ago."

"What are you talking about?" Kensington rested his hand on Anabelle's shoulder.

"It's quite a long story, but Mrs. *Thorbjørnsdóttir* is correct. Her daughter was Anabelle's mother. Anabelle's grandfather runs a white collar-type criminal operation and has for decades. Currently, they deal mostly in Wells Fargo and PayPal scams as well as identity theft and sales."

Anabelle gasped. "I've never been fond of my grandfather, but truly?"

"Yes. Many years ago, your parents wanted to get out altogether, but the only way he would let them was for them to virtually disappear."

"What about Gracie?" the king asked. "What does he want with her?"

Esme stared at her hands. "I was at an event in Eyjania about two years ago. I met your parents by chance I thought, but later found out they'd been sort of stalking me because they needed my help. After due diligence, we discovered they were telling the truth. This year, when you and your family came to the Games, all of you were going to disappear, first to Sargasso then likely Athmetis for a time."

Anabelle's grip on his hand tightened. "But why?"

"Because of Gracie. Gracie is actually your cousin. Your grandfather had an illegitimate daughter. When she gave birth, and subsequently died, he convinced your parents to raise Gracie until she was old enough to send to the boarding school of his choice."

Esme did reach out and rest her hand on Anabelle's arm. "Your grandfather found out, and we believe he somehow made their car run off the road."

"How could he do that? There was no evidence of foul play." Anabelle's cheeks were wet and her eyes red. Kensington knew she was holding back sobs.

"It's possible he has enough clout to influence the investigation or to manage it somehow so there isn't any evidence."

Esme looked up at Kensington. "But that's not all of it."

"Tell us the rest." The king's words were a demand despite his quiet tone.

"They believed, though they didn't have definitive evidence to back it up, that Gracie's biological father is King Benjamin."

16

Stunned silence greeted the princess's pronouncement, but after all of the other revelations, Anabelle found herself numb.

Her grandfather was a criminal mastermind.

Her adopted sister was really her cousin.

Her parents planned to run away during the Games, taking Anabelle and Gracie with them.

Her grandfather likely had her parents killed.

But perhaps most surprising, even more so than the presumption about King Benjamin's relationship to Gracie, was the revelation that Mrs. T was her biological grandmother.

Ignoring all the other implications about everything, she turned to her favorite yarn customer. "You're my grandmother?" she whispered.

Mrs. T nodded. "I can't knit or crochet to save my life, but once I knew, I had to have a reason to keep coming."

More tears streaked down Anabelle's cheeks. "You didn't need to buy yarn. All you had to do was be yourself."

"I know. *Now* will you call me Amma?"

Anabelle did a sniffle-laugh thing through her tears. "Of course."

"I know all of you want to catch up, but it will have to be later." The king turned to look at this new princess, one Anabelle couldn't quite place. "Esme, what makes you think Benjamin is Gracie's father?"

"Gracie's biological mother worked at the palace until a few weeks before she was born."

King Edward crossed his arms. "I've never heard any allegations that Benjamin takes advantage of the women living in the palace."

"Neither have we," the princess told them. "But for whatever reason, one I'm not privy to, they believed he is Gracie's biological father."

"Does Benjamin know?"

The princess shook her head. "I have no idea."

"He has to." It all suddenly made sense to Anabelle. "My grandfather wanted me to marry Benjamin so he could get his hands on Gracie by volunteering to take care of her for the first while when we got married. But Benjamin wanted the marriage so he could get Gracie into the palace as his supposed sister-in-law and ward. Isaiah was quite insistent that Benjamin wanted her to live with us and would find someone to take care of her."

The king gave a sort of half nod. "That would seem to indicate that he does know."

Anabelle wiped her cheeks. "So which one of them took Gracie? And where is she?"

"That's the question, isn't it?" The king turned to his head of security. "Make sure those who need to know are aware, but we don't want to spread this unnecessarily. Until we know for certain Benjamin is Gracie's father, no one needs to know. And it's quite serious for us to even insinuate he might have had something to do with the kidnapping without proof, so it's best that everything we said is kept within this room and only tell those I deem necessary." He turned to the princess. "Does anyone know in Sargasso, Esme?"

"Not the full story. Mother knew there was a couple from Eyjania who wanted to defect and might be able to help bring down the crime boss who stole credit card and other personal information from a large portion of our population a couple of years ago. I saw no reason to share the information about Gracie unless I needed to."

Anabelle tuned out. The conversation revolved around political implications and things she didn't much care about. All she cared about was getting Gracie back and keeping the little girl away from both their grandfather and King Benjamin.

The foreign princess stood and started a quiet but earnest conversation with the king. Several other members of the family, including Kensington, joined them.

Mrs. T and Rachel came to sit by Anabelle. Anabelle let Mrs. T envelop her in a grandmotherly embrace far too long coming.

"It makes me so happy to know you're my grandmother," Anabelle whispered.

Mrs. T moved back and brushed a bit of hair off Anabelle's face. "I wish I'd told you what I knew sooner. I don't know that it would have made any difference, but maybe it would have."

"We've been on the lookout for anything grandfather might try since we eloped. They've never found any indication he was going to do something, much less something like this."

Anabelle slumped back against the sofa in a decidedly unprincesslike position. Rachel slumped next to her.

"I think you need to get some sleep." She leaned her head against Anabelle's shoulder. "I know I need some. So does Mrs. T. Maybe you can show us where we can rest?"

Giving a half-shrug, Anabelle let her head fall against Rachel's. "I don't know my way around this place. Kensington and I don't live here. This is only the second time I've actually been in the palace, I think."

Jacqueline Grace reached a hand out to Anabelle. "Come on. I'll show you where all three of you can get some rest."

With Rachel helping hold an exhausted Anabelle on her feet and Jacqueline Grace guiding Mrs. T, they went up the wide staircase and passed a guard into what seemed to be the family's private quarters.

"This is Kensington's apartment." Jacqueline Grace opened the door and let them in. "There's plenty of room for all three of you. I believe your things have already been brought here, Mrs. T and Ms. Christiansen. Anabelle, I know some of your things were brought over earlier, just in case this dragged on and you needed them."

"Thank you, Jacqueline Grace." Anabelle nodded as she stumbled over the threshold. "Will you let Kensington know where we are?"

"Of course." Jacqueline Grace reached out and pulled Anabelle close. "We're doing everything we can," she whispered. "They all are."

"I know."

After Jacqueline Grace let her go, the princess left the room and closed the door behind her.

The three of them explored just long enough to find a room that had to be Kensington's and then two more for Rachel and Mrs. T.

Once they were settled, Anabelle returned to Kensington's room and collapsed onto the bed.

Overwhelmed by everything the day had wrought and the information overload in the last couple of hours, Anabelle let the sobs finally break free again.

With shoulders heaving, she cried herself into hiccups and eventually, sleep.

He didn't mean to fall asleep in his chair in the security office, but that's just what Kensington did.

"Sir?"

Someone shook him awake. "What is it?" Kensington growled.

"There's news, sir."

Kensington bolted out of the chair and looked around. "What time is it?"

"Just after ten."

"How long did I sleep?"

"I'm not certain. I believe you fell asleep sometime after four this morning."

"So what's the news?"

"Jenny has been found."

Together they started for the door. "Where is she?"

"On her way here with Cabo Juan-Eduardo police. That's all I know."

A few minutes later, Kensington waited inside the palace near the portico where the car would arrive. Anabelle ran in with Rachel close behind her. "Where are they?"

Kensington wrapped her in his arms. "On their way."

Close behind, came Caitlin and her family. They'd been given accommodations away from the hubbub around his family, but with a liason to help with anything they might need.

"Did they find Gracie yet?" Caitlin asked. "Where's Jenny?"

"No word on Gracie," Kensington answered. "Jenny should be here in a couple of minutes."

The rest of his family, Esme, and a security contingent all swarmed in. The door opened and a member of the local police force carried in a little girl.

"Jenny!" Caitlin and her whole family swarmed the little girl who reached for her mother.

"Mama!"

A group of security guards encircled them and whisked them

toward the security offices. Kensington left his arm around Anabelle's shoulders as they followed behind.

Caitlin and Jenny were taken into an interrogation room, though it had been made more homey. Kensington left Anabelle with his mother and sister then went into the other room to watch through the mirror.

Jenny sat on Caitlin's lap, holding her favorite stuffed animal.

A woman Kensington recognized as a prominent local psychologist who often worked with the authorities in cases involving children sat on the floor with them.

Over the course of what seemed like an eternity to Kensington, she got some information out of Jenny, though not much of use. There were several men. All of them were nice to her and Gracie. They had sandwiches for dinner and some sort of sweet cake for breakfast. They took her to the park, but Jenny wished Gracie had gone, too. They took her out of her car seat, told her Caitlin was waiting by the swings, so Jenny ran to the swings only to find Caitlin wasn't there. Another mom helped her and called the police after reading the note Jenny had been given.

"None of that helps us find Gracie." Kensington sat in one of the chairs and looked at his father. "Nothing about where they were or whether they could see the ocean from the house or the palace or anything to give us a direction. What did the note say?" He hadn't heard.

"That they don't plan to hurt Gracie, but we'll never see her again."

"No indication if it's their grandfather or Benjamin behind this?"

"No, but I did speak with Benjamin earlier. If he's behind it, his acting skills are better than we give him credit for. He'll be here in a few weeks for the Games. I told him I wanted to meet with him. He asked what about, but didn't press. He offered his thoughts and prayers for Gracie's safe return, but didn't seem overly interested or concerned. No more so than we would be about his child being abducted." His father shrugged. "Well, maybe we'd be more concerned, but Benjamin has never been particularly demonstrative or emotional."

"No, he hasn't. Is it possible he's using his unemotional side to make it look like he doesn't care very much?"

"I don't think so. I think either he doesn't know she's his daughter, or she isn't his daughter, and he has no idea anyone thinks she is. It's not outside the realm of possibility that he's faking it, but I doubt it."

"So Gregorson it is."

"That seems most likely. We've talked with some contacts in Eyjania who will keep it under wraps so Benjamin doesn't find out just yet. If we determine it was Mr. Gregorson, then we may go to Benjamin for help, but not yet."

"What's the next move?" He wanted to be out in the city, looking for Gracie, but they wouldn't let him.

"The next move is to let the authorities do their jobs. I know you have a team working for you, and they're quite competent, but you need to stay in the loop with the Games. We're just over a month from Opening Day."

Kensington nodded. "I know. I've been getting updates the whole time."

"That's not enough, and you know it. Today you get a pass, but tomorrow, you need to be back in the office because you have work to do that can't be passed off to others. Fortunately, the entire country is looking for Gracie. We don't *need* you to look, though I understand your desire to."

When his phone buzzed in his pocket, Kensington pulled it out. "That's Anabelle asking for an update." He nodded toward the room where Jenny still clung to Caitlin. "Will we learn anything else from Jenny?"

His father turned to the official sitting there. "What do you think?"

"Unlikely, but we may learn a thing or two. They're going to stay in guest quarters for a few days. It's got audio and video monitoring throughout most of it, which they know is in place. That way we can catch anything else she might say in passing that her parents might not pick up on or might not remember word for word when we need them to."

Kensington put his phone back in his pocket and started for the door. "When's the press conference?"

"An hour."

"Do we need to be there?"

"Yes, and you need to change clothes before then. You can't be seen in yesterday's wrinkles."

Weary, he gave a single nod. "Yes, sir." He needed to find his wife, tell her there wasn't anything to tell, and hold on tight.

17

A nabelle clutched Kensington's hand with both of hers. Despite what Jacqueline Grace's stylist had tried to do, her red-rimmed eyes and splotchy cheeks couldn't be hidden for this press conference. At least she wore clean clothes and had been able to take a quick shower. She *felt* better, physically, even if she was still an emotional basket case.

"We will take a few questions at this time," the police chief told the assembled press.

One of them stood and shouted louder than the others. "Princess Esmeralda of Islas del Sargasso was seen entering the palace grounds yesterday. Why is she here and does it have anything to do with the investigation?"

King Edward stepped forward. "She came to extend her family's support and her country's resources, as well as access to any information they may have to help in the search, should it lead us outside the borders."

The truth, but not all of it.

"Duchess Anabelle, is there any truth to the rumor that Gracie is your daughter?"

With great effort, Anabelle managed to control her reaction as she leaned toward a microphone. "No. I didn't even know my parents were adopting her until they showed up at home with her one day. I'm not sure of the circumstances of her birth, but I believe her biological mother passed when she was a few days old. I'm not sure how my parents knew she needed a home, but they offered it to her, no strings attached. She's not my biological daughter or sister, but, since the death of our parents, I love her as both."

Kensington squeezed her hand as she held tight.

"Why haven't you adopted her?" another reporter asked.

Before Anabelle could answer, the king stepped forward. "I am certain my daughter-in-law will be happy to answer some of those questions at a later date. For now, our focus is on finding Lady Grace and her safe return. Thank you for your time."

He turned to leave, with Anabelle and Kensington falling in behind him and the assorted officials following in their wake. When they reached a safe place, out of the way of prying eyes, Kensington pulled her close, his arms enveloping her. Only exhaustion prevented her from dissolving into sobs again.

"I hate to do this to you, love, but something's come up with the Games and needs my attention. I can't let anyone else do it, unfortunately." His whisper against her hair cut through to her heart.

Swallowing deeply, she took a step back. "I understand."

"I should be able to come find you in an hour or so." His head dropped. "But tomorrow, unless something changes, I need to be at work all day. The Games are in less than a month, and there's a lot I can't leave to others."

She nodded. "I understand." She hated it, but she understood. Some things didn't wait for personal trauma. Her grandfather had taught her that.

The irony wasn't lost on Anabelle.

His hand wrapped around the back of her neck as his other

arm held her close again for a moment. With a kiss to her fore-head, Kensington stepped away. "Be sure you tell someone what you need. My mother or sisters, or anyone. They'll take care of you until I get back."

"I know."

He gave her a kiss then turned to walk away, pulling his phone from his pocket as he did. It wasn't his fault, Anabelle knew that, but she couldn't help but feel a bit abandoned at the same time.

Someone else took her elbow and led her to a sitting room where some snacks waited. She wouldn't be able to eat much, but Anabelle knew she needed to keep her strength up.

Nibbling on a sandwich took most of her energy as conversa-tion went on around her, though she didn't pay any attention to any of it.

Motions.

She had to go through them.

Eating. Drinking. Sleeping. Showering.

For two days that's what she did at the palace.

Then Amma and Rachel went home, and she spent most of two more at the Lowery House while overseeing the packing up of her things along with Kensington's and Gracie's. Until she was found, they would use the palace as their home base.

Kensington had thrown himself into his work with the Games. Anabelle needed to do the same. At home, even if it was a palace, all she did was stew. Despite the circumstances around her being outed as Kensington's wife, she'd been receiving requests for appearances and support and everything else. She'd been assigned an assistant from the palace pool who was responding to everything with a kind, but firm, thank you but not at this time.

Six days after Gracie disappeared, Anabelle decided it was time to change things up. After speaking with the assistant, whose name she couldn't quite remember, Anabelle decided it was time to visit an assisted living and nursing home facility. Part of her wanted to choose an early childhood venue, but she feared it would be too difficult.

The invitation had come four days earlier, with apologies for the timing, the belief Gracie would be found long before the event took place, and the promise of good food and warm companionship to take her mind off whatever it needed taking off of.

A car drove her to the facility ten miles from the palace. Anabelle was certain it took longer than it should have. When she'd looked it up on her phone, the route should have taken them right by the Turtle Sanctuary, but she hadn't seen so much as a sign for it. That couldn't be an accident.

No one but the director of the facility had been told she would be in attendance, so there were no hordes of photographers waiting as she emerged from the car.

Instead, a middle-aged woman greeted her and then ushered her inside. Inside the building, several elderly men and women waited. Each seemed torn as they bowed or curtsied, which she thought was completely unnecessary.

Finally, she had to ask. "What is it? Do I have something in my hair? Something in my teeth?"

One of them, a man about her grandfather's age and bearing a slight resemblance to him, stepped forward. "Nothing like that, Your Royal Highness."

"Then what is it?"

Without another word, the man wrapped her in a bear hug, the kind she'd always imagined little girls would get from their grandfathers. "We all really want to do this," he told her. "Hug away as much of the hurt as we can. We're all grandparents. Some of us are great-grandparents, and we wish we could treat you like we would if you were our granddaughter, and it was our great-granddaughter who was still missing after all these days."

The tears that flowed weren't the sobs Anabelle had experienced so often over the last several days, but cleansing tears. They hadn't found Gracie yet, but the soul-deep belief that somehow it would all work out enveloped her, like the hug the man gave her did.

It would.

It would work out.

It wouldn't be easy, but in the end, it would all be okay.

It had to be.

"What exactly is the issue?" Kensington pinched the bridge of his nose as he spoke into the phone.

"The plumbing in one of the dorms isn't working right. Something about the sewer. I don't have the details yet, but I'll let you know more when I do."

"So no estimate on when it'll be fixed then, is there?"

"No, sir."

"Keep me posted."

"You'll be my first call when I know more."

Kensington hung up his phone. Great. Focus was already difficult when all he wanted to do was a house-by-house search for Gracie, but at least when it was all normal things, he could do it somewhat on autopilot. Problems required more mental energy than he had.

"You'll want to see this, sir." Bertrand held out a tablet.

"What is it?"

He smiled. "Just look."

Kensington saw a photo of Anabelle.

Smiling.

With a small group of grandparent-looking men and women around her.

"Where is this?"

"She was invited to attend a small garden party at a local assisted living community. They didn't decide until this morning that she was going to go."

"So no camera crews?"

"Not until the end. Word got out during the event. There were half a dozen or so waiting as she left. One of them snapped this picture as she was walking toward the exit."

He flipped through several others and could tell when she realized her trip was being documented. Her smile dimmed a bit and didn't quite reach her eyes anymore.

There was a video where she stopped and said a few words about how lovely the garden party was, but as soon as the shouted questions about Gracie became too loud, she waved and left.

"Good. I'm glad she's getting out. Sitting around just gives her too much time to stew and mope and dwell. Being with people is good for her. I've got my work with the Games to keep me occupied. Anabelle needs something, too."

"Speaking of the Games, you have another call on line three."

Kensington nodded to dismiss Bertrand and reached for the phone. "Kensington." The manager of the track and field facility was having an issue with the employee management companies who were supposed to work at her venue and several others. She'd done everything she could, but the vendor refused to cooperate with the terms of their signed contract. At the late date, it would be nearly impossible to get another one. "I don't have the paperwork in front of me, but am I correct in remembering the products have been purchased by the venues, and this company simply manages the employees who sell the merchandise?"

"Yes, sir."

"Who actually employs them?"

"Their paychecks come from my office, but we don't actually hire or fire them. It's a bit of an odd arrangement, but that's the way it is."

"So, what we really need is someone to manage the employees, and the souvenir stores in general?" An idea began to form in his mind. "Do you have anyone who can do that?"

"Not that I can spare, but yes. We need someone in charge, but it's at least a four-person job, minimum. Some of the interviews have already taken place, but no hiring has that we're aware of."

"I'll take care of it. I've got an idea. Once I know if it's going to work and I've got the particulars sorted, I'll give you a call back. Terminate the contract, on my authority if needed."

"Yes, sir. Thank you, sir."

After hanging up, Kensington called for Bertrand. "When is Anabelle available? I need to talk with her as soon as possible."

"Her car is pulling in now."

"Send her in here as soon as she has a minute, please."

He pulled up the contract for the employee management company and started reviewing it while he waited.

"What is it?" Anabelle sounded weary, and when he looked up, she looked even more so.

Kensington stood and went to stand in front of her. "How are you? Did you enjoy your outing?"

Anabelle leaned against him, letting Kensington hold her up. "I did, until the end when the reporters showed up."

"You did an excellent job. I watched a replay of the live feed." He rubbed a hand up and down her back. "I have a proposition for you."

She tensed in his arms.

It made him smile sadly. "Not that kind of proposition. We've had an issue with a company not fulfilling a contract for the Games. I could really use someone to step in and take over the employee management at several venues. You'd work with probably three or four others to hire employees to run the souvenir stands and supervise them during the Games."

"I don't know. That seems like a lot of work and extremely important. I don't know anything about running a business or hiring employees."

"Maybe not, but you know people, and you know how to organize and get things done."

"Who would I be working with?"

"I'm not sure yet. I just found out about it five minutes ago. If you have any suggestions, I'm open to them."

Anabelle shifted her weight until she wrapped her arms around his waist. "Just Rachel, but she can't spare the time away from her shop. Mrs. T went back already, too."

Kensington knew Anabelle missed her newfound grandmother, but the woman had other people counting on her, and they didn't want Gregorson to get suspicious about their knowledge of his activities.

"What if Bertrand worked with you?" It amazed Kensington that he was willing to allow it for two reasons - he actually trusted the man, and Bertrand had become his right-hand man. "I have several other people here who can help with his jobs, but he could be an invaluable asset in helping you figure out what you need to do and how."

Anabelle nodded her head against his chest. "It'll be good to have something productive to do. Has there been any word about anything?"

"No. As soon as I hear anything, as soon as anyone hears anything, we'll let you know."

"When do you need me to start?"

"As soon as possible."

She gave another weary sigh. "Let me go freshen up. I'll come back, and you or Bertrand can help me get it figured out."

Kensington cradled her face in his hands. "Take all the time you need." He gave her a soft kiss. "I'll be waiting."

18

The hot water washed over Anabelle as she leaned against the wall of the shower. She wasn't qualified to do this. She knew nothing about hiring or firing or sales. Not really. Technically, she'd been a salesperson for Rachel, but not really.

She needed something to do, but how could she do this? At least she'd had a good afternoon at the garden party.

Her head snapped up. Was that the answer? Mr. and Mrs. Lachapelle had moved to San Majoria when they retired, wanting to be closer to their grandchildren. In their former lives, they'd owned a successful shop in a tourist town somewhere in the United States. Surely they knew what they needed to about hiring employees.

Feeling a bit more at peace with her new assignment, Anabelle finished her shower and dressed. Once in Kensington's office, Bertrand showed her to a conference room where she could start organizing.

"All of the information we have from the previous contractor is being sent over. They backed out of their contract. You will get paid for this, ma'am, because it's required by law, but if I may, I have a recommendation."

Paid? Really? "Of course."

"Donate the money to charity, one of your choice." He hesitated, as though unsure.

"Go on," she encouraged. He had a point. She didn't need the money. That was a new, and odd, thought for Anabelle.

"Perhaps an organization for missing children."

That brought tears to her eyes. "I think that's a wonderful idea. I also know a couple people I'd like to bring in to help, at least to consult, because I know nothing about any of this."

Bertrand picked up a pen. "What are their names?"

"Millard and Frances Lachapelle. It's not spelled quite like it sounds though." She spelled it for him. Originally, she'd guessed it would end in an i and be Italian in origin. Instead, the single e made the long-e sound, and they believed it to be French for "the chapel." "I met them today, and think they could be assets."

"I'll run a check on them as quickly as possible and get back to you."

"Thank you." With a pen and piece of paper, she began making a list of her questions, things she felt she'd need to know. When she finished, Anabelle took a deep breath and flipped to the news application on her browser. Her face popped up first in the local news section.

New Duchess Makes First Official Outing While Sister Still Missing

Anabelle didn't want to read it, but she had to know. As she feared, they were critical of her attendance at the event while Gracie hadn't been found. She didn't care, though. She needed something to occupy her mind.

Less concerned with what the reporters thought, Anabelle scrolled to the comments. Some were critical, agreeing with the overall tone, but others came to her defense.

Sitting around when there's nothing you can do is a great way to go crazy, one said. *My sister was missing for a year. She ran away, but we didn't know that until later. After a few days, there's nothing more you can actually do, and you have to get on with your life or descend into madness. Everyone responds differently, though. I needed to get back out and live my life normally. My mother spent time volunteering with organizations who helped drug addicted teens. My father started drinking heavily. This kind of thing could be just what Duchess Anabelle needs to keep her sane.*

That was exactly how Anabelle felt. The solitude, even with Kensington's family around her, was too much.

Many of the other comments echoed those sentiments, enough that Anabelle felt she might not be making a fatal *faux pas* after all.

Bertrand came back in with a full-sized tablet. "Here's what I have so far. There's a list of interviews already conducted, along with their notes, but no one's actually been hired yet."

"We have three weeks, don't we? And they hadn't hired anyone?"

"Not officially. It's possible they made some phone calls and verbally offered jobs to some of them, but we have no record of it. This is for the management who will help run the job fair this weekend and hire everyone else."

"In that case, we call those already interviewed, tell them there's been a change in management, and they need to come back in if they're still interested. If nothing else, their reactions will tell us a lot about their character."

Bertrand's lips quirked into a half-smile. "Very good. That was my thought as well. Would you like to start making the calls or shall I?"

"First, we need to determine when and where the interviews will take place, otherwise we can't schedule them."

His smile widened. "I do believe the prince was right. You're perfect for this. Let me make a quick phone call. I think I can get us a place."

Anabelle started looking through the applications and notes.

Something seemed a bit off about them, though she couldn't quite put her finger on it. Bertrand came back in to tell her there were offices at the gymnastics venue they could use indefinitely.

"Why don't I start from the top of this list, and you start from the bottom then? We'll meet in the middle." The documents were shared across the devices, so they'd be able to see when a note about a new time was made and not duplicate calls.

She dialed the first number. When she confirmed she had the right person, a woman named Holly, on the line, she launched into the spiel she'd thought through. "My name is Anabelle, and I'm conducting interviews for the souvenir vendor positions at the Games. Unfortunately, due to circumstances beyond our control, your interview needs to be redone. Could we schedule that for tomorrow?"

"Of course." Holly sounded confused but not upset. "I was told I didn't get the job, though."

Odd. Her qualifications seemed excellent, as had the notes. "I can't comment as to what you were told prior, but the entire process is starting over, and we'd like to complete it as quickly as possible to allow for training and such before the Games commence." In actuality, some of the shops would open a week beforehand as guests began to arrive.

After another minute of pleasantries, Anabelle hung up and made a note.

Maybe she could do this after all.

"Who is with her?" Kensington rested his forearms on his desk.

"A couple she met at the event earlier today." Bertrand had come back from the conference room where Anabelle was set up.

"And they passed a background check and are qualified to help her?"

"Yes to both questions."

"So that whole situation is in good hands?"

"It seems so."

There was something more the other man wasn't telling him. "But?"

"Something about the whole thing seems off. We both made phone calls to those who had already been interviewed and noticed the same thing. Some of the best qualified candidates on paper had been told they wouldn't be getting a job, while the opposite was also true." Bertrand shook his head slightly. "I don't get it. Neither does she. The duchess told me she thought it odd, but that she's never really done anything like this before and wasn't sure she really knew what to look for."

Kensington leaned back in his seat. "Is there anything unusual about the company that backed out? Besides going back on this contract at the last minute?"

"Not that we've ever noticed, but we will be looking into it much more closely as soon as possible. We'll be looking into a lot of things as soon as possible."

"Use whatever resources you need without taking away from the search for Gracie. Something weird is going on."

"Agreed."

He flipped to the next folder. "Any word on the residence with the plumbing issue yet?"

"No. The contractor is out there now."

"Any other issues that you know of?"

"Not at the moment."

"All right. What about another assistant, either for me or Anabelle? We can't split your time indefinitely."

"Princess Esther's assistant joined the duchess's team a few minutes ago. The princess doesn't need an assistant at the moment."

That was news to Kensington. He'd have to ask his parents

about it later. Maybe it had something to do with what his father discussed with Benjamin and Isaiah.

"So you're back with me, then."

"Yes, sir." Bertrand gave him the beginnings of a smile. "Thank you."

For allowing him to continue to work for Kensington while away from the Lowery House. It violated both the original agreement and the amended one, but Kensington didn't want to bring someone else up to speed on everything. Bertrand was worth his weight in gold.

For several more hours they worked on the details, the minutia, that never seemed to end.

"How many days?"

"Twenty until the village opens."

Kensington glanced at his watch and realized they'd worked straight through dinner. "I think it's time to wrap up for the night. We'll get back to work in the morning."

"Yes, sir." Bertrand closed his padfolio. "I'll be here first thing."

"Are you still living on San Mediano?" Kensington asked with a frown.

"I have clothes and toiletries here to stay when I need to, but yes. My wife and I live on San Mediano."

"If you'd like, I'll see you get temporary quarters big enough for both of you, at least until this is over." And they found Gracie. Kensington had a feeling Anabelle wouldn't leave Cabo Juan-Eduardo without the little girl.

Relief crossed Bertrand's face. "That would be wonderful. If you don't mind, I'll call my wife. She may join me tonight, she may not, but she can bring everything needed to move here for a few weeks at least."

Kensington picked up the phone. "I'll make the call and see you in the morning."

"Have a good evening, sir." Bertrand left as Kensington made the arrangements.

As soon as he finished, Kensington went to the apartment he'd occupied since he turned eighteen and moved out of the monarch's quarters a floor above. A few lights were on, but the apartment was too still for Anabelle to be there unless she was sleeping. A glance into their room showed she wasn't there.

He called her cell phone only to get the canned I CAN'T TALK RIGHT NOW text in return. As much as Kensington hated to bother Bertrand now that he was off for the night, he sent a text asking where they'd been working. Five minutes later, he found Anabelle along with three others in a conference room.

She held up a finger as she talked into the phone. "Good. I'll see you tomorrow." After hanging up, she gave him the first genuine smile he'd seen from her in days, though it still wasn't a big one. "Hey. What are you doing here?"

"Bertrand and I finished for the day a little while ago, but worked right through dinner. I thought I'd see if you'd eaten yet."

"Not yet, but we're almost done with these calls to set up interviews over the next couple of days."

The other three people were also on the phone and finished up their calls about the same time. They all started to stand, but Kensington waved them off.

"Kensington, this is Mr. and Mrs. Lachapelle, and Brittany, who is actually Princess Esther's assistant but is going to help us out through the Games at least."

Kensington nodded at each of them. "Thank you for your assistance. I appreciate it, and I'm certain my wife does, too. Without your help, the souvenir stands would be unmanned and that simply won't do."

After a few minutes of chit chat, Brittany told them she'd finish the last few phone calls and that the four of them should go get dinner. Though he knew she hadn't meant to imply they should eat together, as they walked out, Kensington invited Mr. and Mrs. Lachappelle to join them. After a moment's hesitation, they agreed.

Kensington made a quick phone call then led them to a small dining area. A member of the staff hurriedly finished setting the table.

He bowed slightly. "Apologies, sir."

"None necessary. I called less than five minutes ago." He held a chair for Anabelle while Mr. Lachappelle held one for his wife. Once seated, he turned to them. "I know you had the opportunity to talk with Anabelle some earlier, but I'd love to know more about you."

A waiter brought them drinks as the conversation began to flow.

W hen Anabelle walked into the bedroom, Kensington was already seated with his back to the headboard and covers pulled up around his waist. As she walked in, he put his book on the side table.

"How're you feeling?" he asked as she sat down.

"Productive." She squirted lotion into her hand and set the container back on her own table. "For the first time since we got here, I feel like I'm contributing something." She hesitated as she rubbed the lotion in. "For a couple hours, it took my mind off Gracie." A tear leaked out of her eye. "I can't believe that I forgot about her, even for a little bit."

Kensington reached for her, wrapping his arm around her shoulder as he pulled her close. "Hey. You didn't forget about her. You just did something else besides sit around and stew for a little while."

Anabelle curled into him.

"You can't just sit here. If you were able to be out searching or something, it might be different, but there's really nothing for you to do in the search right now. Something else to focus on is good for you. Otherwise, you'll worry yourself into an early grave."

"If we don't find Gracie soon, I'll worry myself into an early grave anyway."

"We're going to find her."

"I know." She tried to sound convinced. Despite how she'd felt earlier in the day, Anabelle had a hard time holding onto that conviction.

As she turned her head against Kensington's shoulder to let the tears fall again, he prayed over her. Prayed for peace. Prayed for Gracie. Prayed for Gracie's safety and that their little girl was being well taken care of, despite the circumstances.

Should they instigate adoption proceedings? Would that help anything? She needed to remember to ask Kensington later, but instead Anabelle found herself drifting off, the long days and longer nights catching up with her.

The next day, she was driven, along with Brittany, to the gymnastics venue where they were going to hold the interviews. Anabelle and Mr. Lachapelle would conduct half of them together with Mrs. Lachapelle and Brittany doing the others.

Many of those Anabelle met with expressed their concern for Gracie. Some said they were praying for her, but not all. She chalked that up to differing levels of religious beliefs. A few didn't say anything and seemed a bit off.

After the third such interview, Anabelle turned to Mr. Lachapelle. "He said he'd been verbally offered a job, though there's nothing about it in the notes we've been given, right?"

"That's right." Mr. Lachapelle took a sip of his water. "Something I noticed. Those who say they were told they had jobs haven't inquired about Gracie at all."

Anabelle stood and poured herself another cup of coffee. "I noticed that, too. Is it weird? Or just a coincidence?"

"I don't believe in coincidences."

"I'm not sure I do either." She glanced at her notes. "Our next two interviews are the same. We'll see how those go."

One of the secretaries who worked in the gymnastics venue had been loaned to them for the next couple of days. Anabelle buzzed for her to send the next interviewee in. She seemed surly and put out to be interviewing again. She mentioned Gracie, but there was something off, almost snide, in the remark.

By the time lunch rolled around, Anabelle was willing to admit it wasn't her imagination. She called Bertrand and put him on speaker phone.

"Yes, ma'am?"

"Can I give you a list of names to run background checks on for me? Or you can give to someone else who can?" she asked as she reached for her sandwich.

"Of course. Can you tell me what you're looking for specifically?" She could hear the keys of his computer clacking.

"Nothing we can put our finger on, but some of the people we've interviewed are off. They have some common factors that make me wonder if there's something more going on, but I have no idea what."

"Give me a minute, and I can get a conference call going. There's a man looking into the management agency. He can do this at the same time."

After a series of clicks and a phone ringing, another man answered. Bertrand explained what Anabelle needed. He told them what information she should send him. Bertrand asked to be CC'd on any of it. With a few keystrokes, Anabelle sent the files to both of them and asked to be kept informed.

Once she hung up, she scarfed down her sandwich in a very un-princess-like manner. Mr. Lachapelle just laughed.

"I can't thank you enough for coming out of retirement to help me," she told him as she popped the last bit in her mouth.

"Our pleasure, dear girl. This is temporary anyway. If it was a long-term gig, we might not have, but we can handle a month or so." He stood and stretched his back as his wife and Brittany came in.

They compared notes to find a similar pattern, though none of the other interviewees mentioned Gracie. That didn't surprise Anabelle since they likely didn't know she was even around. The overall attitudes were similar, even without that factor.

"I'll send an updated list in a few minutes." Anabelle sipped some water. "Keep track this afternoon, and I'll send another one later. We won't get through everyone today, will we?"

"No," Brittany answered. "It will take until tomorrow afternoon. We can go through everyone tomorrow evening and make phone calls then, or do it first thing the next morning."

"Why don't we see how we're all feeling by tomorrow night? We may all be worn out and not quite ready to do that. You're making notes, though right?" Suddenly Anabelle worried that she wasn't making enough. "Some sort of rating system so you know which ones you think will be excellent and which ones would be okay if it comes down to it?" That's what she'd been doing, but what if she was wrong?

Mrs. Lachapelle patted her hand. "We've got it under control. But, yes. Everyone gets a number from one to ten. Ones have no chance at getting hired. Tens will be, and on down the list until all the slots are filled."

Good. It wasn't quite how Anabelle had been doing it, but she could tweak her system. Mr. Lachapelle had his own. She suspected it mirrored his wife's.

The intercom buzzed. "Your next interviews are here."

"Thank you," Anabelle called. "Tell them it'll be just a minute." She took a deep breath and blew it out. "Time to do some more of this."

The security office buzzed with activity. Until recently, that wasn't normal. It had always been active, but not like this. Not until Gracie disappeared.

"What's new?" Kensington asked the security chief.

The man shook his head. "Nothing. That's puzzling. We'd have expected some movement or something that would give us some indication she was being taken out of the country, but nothing."

Kensington's father sat at the head of the conference room table. "What do we think that is indicative of?"

"That they're laying low. Perhaps waiting for the initial furor to die down before trying to move her. Based on the note we found with Jenny, they're likely taking good care of her, but want her in their physical custody."

Kensington tapped a pen against his other hand. "Anabelle asked me something the other night. Is there any reason why we can't or shouldn't pursue adoption? Legally, in Eyjania, Anabelle has guardianship, I think, but Gracie has no legal parents. Would doing that give us some sort of benefit? Can we adopt her?"

The head of security shook his head. "That's a question for lawyers, not me. I suppose, when she's found, whoever has her could claim they're the rightful guardians and having legal paper-work here in San Majoria could help mitigate any claims of that nature, but that's really outside my purview."

His father scratched something onto a piece of paper. "I'll have my attorneys on it as soon as this meeting ends."

"Thanks." Kensington wasn't sure what the point of the meeting was. All they did was sit around, find out there was nothing to report, occasionally a specific lead that didn't pan out was mentioned, but nothing else.

A knock on the glass caused them all to turn. The man Bertrand had told him was in charge of the employment agency investigation walked in. He gave a slight bow in the direction of the king. "I have something I think you should see, but I'm not sure yet what to make of it."

He plugged his computer in to the projector and the screen popped up. "It's not in a presentation or anything. I'll just be clicking around and showing you what I've found so far."

"It will be fine," the king said.

"I haven't gotten very far on the owners of the agency yet. I'm waiting on some information to come back on them, but since lunchtime yesterday, the duchess has sent me a list of about fifteen names. All of them are suspicious. Petty criminals associated with a local gang. Nothing outrageous. Mostly stealing credit card information and petty theft, things like that."

"Stealing identities?" Kensington asked.

"Nothing that elaborate, that they've been caught for, anyway. What they've been convicted of is more along the lines of using card skimmers to obtain data then use the data to buy gift cards or other things easy to resell. Why? Have you heard something?"

Kensington shook his head. "No. Just curious after learning that Anabelle's grandfather is likely involved in more elaborate crimes of a similar nature."

"I do know one of the owners of the management agency has some connections in Eyjania, but that's as far as we've gotten at this point."

"Keep pursuing all of it," Kensington's father told the man. "I'd like you in these update meetings from now on as well."

"Yes, sir."

A minute later, Kensington and his father were walking back toward the offices. "I know we think she's being well taken care of, but I hate the thought of her alone and scared."

"We all do." They reached the king's office, and he motioned for his assistant to follow them in. "I need to speak with my attorneys and the best family attorney in the country as soon as possible."

"Yes, sir." The man hurried out of the office to make some calls, Kensington presumed.

"Is it legal for me to adopt her?" he asked his father as they took a seat on either side of the desk.

"I need to check the legislation passed last year after Jordan married Astrid. I believe it included language that said a member of the family a certain number of spots down the line of succession could adopt, but the child would not be added to the line. I'm not sure what that number was, though. You're third right now. It may need to wait until after the baby is born." He typed on his computer and scanned the screen. "This is one of the articles written about it, so we'll have to verify it, but I think you're okay."

A small weight lifted off Kensington. "I am?"

"According to the article, Astrid, as the heir apparent, cannot adopt regardless. A royal child can be adopted by the other non-royal parent. If something were to happen to Astrid, Sofia and any other children could not be adopted by Jordan's new wife. Since you are not the heir apparent, you can adopt Gracie, but she will not be added to the line of succession."

"I'd like to start that process right away. I'm sure Anabelle will, too."

"I'll get in touch with Benjamin and make certain any legalities are dealt with expeditiously."

"His reaction could tell us for certain if he's Gracie's biological father. If he's not, but someone close to him is, we might figure that out too."

"Good point." With a smile, his father leaned back in his chair. "You'll figure this diplomatic thing out yet, even if you did run off and elope, causing a minor international incident."

"What did you say to Benjamin and Isaiah to get them to back off?"

His father rocked softly in his chair as he stared into space. "You know, I'm not sure Benjamin actually cared."

"That fits with what Anabelle told me about their meeting. He looked her up and down, shrugged, and said she'd do."

His father's eyebrows knit together. "That's what he said?"

"That's Anabelle's version. I have no reason not to believe her."

"Odd," his father muttered. "Regardless, the terms of the deal are between myself and Benjamin for the time being."

"Is that why Esther hasn't been around? Did she have something to do with it?"

The sharp glance told Kensington not to question it any further.

They discussed several other matters of interest regarding the Games. His father was impressed with the way Anabelle was handling her new role. As they wrapped up, two men entered the room. Kensington wasn't sure of their names, but knew they were two of his father's lawyers.

Once they were all seated, the king outlined the issues at hand.

"Yes," the older one confirmed. "That is how the adoption rules were written. There's no legal issue with Prince Kensington adopting the Lady, at least not as far as his royal stature is concerned."

"If something should happen to Astrid and her children, making Kensington the heir apparent, would he, in effect, need to unadopt Gracie?"

The morbid thought wouldn't have occurred to Kensington, but he supposed it was his father's job to think of those things.

"Once the adoption is final, there would be no reason for him to disown her, as it were. However, the Lady would not be the heir apparent, or even the heir presumptive. Princess Jacqueline Grace would become the heir presumptive until such a time as Prince Kensington has a child who would become the heir apparent."

Clear as mud.

But it meant Kensington could adopt Gracie.

He needed to tell Anabelle.

THE INADVERTENT PRINCESS

Holding up a hand, Anabelle stopped Kensington mid-sentence. "Let's start with what's the difference between heir apparent and heir presumptive?" As a member of the royal family, she should probably know this.

"Heir apparent is next in line for the throne," Kensington explained.

"I knew that much."

"*But*," he went on, "Astrid, for instance, can't be pushed down the line by someone else's birth."

"Right."

"Queen Elizabeth was always her father's heir presumptive. It was *presumed* she would be the heir, but Great Britain had male primogeniture until a few years ago. *If* her father had a legitimate son before his death, or even after his death, that son would have supplanted Princess Elizabeth as the heir. They passed absolute primogeniture shortly before Prince George was born. If he'd been born a girl, she would have retained her place in line, regardless of any younger male siblings. As it stands it won't come into play until Prince George has children at the earliest."

"Okay." She went back to her home country to see if she understood. "So Princess Genevieve is King Benjamin's heir presumptive, but when he has a child of his own, that child will be the heir apparent."

"Correct. If it's a boy. If it's a girl, it depends on if they've adopted absolute primogeniture yet, and I'm not sure if they have. San Majoria did when my mother was pregnant with Astrid. In Sweden, Princess Victoria was heir presumptive until Prince Carl Philip was born. He was the heir apparent for a few months. They passed retroactive absolute primogeniture, promoting Princess Victoria to heir apparent."

Anabelle waved a hand. "I'm kind of sorry I asked. What does it boil down to?"

"Since Astrid is the heir apparent, and has a child who is her heir apparent, I can adopt Gracie. She will not be added to the line

159

of succession despite the adoption, but otherwise, she'll be considered my daughter in all other aspects."

"Good. When can we file the paperwork? What has to happen?"

"My father's lawyers are figuring it out. He's going to call Benjamin and make sure there's no legal sticking points."

"And if he is Gracie's father?"

"This should smoke out that information."

Anabelle nodded and tried to get her shoulders to relax. "Good."

"Tell me how your day went."

"I think we've got our list of people to hire together. These people will be managers, more or less, and will take care of the hiring fair for the general staff members this weekend. That means we have less than two days to get them up to speed on what everything entails. That won't be easy since I have no idea what all is involved. There's some information in the files, but I haven't looked at it yet."

"Let me know if you need any more assistants."

"I don't think so. We interviewed just over a hundred people between us. We need ten venue managers and thirty assistant managers. Most of the ones who made it to the list were well-qualified, except for the names I already passed on." She kicked off her shoes and sank into a chair. "I'm already ready for it to be over. I can't imagine how long you've been working on this."

"Fortunately, my aunt took care of it the last round, and we don't have another Games here for six years. The next two will be in Islas del Sargasso." Kensington leaned back and closed his eyes. "There isn't any news on the Gracie front."

Anabelle's heart ached. "I didn't figure there was. You would have told me."

"Immediately," he confirmed. "I have a question, though. As far as you know, does your grandfather have any connections here in San Majoria? Business associates, that kind of thing?"

She thought about it as she tucked her feet underneath her. "I'm sure he does. He would have dinner parties that I had to attend. There were often business associates from around the world, but always from the four countries." One in particular sprang to mind. "There was this one guy. He always seemed creepy to me."

"Do you know his name?"

Anabelle shook her head. "He had a big scar on the back of his right hand that disappeared under his long sleeve dress shirts. A thick one."

Kensington made a note in his phone. "I'll let them know. It may ring a bell for someone and give us some direction."

She pulled a blanket over her legs. "I'll keep thinking. If I remember anything else, I'll let you know."

"How're you feeling?"

Such a loaded question. "About what?"

"Anything. Everything."

"I miss Gracie so much it physically hurts when I have the time to think about it. I'm glad for this job because it gives me something productive to occupy my mind and my time, but it also overwhelms me to be in charge of staffing for all these venues. I know the revenue from the Games is huge for the local economy, and I really don't want to screw it all up."

"You won't." Kensington's voice was firm, but his look was surprisingly gentle. "Truth is that if we didn't sell one souvenir, it wouldn't grossly affect the overall income from tourism. Yes, it's a lot of money, but the food and hotels and everything else has a much greater impact than the souvenirs."

Relief washed over Anabelle. "That makes me feel better."

He stood up and stopped in front of her, holding out his hands to help her up. Once she stood in front of him, he wrapped his arms around her. "I wouldn't have asked if I didn't have complete faith in you. You can do this."

"I know." She thought she knew. How could he be so certain of her abilities? They'd only known each other a couple of months, and really hadn't spent much time together for most of that.

Kensington crooked a finger under her chin and tilted her face toward his. "I'm proud of you for so many things, love. I'm so glad you're here." He kissed her softly. "I'm so glad you're my wife."

Overwhelmed, Anabelle kissed him back, letting the intensity build until it was just the two of them in her world, and she could forget about the crippling fear over Gracie and the anxiety over this job, and everything else except Kensington and the good between them.

Despite all the work he had to do, Kensington couldn't say no to an engagement that had been on his calendar for years. Every summer, a surf competition took an afternoon where the competitors taught local kids how to surf, kids who wouldn't otherwise have the opportunity. Even in an island nation there were those who couldn't afford it or for a myriad of other reasons didn't have the chance.

Since he was old enough to hold a boogie board, Kensington had been on the waves. By six, he was surfing on his own, though he didn't have the strength to paddle out by himself for a few more years. At thirteen, he'd been a guest at the exhibition. That's when he first learned about the San Majorian Surfers Give Back afternoon.

Every year, he spent time with the kids and took part in the exhibition. But as he grew older, he wasn't able to just put on a pair of board shorts and a t-shirt and show up. Eventually, he had to arrive in dress slacks and a button-down shirt with loafers and change into a wetsuit right before going into the water. Part of the whole formal public persona of the royal family.

He tugged the zipper all the way up his back and went outside, scanning the beach as the organizer stood next to him with a clipboard.

"As usual, we have you working with the young teens today, sir." The organizer had become something of a friend over the years.

Kensington hesitated. Rarely did he throw his weight around, but he also knew if he requested it, he could get pretty much whatever he wanted.

"Is something wrong, sir?"

"I'd rather work with the boogie boarders this year, if it's all the same." He couldn't explain it but as he saw the smaller children, something called to him.

"Of course, sir." She made a few notes on her clipboard. "Whenever you're ready."

Kensington walked toward the younger children as applause sounded around the beach. He waved to the scattered crowds until he reached the younger children.

"Who wants to boogie board?" he asked the eager young ones.

"Me!" came from all of them except for one little girl. She bit her lip and looked scared.

In fact, though she was a little older, her skin was naturally a little darker, and her hair so brown it was nearly black, she reminded him of Gracie when he first met her.

"Boogie boards to the water!" one of the other instructors called. "Right at the edge. Don't go in yet."

The little girl hung back. Kensington knelt next to her. "Do you want to boogie board?"

She nodded.

He held out a hand. "I'm Kenny. What's your name?"

Her small fingers gripped his. "Mary."

"Hi, Mary." He sat on the sand next to her. "You want to boogie board?"

Mary nodded again.

Kensington leaned toward her. "Are you a little scared?"

Another nod.

"Would you like me to go with you?"

One more nod.

Kensington stood and reached out his hands. "Come on then."

She took both hands, and he made a big show of helping her stand. Mary gripped his hand as they started toward the ocean. His feet dug into the soft sand until it gave way to the wet hard packed sand near the waves.

Mary stopped walking as they neared the ripples of water.

"You don't want to go any further yet?"

She shook her head.

"How about just a tiny bit, and we'll get our feet wet?"

Mary shuffled forward until the water just barely lapped at her feet. The "big" wave came all the way to her ankles.

"Look." He pointed at their feet. "It's kind of like it's burying our toes, isn't it?"

Another nod.

So the girl didn't talk much, at least not to strangers.

Then it hit him. Kensington knelt next to her. "Mary, have you ever been to the beach before?"

"No." The tiny voice nearly broke him.

"You want to boogie board, because it looks fun, but you're not so sure about the waves and everything because you've never been here before."

"Yes."

That settled it. They wouldn't boogie board, not today, but they'd work on getting her comfortable with the water, and someday, he'd teach her. "Then why don't we just sit here and let it get our feet. If you want to go out a little further, let me know."

They moved a few inches closer to the waves and sat down, with their feet in front of them.

"Do you live in Cabo Juan-Eduardo?" he asked as the remnants of another wave rolled in.

"No."

That surprised him. "Where do you live?"

"Tiptonvillia."

Right in the middle of the big island. "That's far."

"My school came."

That made sense. Some of the schools from lower income areas would have their children apply or be nominated to come to this event.

"What's your favorite thing to do?"

Mary drew in the sand with her finger. "Paint."

"I bet you're a good artist."

She shrugged.

"Do you have friends you like to play with?"

"Sometimes. All the kids in my class are bigger than me. They make me be the baby when we play family because I'm little."

"And you don't like being the baby?"

"No." She leaned her head against the neoprene of his wetsuit.

His head dropped as tears filled his eyes.

"What's wrong, Mr. Kenny?"

He used his other hand to give her head a bit of a hug against his arm. "I have a little girl. She's littler than you are, but she went away for a little while, and I miss her a lot."

"Does she miss you?"

"I think she probably does. I haven't known her very long."

The little girl nodded, far too wise for her age. "You're her new daddy."

"Kind of. Her mummy and daddy were in an accident so she lives with her grown-up big sister. When I married her sister, she became my little girl, too."

"Then I bet she misses you as much as you miss her."

Kensington wrapped his arm around Mary's shoulders. "Hopefully, she'll get to come home soon, and we won't have to miss each other at all."

"Prince Kensington took some time away from preparation for the Games and looking for his sister-in-law to spend time with children at the San Majorian Surf Festival." The news anchor smiled. *"One little girl in particular seemed to capture his attention."*

Anabelle watched him walk into the surf holding the little girl's hand. They only made it about to her knees before she started to shy away. Kensington picked her up and carried her out a little further. Anabelle would have to ask him about it later.

She turned back to the lunch meeting. "So, we're agreed on everyone?" she asked. Murmurs of assent came from the other three at the table.

Holly, the first person she'd talked to, would be in charge of track and field, the largest venue. That decision lent credence to the idea that something wasn't quite right about the agency. She was the manager of a large boutique that started on San Mediano and expanded to every major city in San Majoria, and a few minor ones, plus several stores in Islas del Sargasso. Her boss had approved six weeks off, if she needed that much time, to work for the Games. Holly wouldn't get a salary from the boutique, but they were going to give the money to charity.

It was a marketing coup and would generate goodwill around the country. They already had a reputation as a good place to work and reasonable prices for high quality products. This would only serve to improve on that, while enabling the souvenir stands to be run competently.

Anabelle began making phone calls, asking all of their new managers to come in for a meeting first thing in the morning and plan to hit the ground running.

When she finished, she turned to the others. "What else do we need to accomplish today?" Anabelle was overwhelmed by all of it.

Mr. Lachappelle smiled gently at her. "Go home and get some rest. We'll finish getting these schedules done and send them to you this afternoon. You can look over them after you take a nap. You're exhausted."

He wasn't wrong. Despite falling asleep quickly in Kensington's arms, Anabelle hadn't slept well. After a few more minutes of discussion, she left, driven by her security team.

Once at the palace, she started for Kensington's quarters, but instead went to his office. Bertrand sent her in. He was on the phone but motioned for her to have a seat.

"Good! I'll talk to you tomorrow. Thanks." He hung up. "What are you doing here?"

"The calls were made, and they sent me home to rest. I stopped here first to see how your day is going."

"It's going well." He pointed to the phone. "That was an update on a plumbing issue in the Athletes' Village. It should be fixed by the middle of next week. I spent the morning at the beach, so I'd say it's a good day, all things considered."

"I saw the video of you with a little girl."

He sighed and nodded. "I usually work with older kids on surfing, but today, I saw her standing there, and she reminded me so much of Gracie the first time I saw her. I worked with her instead. I don't know how much they showed, but eventually, I got her to sit on a long board with her feet in the water. I was only in up to my knees or so, but she'd never even seen the ocean before."

"And she lives here?"

"Almost the exact center of the island." He tapped his pen against the blotter on his desk. "I got the impression she has a difficult life. Her school nominated her to come which means she likely comes from a poor family. She doesn't seem to have many friends, and when I said I hadn't known Gracie very long, she just sort of nodded like she knew what it was like to have new men in her life. When I told her we were married and that made Gracie my sister, she almost seemed jealous for a second."

He exhaled slowly. "It made me miss Gracie even more." His phone began to vibrate. "And that means it's time for the daily briefing. Do you want to come with me?"

Did she? The nap sounded much nicer than sitting in a conference room and listening to some men say they didn't know anything new, but she also knew she wouldn't actually get any rest. She nodded and stood when he did. With her hand snug in Kensington's they left his office and went to the security conference room.

His father was already there. "Anabelle! Hello, dear. How are you?" He gave her a kiss on the cheek.

"I'm okay. Trying to stay busy with the stuff for the Games to keep my mind off everything else."

"I'm glad. I've heard good things about the work you've already done."

Before Anabelle could reply, the head of security cleared his throat. She took a seat next to Kensington.

"Unfortunately, as with the last few days, there isn't much to report. We've tracked down a few leads and are working on many others. Dozens of new ones come in every day. Most of those are suspected sightings that turn out to be nothing."

Maybe she should have just gone to their room. To hear there was nothing really going on was far different than just thinking there probably wasn't.

"What about the employment agency?" the king asked.

"Possibly," another man answered. "Duchess, I'm glad you're here today." He tapped on a tablet. "Do you know this man?" There was a picture on the screen he held up.

Anabelle gasped. "That's him."

"Who?"

"One of the men who would be at my grandfather's house. Not

the one with the scar I told Kensington about, but he definitely knows my grandfather."

"He's one of the owners of the agency. With your confirmation of a connection we only suspected, it seems likely they were planning to use the Games as a front for fraud and identity theft."

Anabelle's heart ached. Was there no end to her grandfather's tentacles?

"**D**oes he have any connection to Gracie?" The heartbreak in Anabelle's voice nearly overwhelmed Kensington.

"Not that we've found yet," the head of security told her gently. "We're looking."

"It's been almost two weeks." Kensington put a hand on the back of Anabelle's neck as she swiped at tears. "She has to be so scared."

"I know, but we have to keep believing that they're taking care of her. Even if she's not allowed to play outside, she's getting enough to eat and drink and likely has toys to play with and a safe place to sleep."

"Safe except that she's not home."

"I know. I meant she's not in some run-down warehouse with a roof that might collapse in a couple days. She's probably in a nice, suburban house with a nice bathtub and her favorite foods."

"It's not the same."

Kensington massaged her neck lightly. "I know it's not, sweetheart, but at least she's safe otherwise."

Anabelle pushed back from the table. "Is there anything else I need to know?"

The head of security shook his head. "I'm afraid that's all we have to report, ma'am."

Kensington suspected they would go into more detail with his father after Anabelle left. She walked quickly to the door, with Kensington in her wake. Before they reached the outer door of the security office, she'd broken down. Kensington pulled her close, her sobs breaking his heart.

"She needs me, Kenny. I need her."

"I know, love." Holding her upright, he urged her out of the offices and toward a nearby stairwell. Though not the quickest way to access his apartments, it would get them there.

Once in their room, Anabelle laid on the bed and cried herself to sleep. Kensington didn't know what to do but sit next to her and brush the hair off of her temples.

Jacqueline Grace texted him, and he let her into the sitting room while Anabelle slept.

"I had a thought," Jacqueline told him.

"You've been thinking?" He tried to make light of something. "Sounds dangerous."

She rolled her eyes. "I know working on the Games has been good for both of you, but what about a support group? People who've been there, and really understand what you're going through. I read some of the comments on the article about Anabelle attending that garden party. Someone mentioned they'd attended a group for parents whose children had gone missing. I wondered if that might help both of you."

Kensington went to look out the window. "We're a fairly small country. Are there really enough kidnappings and runaways for support groups?"

"Unfortunately, yes. Many of the children who are abducted are abducted by a non-custodial parent or other disgruntled relative. Some of the teens are runaways. Some are lured into leaving 'voluntarily' by predators. There are several support groups in the city. Some focus on just one kind of missing child. Some are open to anyone. I can send you the links."

"Thanks. I don't know that either of us will have time until after the Games, and I pray to God she's home long before then."

Jacqueline Grace slid her arm around his waist as she stood at his side. "I pray for that constantly."

Kensington looped his arm over her shoulders and gave her a squeeze. "Thank you."

They stood looking out the window for several minutes until Jacqueline Grace broke the silence. "Do you know what's going on with Esther? I think it's odd she hasn't come home since all of this started. Even Esme came."

"All I know is she was acting odd in Eyjania before Anabelle and I flew off to Athmetis. Other than that, I don't know."

"Father won't say."

"He won't tell me either. If Mum knows anything, she's not talking."

"I'm sure she knows. He wouldn't keep something like that from her. They'll tell us when they're ready, I suppose."

"I guess." Jacqueline Grace leaned her head against him. "I miss her, though. Harrison, too."

He'd left the day after Gracie went missing to attend a summer program at Serenity Landing University. He would be home in time for the Games, but until then only two of the five children were actually living in the palace. It would have been just Jacqueline Grace if Kensington and Anabelle remained at Lowery House.

"I must admit," Jacqueline Grace said softly, "sometimes I fear becoming like Prince Harry."

Kensington blinked. "He's grown up quite a bit in the last decade or so, but why would you be like he was in his younger days?"

"Not then. Now. I'm quite certain William and Catherine both love him and vice versa, and they certainly seem to get along well, but to an outsider at least, sometimes he seems like the third taga-long, you know?"

"You're afraid of becoming a third, or fifth perhaps, wheel?"

She nodded.

"I find that highly unlikely. Some smart man is going to run into you somewhere, sparks will fly, and that will be the end of you as a single woman. Or maybe you won't find him right away, but until then, you will continue to be the smart, successful, confi-dent woman you already are. You'll find a way to make a differ-ence in causes that are important to you, with or without a man at your side. And I can guarantee that neither Astrid nor I, or our spouses, will ever see you as a third wheel."

"Thank you for saying so. I appreciate that."

He winked at her. "Besides, Prince Harry has a girlfriend, and by all accounts, is quite happy." Kensington's phone buzzed. "Duty calls. Do you have anything going on this afternoon?"

She shook her head. "Nothing I can't do from here. I'll have my assistant bring my laptop over and work out here while Anabelle sleeps."

"Thank you." He squeezed her shoulders again. "Love you."

"I know you do."

His phone buzzed again, but this time indicated a phone call. He stepped away from Jacqueline Grace and pulled it out of his pocket, stifling a groan when he saw who it was from.

Another problem.

It shouldn't surprise him, but it didn't mean he liked it. At least it hadn't happened while he was sitting with a crying Anabelle.

Thank God for small favors.

Blinking, Anabelle pushed herself into a seated position. Her eyes burned from crying herself to sleep, and she knew Kensington was nowhere to be found.

"Hey."

She turned to see Jacqueline Grace sitting in a chair near the window, working on her laptop. "Hi."

"Kensington had a call he had to take. Something about the Games."

She nodded. "I'm not surprised. It's only a couple weeks away."

"How'd you sleep?"

Anabelle managed a one-shouldered shrug. "Okay. Nightmares. Daymares. Napmares. Bad dreams."

Jacqueline Grace nodded. "I understand. I've had my share, though never in quite this situation."

Something about the way she said it made Anabelle wonder what kind of hurt her sister-in-law had experienced to make the pain sound so real. "It didn't lend itself to a refreshing nap." Anabelle reached for her phone. "I wonder if they've emailed me the information about the scheduling yet." The message waited in her inbox. "Guess I need to get back to work."

"Perhaps, but Kensington did say something about having dinner with you tonight. I think there's an event or something, but I'm really not sure. He hasn't committed to much outside of the Games for the next few weeks, though there are a few things he would like to attend, I'm sure."

"I don't think I'll be up for going out in public." She swung her legs over the side of the bed. "Besides, I've got work to do."

She headed into the bathroom then to the sitting area when she realized Jacqueline Grace had moved out there.

"What can I do to help?" the other woman asked.

Anabelle shook her head. "Nothing, really, but thank you."

"You need to ask when you need the help," Jacqueline Grace told her gently. "That's part of why we're here, why you have an extensive staff at your disposal when you need it."

Anabelle nodded, but wasn't sure how she felt about that. She had a job, finally, and needed to do it herself, not pawn it off on someone else.

Jacqueline Grace looked at her cell phone. "That's Kensington. He said to let him know when you wake up because you do have dinner plans tonight."

Stifling a sigh, Anabelle reached for her phone to call him, only to be sent to voice mail. A text came in telling her he couldn't talk but that they were having dinner with some important guests in about an hour and a half. She needed to dress nice, but not formal, and they wouldn't be leaving the palace.

Anabelle couldn't back out. She knew that. No more than she could have backed out of dinner with her grandfather at home. Such was part of the life with important people.

I'LL BE THERE, she texted back. JUST TELL ME WHERE I NEED TO BE.

It took a few minutes for him to reply, but when he did he said he'd meet her in their quarters, and they'd walk over together.

"Ma'am?" Brittany walked in.

Anabelle looked up from where she was downloading the information into the scheduling program. "Yes?"

"I'm here to help you with the program if you need it. Just let me know if you do."

"I will." Anabelle thought she understood how it worked. She could see how many people they needed per day, then zoom in and see how many people they needed per day per venue. Zooming in more would show her how many people per day per venue per stand or store. Further in broke that down by shifts. "I think I understand how this works, but how do we know three people at a time is enough for this kiosk?" she asked pointing to one of the lines.

"It's a small kiosk." Brittany showed her the star next to the name. "That means there's only one register, so two or three people at a time is all there's room for. More than that and they're walking all over each other. The dot means two registers so four to six people at a time. The plus sign means it's one of the actual stores. Those are a whole different thing. They'll have anywhere from six or seven people early and late to a dozen or more during the peak hours."

Anabelle nodded. "Okay. Do I just need to look over the schedule for each kiosk, stand, and store for each day and make sure there's enough people?"

"Yes and no. Each day at each venue is given a busy rating from one to five. We did five sample days, one for each. You need to look over each one and make sure it looks adequate. If you have questions, ask. Once the sample days are done, we'll copy them into the actual days based on expected volume."

Thank goodness. She didn't have to stare at this endlessly.

"Also, you're only looking at each *kind* of location. You don't have to look at each kiosk, just one per venue. That will also be copied as many times as appropriate."

More sighs of relief. She could handle this.

For forty-five minutes, Anabelle stared at the screen until her eyes started to cross. "Is there a way to print this out?" she finally asked. "I think I could work better on paper."

"Of course."

Sensing some hesitation in Brittany's voice, Anabelle looked up to see her holding an envelope. "What is it?"

"This was just delivered. It's from Caitlin." Brittany fingered the corner of it. "Would you like me to screen it for you?"

Anabelle didn't know how to answer that question. Finally, she shook her head and held out her hand. "I would appreciate it if you could go to the offices and print out the schedules for me."

Brittany handed it to her and nodded. "I'll be back shortly."

Looking around, Anabelle realized Jacqueline Grace had packed up her things and left at some point. When?

Taking a deep breath, she slid her finger under the flap and tore the envelope open.

With her hands shaking slightly, she slid the card out. A simple "thinking of you" adorned the front. Opening it, she found a short verse about being in their thoughts and prayers. The blank side was filled with a note from Caitlin.

Anabelle would have expected more pain at the words about how Jenny was settling back into life. How Caitlin hung on her every word praying she'd hear something new that would help find Gracie. That Jenny talked about her friend all the time.

Instead, that peace came back and settled over Anabelle as it had several times before. Why wouldn't it stick around? For now, she grasped hold. Jenny was okay. That was important to Anabelle. Knowing she was gave her continued hope that Gracie would be, too, once this ordeal was over.

The door to the suite opened and Anabelle looked up to see Kensington walking in. Lines around his eyes told her all she needed to know. He was as stressed about this as she was. He simply had more experience hiding it.

The smile he gave her was genuine. "It's time to quit working for a while, love. I think you're going to love this surprise."

22

Kensington kept the grin on his face as Anabelle blinked. "Surprise? I thought we were having dinner."

"We are. The guests are the surprise."

"Guests?" She shook her head and held up a card. "Caitlin sent this. Jenny is doing well."

"I'm glad. I have no doubt she's bouncing right back."

"Caitlin promised to let us know if she says anything new, anything that might help find Gracie."

"Good." Kensington tugged his tie off and walked toward the bedroom. "You might want to change into something a bit more comfortable. We're not formal tonight."

He heard her following him. "What are you wearing?"

"Probably jeans and a shirt with no collar."

"Think leggings and a tunic is too casual?"

Kensington chuckled. "I'm not sure what that is, but it'll be fine. We're not leaving the floor." Or were they? "Maybe. I'm not sure where dinner is yet, but it won't be fancy."

They both ended up in the closet at the same time. Anabelle took her clothes and moved into the dressing room. Kensington quickly changed then went back to the sitting room. The card from Caitlin caught his eye, and he scanned her note.

Something in it niggled at the back of his mind, but he couldn't put his finger on what it was. With Anabelle's permission, he'd turn it over to security so they could read between the lines and make sure there wasn't something being missed by everyone else.

"I'm ready if you are."

He turned to see Anabelle putting in an earring. So that's what leggings and a tunic meant. She wore sparkly sandals, form fitting pants that must be leggings, and a long, flowing shirt that kind of reminded him of one his older sister wore sometimes. "I like the shirt."

"Holly sent it to me."

"Who's Holly?"

"She's the head of the stores in the track and field venue for the next month. She runs a chain of boutiques. When we met the other day, she told me she'd had a shirt come in that she thought would be perfect for me and I would love. She was right."

Kensington took her hand as they walked toward the door. A text informed him where they were meeting. One of the balconies near the kitchen had a table that could be used. He kept the conversation light as they made their way through the building.

He could see movement on the balcony as he held the door open for Anabelle to exit the building before him.

"Mrs. T?" Confusion filled her voice. "What are you doing here?"

Mrs. T held her arms open for Anabelle to walk into. "Please, dear one, call me Amma. I've been asking you to for years. Now you know why."

"Amma, what are you doing here?" Anabelle asked again as she clung to the smaller woman.

"I thought it was time you met Afi." She let go. "This is my husband, your grandfather."

Kensington watched as Anabelle was enveloped in another hug. Once they let go, she turned to him.

"Afi, this is my husband, Prince Kensington of San Majoria."

He extended a hand. "Please, call me Kensington when we're not in public. It's a pleasure to meet you, Mr. T. I'm afraid I'm not quite prepared to pronounce your last name yet." He winked at Mrs. T. "But I have been practicing."

Her grandfather chuckled. "Then it's a good thing she retained her last name when we got married. My last name is Sørensen."

Kensington grinned as they started for the railing at the edge of the balcony. "Then it's a pleasure to meet you, Mr. Sørensen."

"Call me Afi, and I am certain my wife will be offended if you don't call her Amma."

"He's right," Mrs. T confirmed. "You're our grandson now, too, you know."

"My grandmother will be quite pleased to hear that I have other grandparents to annoy now." Kensington made a mental note to find his grandmother and spend a few minutes with her in the next few days. He hadn't seen her in quite a while, not since the lunch with Anabelle and Gracie. Their weekly lunches had become a thing of the past since his return from Eyjania. Once the Games were over...

"I do have something for you, dear." Amma pointed toward a gift box sitting on a side table.

Kensington watched Anabelle walk over to get it then opened it back at the table. She gasped when she saw it. "Amma! Is this the quilt?"

Tears pooled in Amma's eyes. "I started it for your mother many years ago, while she dated your father. I didn't get it finished before they died the first time. When I realized you were their child, I knew I wanted you to have it someday."

Anabelle ran her fingers lightly over the white, blue, and green fabric. "Oh, Amma. It's beautiful." Kensington didn't know where she would put it, but it would get used often and be well taken care of. He knew that much.

The meal wouldn't be served for another fifteen minutes, giving them a little time to chat while looking over the bay. Kensington found them easy to talk to and hoped Anabelle felt the same way.

A member of the staff came told them dinner was ready to be served. Kensington held Amma's chair for her, while Afi sat Anabelle.

"What are we having tonight?" Amma asked.

Concern crossed Anabelle's face. "You don't have any allergies, do you? Either one of you?"

He hadn't thought about that, and breathed a sigh of relief when they both shook their heads.

"No," Amma told them. "I am hoping for some delightfully local cuisine though. I do hope no one went to the trouble of preparing something Eyjanian or even Icelandic. I can have that any time."

"Not at all," Kensington reassured her. "I believe we're having seafood, though I'm not certain exactly what kind. I told Cook just to make it delicious, something she always does."

"Then I'm certain it will be lovely."

Kensington took a sip of his water. "So, tell me. Amma, you are Icelandic, correct?"

She nodded. "Yes. My family moved from Iceland to Eyjania when I was about ten. When I was fifteen, I met a very handsome young man and knew I would never leave."

"They have a large family," Anabelle told him. "But only one girl, Clari. She's married to Rachel's brother."

Amma shook her head. "That was true at one time, dear, but no longer. I have you and Gracie."

Kensington could see it register on Anabelle's face.

"I suppose that's right."

She waved a hand. "Of course it's right. I had your mother, too, but I could never be certain she was alive until she wasn't anymore. Instead, I've gotten to know you, and I will get to know your sister as soon as she's returned to us."

Salads were set in front of them. Anabelle took a bite of hers and swallowed before speaking. "We've started the process to adopt Gracie. The king has told King Benjamin he expects the proceedings to be expedited as much as possible."

Kensington was going to tell her his father hadn't had a chance to talk to Benjamin yet, but before he could Amma was hugging her again and exclaiming how wonderful it all was. Never mind. It could wait.

Nothing would be hurt by waiting a bit longer to tell her that part.

Dinner wasn't the jolliest of affairs, with the pall of missing Gracie, but Anabelle did enjoy getting to know Mrs. T - Amma - and Afi better. They told her all about the rest of their extended family. Anabelle had met a couple of them, including Clari, the only other girl born into the family, who was married to Rachel's brother, Joel.

"Then there's Thor," Amma told her. "He works in security at the palace. I'm not certain exactly what he does, but I do know he's one of the key men."

Kensington held up a hand. "Wait. You have a son named Thor who works for Benjamin's security detail?"

Afi nodded. "He's worked for the palace since he turned eighteen and for security for well over a decade. Worked his way up through the ranks."

"Things got harder for him after his wife passed a while ago." Amma pushed her plate back. "She was a lovely girl. Thor and their boys miss her something fierce. They miss having a wife and mother in their lives."

"Perhaps someday they'll find someone new," Kensington offered.

"Perhaps." Afi took a sip of his coffee. "He's said things a few times that makes me wonder if there already is someone, but he's not ready to tell anyone, perhaps even her, just yet."

A throat cleared behind them. Anabelle turned in unison with Kensington to see Bertrand standing there.

"Sir, you have a phone call."

Kensington wiped his mouth with his napkin and pushed away from the table. "Excuse me."

Anabelle spent another half hour talking with her new grandparents before they needed to leave for the airport.

Bertrand returned and turned to Amma and Afi. "I will be happy to escort you out, Mr. Sørensen and Mrs. *Thorbjørnsdóttir.*"

Amma clapped her hands together. "You say that quite wonderfully."

Bertrand smiled. "I worked quite hard on it, ma'am."

"I did, too," Anabelle chimed in, "but I still haven't managed."

After a round of hugs, Anabelle's newfound grandparents left for the airport.

The next few weeks were a blur of activity as Anabelle threw herself into her work. Kensington's parents went to a wedding in Ravenzario where a long-lost prince suddenly reappeared, but she couldn't focus on anything but her job and the search for Gracie long enough to figure out what happened there.

Thirty-six hours before the opening of Athlete's Village, she met with Mr. and Mrs. Lachapelle and Holly to go over the schedule. They were in Kensington's office in the palace.

As they were about to wrap up, Kensington came in. He listened intently as Holly explained some of the things Anabelle had learned in the last few weeks.

"We're quite proud of her," Holly finished. "She's come a long way."

"Sir?" Bertrand interrupted the conversation.

"Yes?" Kensington looked over at him.

"I need you both to come with me." He looked at the others in the room. "Someone will escort you out, with our apologies."

Anabelle pushed back from the table. Kensington grabbed her hand and started for the door. "Where?" Kensington asked.

"Security." Bertrand fell into step behind them.

Their pace quickened.

"Is there news?" Anabelle asked as they broke into a trot.

"I'm not certain what's going on, ma'am."

The security office was a flurry of activity. Anabelle followed Kensington into the conference room.

"Can someone please tell us what's going on?" he barked.

The king motioned for them to have a seat. "We may have news on Gracie."

"May?" Kensington asked.

"A couple arrived at the hospital with a little girl. They claim she's Gracie..."

Anabelle jumped up. "Then why are we here? Let's go."

"Sit down." The commanding tone of the king's voice compelled Anabelle to follow his instructions. "We don't know what's going on just yet. They brought a little girl in. She matches the general description of Gracie, but there's an issue."

"General description?" Kensington asked. "You mean you can't tell for certain if it's her or not? Is she injured?"

"We're not really sure just yet. Her face and hands are bandaged. The doctor isn't ready to take them off, so we can get a better look. She's drugged right now, so we can't even talk to her yet."

Anabelle clutched her stomach. "What? Why?"

The king gave her a look. "We don't know. We don't know if it's her. We don't know what the injuries are. We debated not telling you until we know more, but decided it was best to go ahead. We want you to visit her. There may be something you see that we can't. A noticeable freckle that you didn't think to mention but will know when you see it or some other minor identifying mark. You'll be able to see her in about half an hour. We wanted you to have time to compose yourself before you go."

Kensington's hand over hers brought slight comfort. "Why is there even any question?" she asked. "Why wouldn't it be Gracie?"

"Because people are greedy," her husband answered. "Given that we're not able to immediately, definitively identify her, it raises the question about why. Is it really Gracie, but she has been injured, or is it a little girl they're trying to pass off as Gracie long enough to get the reward money and disappear?"

Her stomach twisted. "People would really do that?"

"People would do all kinds of things." The weariness in the king's voice saddened Anabelle. This was the life she'd signed up for when she married Kensington?

The door to the conference room opened. "It's time," Rob told them.

"You'll be taken in through a back entrance. You shouldn't be seen by anyone." The king gave Kensington a hug then turned to Anabelle and held open his arms. "Come here, dear one."

With the hug from the king, Anabelle found herself missing her father. And her mother. And her new grandparents.

And Gracie.

The tears began to flow. She clung to her father-in-law as the sobs shook her shoulders.

"Shh." He let her cry. "We're going to find her. If this isn't Gracie, we still won't stop looking until we find her."

Anabelle willed herself to stop, and took a couple deep breaths to steady herself. "I'm sorry. I've been doing so much better."

"It's completely understandable, my dear. It's an overwhelming time." With a final squeeze, he let her go. "Go to the hospital, find out if it's our girl."

23

Kensington wished, more than anything, that he could fix this for his wife, but sometimes even a prince couldn't make things work the way he wanted.

The car pulled into a parking garage and up to a service entrance. From there, he and Anabelle were ushered inside. He kept his hand tight around hers as they were taken upstairs to a private room across from the nurse's station.

"Is the doctor here?" Kensington asked the nurse who met them.

"Not right now. He'll be back later." She looked at the chart she held. "I'm afraid there's not much I can tell you, except that she's sedated."

"Can we see her?" Anabelle asked.

From the way she clutched Kensington's hand, he knew her apprehension outpaced his.

"This way." The nurse hesitated. "I really hope this is the Lady."

"Thank you," Kensington told her. After they washed up thoroughly and put on masks along with other protective gear, they went into the room, past two security guards on either side of the door.

Anabelle's gasp could be heard through her mask. "Gracie," she whispered.

"Maybe," he cautioned.

She went to one side of the bed and perched on the edge of the chair. "Gracie?"

Kensington stood on the other side and watched as the little girl didn't respond. He turned to the nurse. "What exactly is wrong with her? What are her injuries?"

The nurse shrugged her shoulders. "I'm not sure. It's not in the chart. Her medications are, but no mention of why she's in so much pain."

"Is that unusual?" Anabelle asked.

"Extremely."

"Can I hold her hand?" Anabelle reached toward the bandages. "I don't want to hurt her."

"Please don't touch where she's bandaged."

Kensington watched as Anabelle ran her finger along the little girl's arm.

"Oh, Gracie."

He sat on a chair opposite Anabelle. If only he could pick the little girl up, grab his wife's hand and take them both back to the airport and fly away to a place where they'd never be bothered again.

"Kensington?" Anabelle's urgent whisper caught his attention.

"What is it?" He looked over to see her eyes wide and frightened.

"This isn't Gracie."

"How can you be sure?"

"I just am."

He leaned over the hospital bed. "We need some sort of proof, love."

"Look at the bottom of her right foot. We can't see if she's got the scar near her hair on her forehead or the stork bite on the back of her neck, but she scraped her foot about a year ago. There was a scar on the bottom of her foot."

Apprehension filled Kensington as he moved to the end of the bed. He lifted the blankets until he could see her foot.

Socks.

Carefully, he removed it and lifted her foot by cupping his hand under the heel. "I don't see anything."

"I knew it." She pushed back and went around to the other side of the bed and studied the bottom of the girl's foot. "I don't see anything either. Is there a freckle on the side of her ankle?"

He leaned closer. "I don't think so."

"It's very noticeable."

"Then definitely not."

She moved the blanket further to the side. "Check the other foot, just to make sure."

A minute later, he knew she was certain.

"It's not her."

Kensington looked over at the security guard who was already tapping furiously on his phone.

"Then who is this?" Anabelle's hands splayed across her stomach. "Who could do such a thing to a little girl, just for the money?"

"There's more good people than bad in the world," Kensington reassured her. "But there's enough bad people that, unfortunately, sometimes these things cease to amaze you. Especially when you're in the public eye and have money."

He could see the continued disbelief in her eyes, as well as her reluctance to leave the little girl, whoever she might be.

"I'll stay with her, ma'am." The nurse spoke gently to Anabelle. "My shift is over, but I don't have anywhere to be tonight. I don't want her to be alone any more than you do."

Anabelle nodded. "Thank you."

But she didn't move. As though, if she left, she would be

admitting this wasn't Gracie, giving up the last shred of hope that it might be.

He walked to her side and wrapped an arm around her waist, turning her partly into him. His wife buried her head in his shoulder, holding back her sobs as evidenced by the stiff set of her back.

"We're praying for you," the nurse told them. "All of us. We're praying for both of you and little Gracie. She's still out there. She's okay. I don't know how I know that, but I do. We all have this unexplainable conviction that she's okay."

"So do we," Kensington told her. "But it's hard to stay upbeat and convinced of that all the time."

The nurse nodded and walked toward the door. "Let me go clock out, and I'll be right back to sit with her."

He stood there, holding his wife in his arms, heart breaking for her, for this little girl and her family, and for Gracie.

Breaking at his impotence to fix this. To make it right.

True to her word, the nurse returned a few minutes later with her bags. "I know you don't want her left alone, so I'm here. I won't leave. I know you both have a million things to do with the Games starting next week, and the ball tomorrow night, and everything else. Go. Do what you need to. We'll take good care of this girl."

"Thank you." Kensington would see she was compensated somehow for her time.

Anabelle managed to walk out under her own power, but Kensington knew it was only his arm around her that kept her upright. She managed to hold it together until they reached their apartment. Then she crumpled and let the sobs overtake her.

With tears of his own streaking down his cheeks, Kensington gathered her into his arms and prayed once again for peace.

Anabelle hated wearing heels, especially spiky ones, but at a formal event, she had little choice in the matter. Her dress, also from Holly's boutique, shimmered and sparkled, and her shoes had to match.

As she walked out of the dressing room, the weight of the world still on her shoulders, a low whistle greeted her.

"You clean up quite nice," Kensington told her.

She cracked a small smile as she looked him up and down. "You do, too." His tuxedo fit him perfectly. "I will be the envy of every woman there tonight."

"And I will be the envy of every man." He extended his elbow. "Shall we?"

Her hand slid perfectly into the crook. "Let's go."

With every step, her heart ached, but she knew she had to put on a happy face. This was the ball to kick off the Games. Kensington, though young, had put the whole thing together, and needed to look the part tonight. As his wife, she did, too.

Photographers and reporters of all kinds would be waiting for them at the venue. Despite near-daily press conferences, questions about the search for Gracie were certain to be shouted their direction.

She breathed a sigh of relief when she realized they wouldn't be arriving alone. Three cars were visible under the portico through doors already opened for them to go through.

"Princess Jacqueline Grace and Prince Harrison, Their Majesties will arrive momentarily for you to accompany them in the first car." The footman spoke to Kensington's younger siblings then snapped his heels together and bowed at the waist as he finished the statement.

Anabelle turned to see the king and queen walking into the room. Would she ever have such effortless grace as her mother-in-law? Since she hadn't seen either one of them yet that day, she bowed her head and curtsied.

The king gave her a sly wink. "Tonight is going to be wonderful. I'm quite looking forward to what the two of you have put together."

Though Kensington was in charge of the Games, Astrid was in charge of the pre-opening ball. That's why the four of them would be the last to arrive.

A few moments after the other car pulled away, the door was opened for Anabelle, Kensington, Astrid, and Jordan to climb into their own vehicle.

"How are you feeling?" Anabelle asked the Crown Princess. "Are you getting miserable yet?"

Astrid rubbed a hand across her stomach. "Not quite, though I have my moments. This little one is harder on me than Sofia was."

Sofia was Astrid's daughter from her first marriage, adopted by Jordan, and not quite two-and-a-half years old.

"He'll be here before you know it," Jordan promised.

"He?" Anabelle asked.

Astrid shook her head. "We don't know so we alternate between he and she. We haven't confirmed to the press or public if we know or not, though."

"They won't hear it from me," Anabelle promised them.

Astrid stifled a yawn and leaned her head against Jordan's shoulder as they traveled through the streets of Cabo Juan-Eduardo. "I'm ready for this night to be over." She rubbed her hand against her stomach again, though this time discomfort flitted across her face.

"Are you sure you're all right?" Anabelle asked her.

"Braxton-Hicks contractions. I've been having them for weeks. They're nothing to worry about, though they are annoying. I'm under strict orders from my doctor and my husband to stay off my feet as much as possible, which means I get out of dancing for most of the evening."

Anabelle wrinkled her nose. "Lucky doesn't seem to be quite the right word, but it kind of fits. My feet already hurt."

"I can usually sort of tune out the discomfort, but not right now. My ankles swell like balloons on a night like tonight, too. I'll be sitting with my feet up for the next two days, even if I only dance the first dance."

That didn't sound fun. Before she could say anything else, the car slowed to a stop in front of a red carpet. Closer to the other end, Anabelle could see the king and queen, along with Jacqueline Grace and Harrison. She knew he had only been in town since that morning, but he hadn't wanted to miss this. He was back for a few weeks before returning to the States for university.

But Princess Esther's absence felt rather conspicuous. She should ask Kensington about it again, but Anabelle doubted he knew anything else.

As soon as the door opened, the flashbulbs caused spots to appear in front of Anabelle's eyes. Questions were shouted even before they emerged from the vehicle.

Jordan and Kensington climbed out first then turned, each helping his own wife. Hand-in-hand, Anabelle walked next to Kensington, waving to the crown on one side and the press on the other.

"What about Gracie?" one reporter yelled. "Why aren't you searching for her?"

"Ignore him," Kensington murmured. "I'll handle it." They stopped and turned to the man. "I'm sure you know there isn't always much we can actually do. However, you can be assured the authorities are working around the clock to find our little girl." At least the news about the still-anonymous girl in the hospital hadn't been leaked. They'd been in contact with the nurse several times, and there was no change.

"Your little girl? Don't you mean your sister-in-law."

"For now," Kensington conceded, as Anabelle tightened her grip on his hand. "However, adoption proceedings have already begun and, soon, my wife and I will be more than the Lady's legal guardians." He nodded and turned. "If you'll excuse us..."

"His palace credentials are about to be pulled for a while."

Kensington's quiet words were meant only for Anabelle's ears as they walked up the red carpet.

They continued waving until they reached the door.

"Is there somewhere we can step aside for a minute?" Listening to the questions yelled, even though they didn't respond to any more of them, hit her hard.

"Of course." He motioned to an aide and whispered. They were led to a side door and into an office. There were windows into the main area, but the shades were drawn, allowing them some privacy.

Anabelle let her shoulders slump as Kensington wrapped his arms around her. "When will we find her?" she whispered. "When will all of this be over."

"Soon." His hand ran up and down her back, but his voice lacked the conviction she needed to hear.

They'd been saying soon for an eternity.

Maybe one day it would actually be right.

24

For all the privilege he'd been raised with, Kensington couldn't do the one thing he needed to most. Fix his wife's broken heart and find their little girl. He had no idea how many thousands of man hours had gone into the hunt for Gracie, but he knew they were still tracking down leads nearly 24 hours a day.

Anabelle took a deep breath and moved away from him. "I'm okay. I just needed a minute."

"I know." He cradled the side of her face in his hand. "I'm continually amazed by how strong you are." With a kiss to her forehead so he wouldn't mess up her lipstick, he stepped back and offered her his elbow. "Shall we?"

With another deep breath, she nodded.

They emerged from the office into the room filled with dignitaries from San Majoria, Eyjania, Islas del Sargasso, and Auverignon, as well as a couple of other small island nations who participated in the games, but never hosted them. Jacqueline Grace came up and took Anabelle, though he didn't know what for.

Esme found him a moment later. "How are you?"

"As well as can be expected," Kensington answered for both of them.

"Anything from Benjamin yet?"

Kensington shook his head. "No. My father was supposed to talk to him about expediting the adoption on their end, but I haven't heard anything."

"You think he'll let you? If the rumor is true?"

Kensington took a glass of champagne from a passing waiter. "It should tell us if it's true or not. I can't imagine him not putting up a fuss if it is."

Harrison joined them, putting an end to that conversation.

For the next half hour, Kensington made the rounds, accepting the well-wishes and prayers from perfect strangers, business acquaintances, friendly business competitors, and members of other royal families. An announcement was made that dinner would be served in just a few minutes.

Kensington found Anabelle and made sure she hung back with him and several others who would be the last ones in.

They were third-to-last, followed by Astrid and Jordan, and then his parents. As the hostess of the ball, Astrid was in the center. As the coordinator of the Games, Kensington was next to her, one of the few times his father wasn't the main focus.

His other siblings were also at the head table, along with the highest-ranking delegates from Eyjania, Auverignon, and Islas del Sargasso. Esme was actually escorted by Benjamin as they were both unaccompanied. Due to an unforeseen family illness, no one from the Auverignonian royal family was in attendance. Instead, their ambassador and his wife representatived their country.

Whoever arranged the seating made sure the eight members of the San Majorian family were seated so Kensington and Anabelle weren't next to Benjamin, though Kensington did feel sorry for Esme.

After dinner came dancing. Kensington, Anabelle, Astrid, and

Jordan led off with a waltz. Jordan claimed Anabelle for the second dance, while Esme appeared at Kensington's side. Astrid took a seat as promised.

"I'm sorry you ended up with King Cold Shoulder," Kensington said softly after making sure no one was close enough to hear.

Esme glanced to his left where Benjamin remained seated. "You know, he's really not so bad, or not as bad as he likes to act. I get the feeling there's a lot of hurt he's still holding onto. Losing his father so young was bound to have a huge impact. His mother's time would have been split between her eight other children and being pregnant and her own grief. It's no wonder he has a well-deserved reputation for being cold, but there's more there. There has to be."

"I hope so. I hate the thought that he's really that way."

They continued to dance, but Kensington couldn't ask the question at the forefront of his mind.

"He didn't say anything about Gracie," Esme told him. "At least nothing beyond a generic 'hope they find her soon' sort of comment. If what we suspect is the truth, he either doesn't know or is very good at hiding it."

Kensington was inclined to think it was the former. "Thanks for letting me know."

"Of course."

The dance ended a minute later, and Esme was claimed by Benjamin, likely out of obligation. Dance after dance was spent with women Kensington barely knew, occasionally interrupted by a dance with a relative, and once, an ex-girlfriend, albeit one he'd split on good terms with.

"I'm sorry about your little girl," she told him. "We've been praying daily for all of you." She'd started dating another guy the week after they ended things then married him a couple years later. "I'm so glad you finally found your princess."

Kensington glanced over at Anabelle. "She's pretty incredible. I'm thankful for her, but it kills me that we can't find Gracie."

"You will," she said firmly. "I truly believe that."

"Thanks."

The dance ended and with it came a break for dessert. As was customary, Kensington escorted his ex-girlfriend to her table then went back to his own to find the mayor of Cabo Juan-Eduardo seating Anabelle.

As they ate, he turned to his sister. "How are you feeling?"

She shrugged. "Fine. Not fantastic, but not awful. Tired and ready to go home so I can put my feet up."

"You should leave after this. You've put in an appearance, that's all you really needed to do."

Astrid shook her head. "I'm fine. I've got tomorrow off, though. Jordan insisted."

"As well he should."

Kensington took another bite of the fruity concoction and looked out over the crowded ballroom. Did someone in here, someone local, know something about Gracie? About where she was? Were they showing her the videos of him and Anabelle arriving at events like this as proof to her that they didn't care? To show her that they'd moved on, and Gracie wasn't their priority?

Nothing could be further from the truth, but when a little girl had her information controlled, she would believe what she saw.

He closed his eyes and prayed again that they would find her. Soon.

Anabelle had been to dinner parties at her grandfather's house, but nothing compared to this. She'd danced for nearly an hour with one man after another. All were very polite and expressed their concern for Gracie.

But none were Kensington.

She really just wanted to spend the time with him, away from the madness.

Dessert was delicious, but she knew it would be too short. By the time everyone was served, there would be a break of at least half an hour, but it wasn't long enough.

Her feet throbbed. Her head pounded. Her heart ached.

"How much longer?" she asked her husband.

"Another round of dancing," he told her reaching for his glass of wine. "Probably about the same length of time, then we can go home." He put his arm around the back of her chair and leaned closer. "I completely forgot something until a little while ago. Esme will be staying at the palace tonight before tomorrow's ceremony to open the village."

"All right." Why was that a big deal?

"So is Benjamin."

There it was.

"Will we have to see them?"

"Possibly at breakfast, but maybe not. It depends on whether you and I *need* to be somewhere else."

"I do." She didn't know where but she'd find something.

"Annie," he chided. "I'm not saying you have to sit next to him or even that you have to talk to him at all, but if you're not needed somewhere, you need to be there."

"Fine. I will be." Was it wrong to pray for a minor emergency with one of the venues she was responsible for? Nothing big, just enough to get her out of it.

Somehow, she managed to avoid dancing with Benjamin through the next round. As the next to last song drew to a close, Kensington found her.

"We only dance half of this one." He pulled her into his arms, closer than he had for the first dance. "Then all of us from the head table will leave."

"Thank God. I'm ready."

"I know you are." His chin rested against her temple. "Thank you for being here, for being a trooper tonight."

"Right here, this is my favorite place, with you." She sighed the happiest sigh she had in a while. "Of course I'm here."

Kensington backed away and tucked her hand in his elbow. Was the song half over already?

She saw Jordan and Astrid already on their way out the door. That must be the cue no matter how far into the song they were.

A minute later, the four of them were in their car again, but this time something was different.

"What is it?" Kensington asked.

Astrid had both of her hands on either side of her stomach. "I'm not sure these are Braxton-Hicks anymore. We're going to the hospital. The doctor has already been called."

"Not to the palace?" Kensington asked.

Astrid shook her head. "No. If the baby is coming, it's way too early. At least a month before they'd let me deliver without trying to stop it, but really it's just over eight weeks before my due date. If this is something they can't stop and things happen fast, I want to be in the hospital."

"Of course."

"We can drop you at home first," Jordan told them, concern filling his voice. "It's on the way. You have a big day tomorrow."

Anabelle could see the worry on Kensington's face. He was clearly torn.

"Why don't we go home?" she suggested. "We'll get changed into something more comfortable and see what's happening? We can come up to the hospital in an hour or so if necessary. By then you should know more, right?"

Astrid nodded. "I would think so."

Kensington gave his assent. "That will work."

Jordan told the driver, and in a few minutes, they were being let out at the portico.

"We don't have to greet Princess Esmeralda or King Benjamin

do we?" she asked Kensington as they started for the staircase leading in the general direction of the family's quarters.

"No. My parents will."

They reached the top of the stairs and turned a corner. "Good." Anabelle stopped in her tracks, but kept a hand on his arm for balance as she took her shoes off. "Ah! Much better."

Kensington chuckled. "I am so glad men don't have to wear those things."

"At least Astrid doesn't. I know some pregnant women can, but I won't be one of them."

He grew somber. "We haven't talked about that."

"About what?"

"Children. Not since before Easter and that was pretty vague. Just that we'd both like some."

The weariness settled back around Anabelle like a cloak. "Not yet, Kensington. Not until after we find Gracie."

Unless her suspicions were correct.

The day, a few weeks earlier, when she'd just wanted to forget about missing Gracie for a few minutes.

Anabelle wondered if there was going to be a permanent reminder of that day.

Or it could all be a consequence of the stress she'd been under the last few months.

"I understand." Kensington wrapped his arm around her shoulders and pulled her close. "We'll find her, and then we'll talk about it."

Before long, the adoption would be finalized. She hadn't been given a time frame, but surely, given the family's influence, it wouldn't be long. She and Kensington would officially be parents.

"I do want to go to the hospital," he told her. "I know they said it's not necessary, but it doesn't seem right not to."

"Agreed." Concern for Astrid was near the forefront of Anabelle's mind, but with the busy day behind them and the next day sure to be much the same, she really needed sleep. "I'm going to change. Why don't you call and see what Jordan says?"

"They won't even be there yet, so there won't be anything to say." Kensington opened the door to the apartment and stood aside to let her go through first. "Maybe we should wait?"

"Do your parents know?"

"I'm sure they do."

"Then ask them." Could she make it through a few hours at the hospital? There wouldn't be anything to do but sit and wait. Anabelle knew she was likely to fall asleep.

"Good idea. Go change. I'll let you know."

She pulled one pin after another out of her hair. "I'm going to take a quick shower. Keep me posted."

Maybe by the time she was out, he would have decided it was better to stay put for the time being. Anabelle wanted to be there for her sister-in-law, but first she wanted sleep.

25

"When do we head to the hospital?" Kensington held the phone between his shoulder and his ear as he undid a cuff link.

"We don't," his father answered. "Jordan will let us know what's going on. The doctor isn't even there yet. Astrid isn't completely certain these aren't just exceptionally bad Braxton-Hicks, though I understand her rationale for heading to the hospital. If something were to go wrong, delivering the baby there is the best move."

"Will they be able to keep it out of the news?"

He could almost see his father pinch the bridge of his nose. "Hopefully for a while. It's late enough and their car came back here to drop you and Anabelle off. With any luck, the press will have already called it a night. They were going to be able to sneak in a back entrance."

"Good."

"You and Anabelle should get some rest. I'll have someone come get you if you're needed. You both have a big day tomorrow, starting with breakfast with Esme and Benjamin."

"Did you get any kind of vibe from him?"

"Not really. I didn't have a chance to talk with him much. He's been avoiding my calls for weeks, if he's even aware of them. I will discuss that with him tomorrow before he leaves."

Kensington sat on the edge of a chair in the closet. "So you haven't talked to him about the adoption?"

"Not yet. I haven't talked to him at all in over a month of trying. My assistant has talked to his assistant almost every day. If I don't talk to him in the morning, for whatever reason, maybe it's time to skip the assistant, and I'll call his office myself. Throw some weight around. I've been trying to give him the benefit of the doubt, but no more."

Through the speaker, Kensington could hear his mother say something, though he couldn't hear what it was.

"Your mother thinks we need to visit the little girl tomorrow. It would give us an excuse to be at the hospital and check up on Astrid if she's still there."

"There's no way I'll be able to. It's one thing for my sister, but not for a random girl who isn't my daughter, no matter how much they wanted her to be."

"Agreed, but we will, perhaps with Jacqueline Grace and Harrison before the ceremony."

He toed off his shoes. "Is there any word on who she is?"

"Not yet. The fingerprints from the toys brought in with her came back without a match, which really isn't surprising, except her prints don't match the ones we took from Gracie's toys. She doesn't match any missing persons report, and the people who had her have been tight-lipped. We're guessing they don't actually know who she is." His father sighed. "It's possible we're dealing with a little girl found by human traffickers, but there's no evidence to back that up."

The thought made Kensington want to lose his dinner. If those were the kind of people mixed up in this, could they be certain the same caliber of human didn't have Gracie, despite the reassurances in the note?

"We're doing everything we can to figure out where she came from," his father assured him. "Tomorrow or Monday, the doctor is going to take off the bandages and maybe we can get a decent picture of her to show the media. If the wounds aren't too bad."

"Let me know how it goes, would you? I hate that this little girl is in pain, possibly from someone scarring her so we would think she was Gracie." He leaned against the back of the chair. "Is there any incentive we're willing to offer to get one of the adults to talk?"

"It's being discussed." There was a noise on the other end of the phone. "We've arrived. I need to greet Esme and Benjamin. If there's anything you need to know, I'll make sure you do."

"Thanks." Kensington hung up and changed into a pair of pajama pants.

Anabelle walked in dressed in a robe and toweling her hair dry. "What did your father say?"

"To get some rest. He'll make sure someone wakes us if necessary."

Her shoulders relaxed in what had to be relief. "As much as I want to be there for Astrid, I need sleep. I'm going to have to be up at an insane hour to get some work done before breakfast."

Kensington filled her in on the rest of the conversation with his father.

By the time he finished, Anabelle emerged from her dressing room in pajamas. "He doesn't think Gracie was taken by human traffickers, does he? No one has ever said anything about that to me."

"No. If she was, they wouldn't have let Jenny go."

Anabelle nodded slowly. "True. They'd have kept both girls."

Kensington put his hands on her hips and pulled her toward him until she rested her forehead on his chest. "She's fine, love. Missing you, but she's being well taken care of, I promise."

"You can't promise that, Kensington, and you know it."

With a sigh, he wrapped his arms around her. "Yes, I can. I can't explain how I know, but it's beyond even believing the note. Somewhere, deep down, I just know that, in general, she's not being mistreated. I can't tell you where that assurance comes from, but it's there. I pray for her constantly, and every time I do, I feel that same thing in my gut."

Her arms slid around his waist. "I do, too." The admission surprised him. "But at the same time, I can't shake the feeling that she's scared and alone and just wants to come home."

"Of course she does. And scared is natural, though if I had to bet, I think our girl is more mad than scared most of the time. She wants her Annie and anyone she perceives is keeping her from you will feel her wrath."

A small chuckle actually came from Anabelle. "Can't you just see her refusing to do something or not cleaning up her toys or eating her breakfast because they've made her mad? She's probably drawing pictures of them with big slashes through their faces to show how mad she is."

The thought made Kensington smile. "They don't know who they're dealing with. She's going to be okay, love. I promise."

He meant it. He believed it with every bone in his body.

If only he could make it come to pass in his own timing.

Bone weary despite the small laugh at the thought of Gracie giving her captors what for, Anabelle let Kensington lead her to their bed, and essentially tuck her in.

Sleep came more quickly than it did many nights, including after the trip to the hospital the night before. Her dreams were plagued with Gracie and the little girl in the hospital. How could

Anabelle protect either one of them like they were begging her to do?

Finally, she knew she couldn't try to sleep any longer. With her Bible in hand, Anabelle made a cup of coffee and settled into a chair near a window where she could just make out the ocean in the moonlight.

Opening to Psalms, Anabelle tried to focus on the passages, first trying one chapter, then another. Nothing seemed to sooth her soul, though. Not like she needed.

Finally, she gave up on the scripture reading and just began to pray. It wasn't like any prayer she'd ever prayed before, though.

She didn't speak out loud, but internally...

Anabelle yelled at God.

Questioned Him.

Accused Him of abandoning Anabelle - and Gracie.

The one-sided conversation in her head seemed to help.

And then she heard a voice, in her head. A still, quiet voice, that sounded eerily like her father's, though deeper.

Are you quite done?

She gave a single nod.

Go to the next chapter.

Obediently, Anabelle turned the page. Psalm 142.

When my spirit grows faint within me, it is you who watch over my way. In the path where I walk people have hidden a snare for me. Look and see, there is no one at my right hand; no one is concerned for me. I have no refuge; no one cares for my life. I cry to you, LORD; I say, "You are my refuge, my portion in the land of the living."

Okay. So even when she felt alone, God was her refuge. Her portion. He was Gracie's too, even if she was too young to really understand.

She started to flip the Bible closed, but it fell open, marked by a scrap of paper she must have stashed there.

Deuteronomy 31:8 was at the top of the page.

The LORD himself goes before you and will be with you; he will never leave you nor forsake you. Do not be afraid; do not be discouraged."

Anabelle felt the peace begin to seep into her bones.

Daniel 3.

This time the little voice sounded like her Sunday school teacher when she was a child. Anabelle skimmed the first part of the chapter.

Then King Nebuchadnezzar leaped to his feet in amazement and asked his advisers, "Weren't there three men that we tied up and threw into the fire?" They replied, "Certainly, Your Majesty." He said, "Look! I see four men walking around in the fire, unbound and unharmed, and the fourth looks like a son of the gods."

This time when she went to close the Bible, another story came to mind. Peter's escape from prison. She had to use her phone, previously tucked under her leg, to remember the story was in Acts 12.

She read the story, how all seemed lost. Herod would likely have sentenced Peter to death. Instead, an angel, protecting Peter, helped him escape despite the secure prison.

Another verse came to mind, though she didn't look it up. Anabelle knew several places in the Bible where it said God would have His angels watch over His children.

That had to include Gracie.

Finally at peace, she stood and went to get ready for the day. When dressed, she spent some time on the computer finishing some work that needed doing before the Games actually started in a few days.

Frustrated when the numbers didn't add up correctly, she slammed the laptop shut.

"What did it do to you?"

One part of her continued to be frustrated at the work problem. Another part of her grew frustrated that the peace hadn't lasted longer, though she knew, deep in her soul, that Gracie was being cared for by beings far more powerful than even the king's men.

"How's your sister?" She skipped the question all together.

"They were real contractions, but with medication, they're under control for the moment. They'll be there until at least tomorrow morning."

Anabelle gave a single nod and blew out a breath. "Okay. Let me know if something changes."

"Of course." Kensington started to turn, but she stopped him.

"I know you were right last night. Gracie's okay."

He smiled at her. "I'm glad you believe so, too." His phone buzzed, and he gave her an apologetic glance as he answered it.

Anabelle finished getting ready then headed out of the dressing room.

Kensington was on the phone, and, from the sounds of it, dealing with another minor emergency related to the opening of Athlete's Village. He whispered that he'd meet her at breakfast.

As much as Anabelle usually loved being around other people, she really didn't want to have breakfast with King Benjamin, especially without Kensington present. At least the rest of the family would be there.

And she was learning her way around the palace. Confident steps carried her toward the breakfast room, but as she neared the last turn, she found the hall roped off.

"I'm sorry, ma'am," a staff member told her. "This hall is unavailable for use at the moment. You'll need to go around."

"Around?" She didn't know any other way.

"Yes, ma'am." The staff member pointed one way then the other, giving her directions.

Anabelle made the first two turns but couldn't remember which direction she needed to go at the next junction. Another staff member sent her upstairs where a third sent her back down another staircase. Frustration rising, she finally made it to the breakfast room, just to discover King Benjamin was the only one present.

He stared out a window with his hands clasped behind his back.

Anabelle started to leave but he stopped her with a word.

"Wait."

She turned but didn't curtsy. Though technically still an Eyjanian citizen, she just didn't feel like it.

"Good morning." But she would be polite.

"I was told breakfast would begin a few minutes ago."

"Everyone else must be running late. I know Kensington is dealing with something about the Village. I'm sure they all have unavoidable delays and will be here momentarily."

"I was sorry to hear about your sister." His tone held no real emotion.

"I'm sure you were."

His eyes narrowed at her snark. "What do you mean by that?"

"You escaped being her legal guardian. Otherwise this wouldn't have happened."

"I did?" He seemed genuinely perplexed at her words.

She didn't buy it. "Yeah. When I married Kensington instead of you."

He blinked. "You did?"

"You don't remember meeting me and telling your uncle I'd do?"

King Benjamin's brows knit together in concentration. "I remember meeting someone Isaiah said he believed might make a good wife for me. I was told it didn't work out, but..." He shrugged. "I barely remember it, and he didn't tell me why."

"Then you won't stand in the way of the adoption? Even if Gracie is your daughter?" Anabelle clamped her lips together. She hadn't meant to say that.

"What are you talking about?"

26

Kensington offered Esme his arm as they walked toward the breakfast room together. "Did you enjoy the ball last night?" he asked, more to be polite than anything.

Before she could answer, shouting reached them.

"What are you talking about?"

"You know what I'm talking about!"

Anabelle and Benjamin?

"You have to know!"

Kensington let go of Esme and bolted ahead. This couldn't be good.

"What's going on?" he asked as he burst into the room.

Anabelle gestured toward Benjamin. "He doesn't even remember being engaged to me, or whatever it was." Her eyes flashed. "And he says he doesn't know anything about Gracie being his daughter. Or why my parents had to die."

"I don't!" Benjamin's exasperation was the most emotion Kensington had ever seen from him. "I have, quite literally, less than no

211

idea what you're talking about. Your sister is not my daughter! How could she be if she's your sister?"

"She was adopted," Kensington explained.

"She's still not my child," Benjamin insisted.

"How can you be so sure?" Anabelle challenged him. "How can you be certain you didn't get her mother pregnant?"

The king's face became impassive. "I am certain. I owe you no other explanation than that."

Could it be that Benjamin wasn't the same sort of philanderer his uncle was?

The pieces clicked into place.

"Benjamin isn't Gracie's father," Kensington told Anabelle. He turned to the other king. "But Isaiah could be."

Benjamin shrugged. "I suppose it's possible."

Anabelle gasped. "That explains it." She turned to Esme. "Everything you said, it could all be just as true if Isaiah is Gracie's biological father instead of Benjamin."

Kensington knew Anabelle had to be flustered if she didn't use Benjamin's title.

"What could be true?" Benjamin folded his arms across his chest.

Esme glanced at Kensington then played it nonchalant. "We were told there was a possibility you were Gracie's father. Her biological mother worked in the palace. It made sense. If you insist you aren't, then that rumor can be laid to rest."

Kensington moved to Anabelle's side and slid his arm around her waist. She needed to let this drop for now.

"That doesn't mean he doesn't know something." Her anger was devolving into desperation. "You're the king. You have to know something about why my parents were killed and where my sister is."

Benjamin shook his head. "I wish I had answers for you, ma'am, but quite simply, I do not."

Kensington needed to shift the focus. "Benjamin, I would

appreciate it, if you have the time, if you would speak with our security team anyway. With the Eyjanian connection, it is always possible you know something you don't realize you know."

"If I have time," he replied, quite noncommittal.

"We would also appreciate it if you would do anything you can on your end to expedite the adoption process. We would like to be Gracie's legal parents as soon as possible."

"If I can."

Kensington didn't hold out much hope of him doing anything, but further conversation was forestalled with the arrival of the rest of the family.

"Good morning!" his father's voice filled the room. "I hope you all slept well after last night's excitement."

Benjamin shifted his focus from Kensington and Anabelle to the new attendees. "I did. However, I do need to get home soon. If we could have breakfast, I would like to speak quickly with your security teams, in case there is some way I can help with the Lady's disappearance, and then I need to take my leave."

"Of course." Kensington's father motioned toward the table. "We appreciate anything you may be able to tell them that could help. Any detail, no matter how small, could be of the utmost importance."

Anabelle didn't wait for others to be seated, but Kensington knew she chose a spot as far away from Benjamin's seat as she could. It wasn't quite where she should have been, but no one would quibble with her.

Conversation around the table remained stilted to non-existent. Jacqueline Grace attempted to keep it going, but eventually she lapsed into silence as well.

As soon as he could, Benjamin excused himself. A member of the staff escorted him toward the security office.

Once he was clear of the room, Kensington's father spoke. "Would someone care to tell me what was going on when we arrived?"

"It's my fault," Anabelle blurted out. "We were the only two here, and I asked him about Gracie, accused him of being her father, and wanted to know why my parents had to die."

"What did he say?"

"He's not Gracie's father," Kensington answered for her. "I believe him when he appeared to have no idea what she was talking about. He categorically denied being her father, and I wondered, out loud, if Isaiah could be. Isaiah is known for his dalliances, but we've never really heard anything about Benjamin taking after him."

His father nodded slowly. "That actually makes a lot more sense. I've never believed Benjamin to be diabolical, but I believe it of Isaiah. I don't know that I think he had anything to do with your parents' death, but Gracie's father? Possibly behind the kidnapping? That I can believe."

Esme nodded as well. "That would fit better with what my family knows as well. I don't know why your parents believed Benjamin to be her father, but that was the information they had. Looking back on a couple things they said, it's possible they weren't even sure, or were going off what your grandfather said - possibly in the hopes of misleading them."

"I'll check in with the security offices later," the king told them. "Kensington, I know you'll be busy with the Athletes' Village opening. Anabelle, I'm sure you'll be occupied as well since the souvenir stands will be in service."

Kensington and Anabelle pushed back from the table at the same time. "We both need to be leaving shortly. Thank you all for your continued support." He rested his hand on Anabelle's back as they left the breakfast room. The confrontation with Benjamin hadn't been enjoyable, but at least it was over. With any luck, they'd have learned something new.

He couldn't focus on that, though. The Village opening had to be at the forefront of his mind. He couldn't dwell on Gracie, no matter how much he wanted to.

Pointing with her middle finger wasn't Anabelle's favorite thing, but sometimes it was the only finger available. That was how she managed not to drop everything she was holding. "Why don't we move that shirt to the bottom and the green one to the top? It makes the colors flow better, I think."

"Good eye." Holly walked up beside her, arms filled with merchandise. "I would have suggested the same thing, despite the layout they sent us to use."

"Thanks. I did a little bit of retail the last couple of years. My best friend owns a yarn store in Akushla. It was a piece of cake compared to what this is going to be."

Holly glanced at the wall clock. "The insanity begins in half an hour. I'm really glad we don't officially open until the Village opens at noon. Trying to get all of this done last night would have been impossible."

"At least I wouldn't have been wearing heels all night," Anabelle pointed out. "And breakfast this morning was a little awkward."

"I thought I heard the family had breakfast with King Benjamin and Princess Esmeralda. It wasn't nice to talk with someone from home, even he is the king?"

Anabelle had to remind herself that Holly wasn't really a friend, not yet. "Exactly. He's the king. We had a not entirely pleasant encounter one time. He doesn't remember it, but when you're in the public eye you meet a lot of people. He unintentionally offended me." She shrugged. "I've moved on, but that doesn't mean I want to hang out with him, and it's just awkward."

"I can understand that."

Twenty minutes later, they were as ready to open as they ever would be. Good thing, because she had ten minutes to get across the complex to the Village and join Kensington at the opening. "I have to go," she told Holly. "You'll officially open as soon as Kensington cuts the ribbon. I doubt you'll have much business for the first half hour. Everyone will be at the ceremony before they start filtering around." Holly knew all of this, but Anabelle couldn't help but tell her again.

Her security team caught her attention and ushered her to a golf cart used to whisk her away.

When she reached Kensington's side, he kissed her cheek despite the crowd milling about to the side of the stage. "My parents want to talk to us immediately after we're done. There's no news," he hurried on, "but it seems to be an issue of some importance. We'll go to the conference room in the building behind the stage."

Anabelle just nodded as their names were announced. Kensington took her hand and led the way up the stairs. They both waved as the crowd cheered then stood in front of their chairs.

They took their seats as the rest of those on stage did. Several people gave short speeches before Kensington took his spot behind the microphones. He kept his address short and sweet. The stage had been situated just to the side of the main walkway leading into the Village. Kensington and several others went down those steps. Anabelle followed, though she hung back. Kensington, along with one of the athletes from San Majoria, used giant scissors to cut the red ribbon and symbolize the opening of the Village and the pre-Games events and venues, like the souvenir stands.

For about ten minutes, they greeted people, mostly athletes, as they streamed into the Village. She noticed her in-laws were further down the line on the same side she and Kensington were stationed. As the crowd surging through dwindled to a trickle, security teams for the five of them surrounded her family and led them to a conference room, but no one said anything until they were all seated.

She watched the king, expectant.

"The nurse you spoke with the other day has stayed with the little girl non-stop, even getting her shift covered so she wouldn't have to leave her side." The king heaved a heavy sigh. "She noticed some oddities no one would have picked up on otherwise. After you left breakfast, we were notified the doctor in charge of her case, along with a nurse he often works closely with, had disappeared. Another doctor met us at the hospital. With our approval, he investigated further."

"And?" Kensington prompted when his father didn't go on.

"There's nothing wrong with that little girl, except sedatives. There are no burns. No wounds of any kind. Blood work is being done to make sure we're not missing anything, but she's quite clearly not Gracie. Photos have been taken and will be distributed to the media today or tomorrow in hopes of identifying her."

Anabelle felt relief wash over her. "She's really all right?"

"She still wasn't awake yet when we left, but they believe once the medication keeping her asleep is out of her system, she'll be just fine."

"How could this happen?" Kensington asked. "How could a doctor manipulate the system so no one else questioned anything?"

"Hospital administration is looking into that very thing. The doctor in question has impeccable credentials. He'd worked for the hospital for decades, won award after award, and no one had any reason to suspect him of anything."

They discussed it until Anabelle asked about something else weighing on her. "What about Astrid? How is she?"

"Fine as can be. She's resting but should be able to go home tomorrow. She'll be out of circulation much earlier than originally planned, though. Her engagements will all be canceled or reassigned."

"The important thing is for her to take care of herself and the baby." Anabelle knew they were all relieved the baby hadn't been born overnight.

The king stood. "That's all we know for now. If anything changes, we'll let you know."

Hugs were exchanged with each of her extended family members holding her tightly and whispering their reassurances.

After a private moment with Kensington, Anabelle returned to the shop where Holly had things well in hand and threw herself into her work.

As he expected, Kensington was so busy he didn't know if he was coming or going. His time with Anabelle had been non-existent, except for a stolen moment or two.

News about the little girl had taken over the airwaves for two days before Astrid's trip to the hospital joined it. The girl hadn't been identified, but seemed to have no lasting effects from the medications. She wasn't talking to anyone at all. Her murmurs in her sleep told them she was capable, but the doctors seemed to think the trauma had caused her to refuse.

The Opening Ceremonies had gone off without a hitch the night before - at least none visible to the public. As with any exhibition of that size, a few glitches occurred, but nothing that couldn't be worked around.

He walked toward the entrance to the track. He wouldn't go out of the tunnel and cause a disturbance with his presence, but wanted to observe for a moment. After watching the high jump for several competitors, he made a few notes about what he saw in the periphery.

Anabelle was working at one of the stores in a nearby venue. He rode in a golf cart to her location, but, once again, didn't want to intrude.

From the back office, he could watch her on the monitors that showed the entire store.

He knew her face by heart. The worry lines much too prominent for someone so young, becoming so much more pronounced in the weeks since Gracie's disappearance. The sparkling hazel eyes dimmed in recent times. The ready smile that made far too few appearances lately.

But here... He could tell she was in her element.

She answered questions, took selfies, hugged little children, gave fist bumps and high fives to kids - mostly boys - who likely deemed themselves too old for hugs.

"She's great at this."

Kensington glanced to the side to see Holly walk in with a stack of papers.

"She was born to be with people. We've talked a bit, but mostly I've observed and read between the lines. Everything with Lady Gracie has taken a toll, but when things settle back down and life returns to normal, she needs to be around people. She's like me."

"In what way?"

"She's very, very good at what she's done the last few weeks. There was a learning curve because she'd never done it before, but I have absolutely no doubt she could do my job if she wanted to, and probably she could do it better. What I really mean, though, is that she's an extrovert. She's renewed and energized by time with people. I hate to say it, sir, but you and your family don't *really* count in that sense. Given her own choice, she'd probably have a wide circle of friends, some closer to her than others, but she finds energy and renewal in times with others."

Kensington nodded. "I understand. I think I'm much the same way, but given my position and family, it's not always possible. Sometimes I chafe at the restrictions. She likely will, too, when things are normal again."

A few comments she'd made back at Lowery House, the frustration in her voice at the limits on her movements, made more sense when viewed in light of extroversion, something he'd never really considered before. "I'll do my best to make sure she has that interaction and the opportunity to work with charities or organizations so she can put those skills to good use. Thank you for helping her find her footing."

"My pleasure." Holly grabbed another stack of papers. "But right now, there's no rest for the weary. Good afternoon." She bowed her head slightly and left.

Kensington took the golf cart back to the track and field stadium and did something his security team would hate, but he didn't much care.

The concourse was filled with spectators, and he wanted to be a part of it, even for a few minutes.

As expected, he was quickly noticed. It was good for him to be with people who didn't really want something from him, just a moment of his time for a handshake and a selfie.

Everyone said nice things about the Games so far, congratulated him on his marriage to Anabelle, and told him they were all in their prayers.

He crouched down and reached for a little girl, to shake her hand, but his arms were grabbed, and he was lifted off his feet and pulled away. The girl's eyes went wide as did her mother's.

Kensington was twisted around and run through corridors he didn't recognize, his shouts for an explanation going unheeded.

He knew it wasn't the little girl or her mother or any of the people around that caused him to be rushed off and hoped someone would take the time to make sure they knew that.

His car waited in one of the underground tunnels. His team practically threw him in it before barreling out of the parking area. The horn blared constantly as they traversed through the back areas of the complex. In just moments, they stopped outside the building he'd been using to house his headquarters for the duration of the Games.

Security here was tight, but also remained tight-lipped. This time, he wasn't being drug away by his upper arms, but he was hurried through hallways just the same.

The path opened into his small, cluttered office area. A man stood there, holding a dark-haired little girl.

He turned.

Bertrand.

"Sir..."

The little girl lifted her head off Bertrand's shoulder.

"Kenny!"

Kensington blinked as she struggled to get down and crossed the few feet. He swung her up into his arms and clung tightly to her before it really registered.

"Gracie," he whispered.

"My miss you, Kenny," she whispered back, her arms so tight around his neck that he worried about breathing, then decided it didn't matter.

His little girl was in his arms, and he wouldn't ever let her go.

27

"**M**a'am, I need you to come with me." The burly security guard had never worked with Anabelle before, but the grip on her arm told her he was quite serious.

"Excuse me," she told the customer she was talking with, as she waved an associate over. "This young man here will help you with any other questions."

The guard hurried her through the back door of the shop and into a waiting car. It sped through a back route to one of the buildings near the track and field venue. She asked repeatedly what this was all about - was Kensington all right? Astrid?

No answers were forthcoming.

She recognized the door to the small office suite Kensington was using. Inside, there were so many people she could barely squeeze through to get into his office. Most of them looked puzzled but one or two seemed to be hiding a smile.

Once in the office, with the door closed behind her, she saw Kensington standing with his back to her, holding a little girl with dark hair.

Sofia?

He turned and she could see the tear tracks still filled with moisture on his cheeks and a trembling smile. "Hey," he said softly to the little girl hidden by a curtain of brown hair. "There's someone else here to see you."

The little girl lifted her head, and Anabelle felt her knees give way.

Bertrand, who she hadn't even realized was there, grabbed her elbow. Otherwise she would have landed on the floor.

"Gracie?" she whispered.

"Annie!"

Stable again, Anabelle reached for her sister and clung tight. Kensington wrapped his arms around them both.

Anabelle couldn't stop the sobs, could feel tears dripping from Kensington's cheeks onto her forehead, and absorbed the warmth of Gracie in her arms.

"Annie, too tight." The whine in the beloved voice made Anabelle laugh through the tears.

"I'm so sorry, sweet girl." She leaned back to look closer. "Are you all right, love? Are you hurt?"

Gracie shook her head. "I fine. My miss you."

Anabelle tightened her hold. "Oh, Gracie. I missed you, too. More than you'll ever know."

The door opened behind her. "It's time to go," a voice told them. "We have a secure route to a vehicle to take you back to the palace."

A crowd of security personnel, both from the palace team as well as the venue surrounded them. The halls were empty, but no one would have been able to tell who was inside the small huddle anyway.

In the back of the limousine, Anabelle refused to let go of Gracie. There was no car seat, so she would hold tightly to her little girl.

Seat belts were buckled regardless, and Kensington's arm around her shoulder reassured her this was real.

"I don't know anything yet," he told her. "I walked into the office to see her with Bertrand a few minutes before you arrived. That's all I know."

Anabelle nodded as Gracie settled her head on Anabelle's chest.

The police escort made the ride blessedly short.

The car came to a stop under the portico. Inside the palace, they were met by the king and queen and ushered to security headquarters.

"No." Anabelle stopped before going through the double doors. "I don't want Gracie in there. We're going to our quarters. They can talk to us there."

The king gave a slight nod and the whole group shifted course. In a few minutes, they were seated in the sitting room of Kensington's apartment.

"Miss Gracie, I have a few questions for you, okay?" The same woman had talked with Jenny. "I just need you to tell me the truth. You will *not* get in trouble for anything you tell me, okay?"

Gracie nodded, but turned to Anabelle first. "Amma say to tell you to find her."

Anabelle's eyes grew wide as she glanced at Kensington. "Amma?"

"Uh huh. Amma took care of me. Not the whole time."

She looked over at the king who met her gaze with an impassive look of his own.

He'd known? If Amma was with Gracie...

"We're already looking," he said softly. "We have been for weeks. We'll update you later."

Amma, Mrs. T, was missing, and no one had thought to tell her.

"We need your help to find Amma," the woman told Gracie.

Anabelle lost track of time as Gracie answered questions.

Before Amma another woman took care of Gracie. She wasn't nice, but wasn't mean.

She was in a house.

There were four bedrooms.

Three bathrooms.

One with a big tub Gracie could swim in.

She couldn't go outside, but she peeked sometimes. There was no playground in the backyard, but there was a tree. In the front she could see a playground but it had a fence around it, and sometimes there were lots of kids on it. She wanted to play with them.

He always said no.

"Who said no?"

Gracie shrugged. "The man."

"Was it the same man who took you at the turtle park?"

"No."

The woman asked a series of questions until they had a general description of the man - dark hair, but like Kensington's so thinning on top. Tall. Something of a stomach.

And a scar on his hand.

The blood drained from Anabelle's face when Gracie pointed to where the scar was.

Anabelle looked at the king who simply nodded and made a pointing motion with his hand. A man scurried out of the room.

"Okay, Miss Gracie, I know you said you're not hurt, but I want my friend to look at you. He's a doctor." She leaned in. "He was Kenny's doctor when he was little. Is that okay with you?"

"Annie stay?"

Grandmother appeared. "Could I stay with you, Miss Gracie? I missed you a whole lot, and Annie needs to answer some questions, too, okay?"

Gracie nodded. "My miss you, too, Gigi. Where 'Fia?"

Anabelle smiled. "Sofia is with Uncle Jordan on San Minoria today, but they'll be back tonight. I know she misses you and can't wait to play."

Gracie went easily to Gigi. Anabelle held tight to Kensington's hand as the doctor started to look Gracie over. They joined a knot of people across the room.

She felt fire flash from her eyes as she looked at her husband, her father-in-law, and the senior members of the security staff. "How long have you known Amma was missing?"

Kensington hadn't known, though he'd wondered if something else was going on for a couple of weeks. He kept his arm around his wife.

His father looked directly at Anabelle. "When your *amma* and *afi* left for Eyjania after you had dinner, they made it as far as the airport. Amma decided to stay here and was on her way back to the palace. That's all we know. Somewhere between the airport and here, she was waylaid. Mr. Sørensen received a note the next day saying she was taking care of her granddaughter and would not be harmed. That lends credence to the theory your grandfather is behind it. Your grandfather, obviously, has known for decades who your mother's family is and would have been keeping an eye on them. For whatever reason, the person taking care of Gracie needed help."

"And no one told me?"

Kensington could feel the tension increasing in Anabelle's shoulders.

"There was nothing you could do. Mr. Sørensen specifically requested it be kept from you unless there was a reason to think you could help us find her. There hasn't been until now. With the information Gracie gave us about the playground and the school, we're mobilizing now to find her."

"And the people who had Gracie won't do something horrible to her now that Gracie's gone?"

"Word hasn't been released. The two men who had her have been arrested. We're hopeful there are no others."

"Are either one of them the man with the scar on his hand?" she asked.

"I don't know."

The doctor walked up to the group. "From a very cursory preliminary exam, the Lady seems to be no worse for wear. She may have nightmares and need to see a psychologist, but there's not much more I can do. I'll have some bloodwork done in a bit, just to make sure there's no drugs in her system, but there doesn't appear to be. She did give me some more details about the playground at the school." He described some different colored slides and other equipment.

One of the security team members passed the information along.

"They already had it narrowed down to a few primary schools," the head of security told them. "Many of them don't have houses near the playgrounds so that helps. She also mentioned hearing bells every day about lunch time so there must be a church nearby. That helps, too."

"Who found her?" Anabelle leaned into him. "How?"

Kensington answered. "Bertrand. That's all we know so far."

"He's being questioned down in security," his father told them. "He's more than redeemed himself for the accidental breech last fall."

Kensington nodded, but the conversation ground to a halt as his mother walked up holding the little girl. "Someone wants her Annie."

Anabelle took Gracie and walked away, toward the room that had been redecorated with Gracie in mind.

"We need a psychologist." The doctor's words had brought that home. "Someone needs to talk to all three of us, to tell me and Anabelle what to expect and how to react."

"There is one on the way. She is the one Astrid spoke with

several times after Andrei's death left her a widow. She has also worked extensively with children."

Kensington's phone buzzed. "As much as I hate to leave, I have a matter that must be attended to. Please keep me posted on the search for Amma."

His father nodded. Kensington kissed Gracie's forehead and Anabelle's temple then headed back to his temporary office.

Word wouldn't be released until later in the day, though enough people had seen him and Anabelle both pulled from their respective locations that the news had to be getting out. In fact, there were probably pictures of him being dragged off all over the social media sites.

Back at the track and field stadium, members of his staff gave him sideways, questioning looks, but he didn't say anything about his sudden, dramatic disappearance. They wouldn't get answers any sooner than anyone else and most of them had been removed from the office before he arrived so only key staff and security were there when the three of them left.

For hours on end, he dealt with issue after issue and finally headed back to the palace about ten at night after the last event for the day had ended.

He found his two favorite females sound asleep in his bed. Gracie had crawled in with him and Anabelle a few times, but usually early in the morning when she was ready to be up for the day, and they weren't. She'd never actually slept with them before.

As quietly as he could, Kensington walked through the room and did what he needed to do before going to bed. He slid under the covers and earnestly sent his thanks heavenward, along with continued prayers for Amma and her safety. The details still hadn't been shared with him, but for the moment it didn't matter.

By eight the next morning, his parents' assistants had been rallied, along with Jacqueline Grace's, to help run the Games for a couple of hours. Anabelle's assistant, Brittany, was working closely with Holly and the Lachapelles to make sure the souvenir stores and stands were running smoothly.

Kensington, along with Anabelle, both of his parents, Bertrand, and several members of the security teams were seated in his father's conference room.

"First things first. Anabelle, your *amma* has been found safe. She's asleep but wants to see you and Gracie as soon as possible. Your *afi* is on his way from Eyjania, along with Rachel, Clari, and Joel."

Anabelle's shoulders slumped in relief. "Oh, thank you, Jesus."

"Second, Bertrand is going to tell us all what he told security yesterday about how he came to have the Lady with him. For the record, before he starts, everything he said has been verified via video surveillance of the areas in question. Everyone we are aware of is in custody with the sole exception of the man with the scar." Kensington's father turned to the side. "Bertrand?"

Bertrand took a deep breath and stared at his clasped hands. "When I took over as Prince Kensington's assistant, I told him my wife and I already had tickets to a gymnastics event. It's been her favorite since she was a child, and I wanted to be able to go with her. He promised to make sure we could go together. As we were walking across the square outside the Athlete's Village, I saw two men carrying a little girl with dark hair who looked familiar, but I couldn't quite figure it out."

He looked between Anabelle and Kensington. "You know how there's that little voice inside that tells you to go a different direction than usual or not to truly trust a person?"

Anabelle nodded. "That's how I've always felt about my grandfather."

"That voice told me to stay close. When she said something, I knew it was her. I just needed to figure out how to get her back, make sure the two men were arrested, and keep her from getting hurt in the process, while making sure my wife stayed safe."

28

Anabelle did her best to relax as Bertrand shared his story. He'd spent some time in the military as a young man and had continued to train for many years, just in case.

He just never knew what for.

Until a day earlier.

Bertrand told how he'd sent his wife to get them a souvenir at a nearby stand. With her out of harm's way, he followed the two men until they neared a narrow alcove.

"I barely remember it, but I grabbed the guy who wasn't holding Gracie. I caught him off-guard and was able to apply a hold to both of his carotid arteries. He was out in a few seconds. I knew it wouldn't take long for him to wake up, though he'd likely be disoriented."

Bertrand closed his eyes. "I saw the other guy looking around for his friend. I knew I needed to get Lady Gracie away from him, but I also knew if anyone saw it happen, they'd think I was the kidnapper so I needed him closer to a secure area where I could get behind-the-scenes as it were. I told him his buddy had gone around a corner while attaching my swipe card to my lanyard."

Anabelle's heart resided in her throat while he spoke. It hurt to hear.

His shoulders hunched over. "I didn't want to hurt him too badly, just get the Lady. Once he went around the corner, I kidney punched him in the back. Gracie slipped out of his hold, but she didn't land hard. I grabbed his hair and hit his head against the wall. Gracie started to cry, but I picked her up and ran to the gate, swiping my card to get behind the locked entry as quick as I could. Once on the other side, I called security, then started for Prince Kensington's office. She knew who I was from Easter, so she wasn't scared, but just said she wanted to go home. We'd only been in there a couple of minutes when you arrived."

"Thank you." Anabelle reached across the table to grip his hands. "Thank you for getting Gracie back."

Bertrand bowed his head. "It was my privilege, ma'am."

"Do we know why they ventured out with her?" Kensington asked security.

"From the little they've said, we believe it to be arrogance, pure and simple. With the news about Astrid and the baby plus the other little girl and dyeing Gracie's hair, they figured it was safe enough."

Anabelle chuckled. "I bet she threw an absolute fit until they agreed to take her. We've been talking about this for two years. She would have wanted to be there."

"Whatever the reason, she's home now." The king looked past all of them. "And I believe your *amma* is awake and looking for both of you."

Without waiting to be officially dismissed, Anabelle hurried out the door. "Where is she?" she called over her shoulder.

"Esther's quarters," came the answer combined with a chuckle.

Of course. The family would want to make certain Amma was

well taken care of, and Esther wasn't home. Her quarters would be available, or at least one of the other bedrooms would be.

Anabelle nearly sprinted up several sets of stairs and down even more corridors, slowing only when she reached the heavy wooden door. Pushing it open slowly, she stepped out of the hall and into the dimly lit sitting room.

"Amma?" she called softly.

"I'm in here, darling!" The strong voice reassured Anabelle as she crossed to the bedroom, smiling at the sight of the quilt covering her *amma*. "Is Gracie with you?"

"No. She's with Jacqueline Grace right now." Anabelle stopped as she crossed into the bedroom. Amma sat upright in the bed, covers pulled up to her waist. "Oh, Amma!" It only took a couple seconds to cross the room and wrap her grandmother in a hug. "I didn't even know you were missing," she whispered. "How could I not know?"

"You've been very busy, child. Looking for Gracie, running the Games, and everything else on your plate." Amma held her close. "I am very glad you didn't know. You didn't need to be worried about me when your mind was already so overloaded. I was just fine."

"They didn't hurt you?"

Amma motioned for Anabelle to join her on the bed. Anabelle kicked off her shoes and stuck her legs under the covers, pulling them up as she sat next to Amma.

"No, they didn't hurt me. They needed someone Gracie would trust. She'd been giving the other person, a woman, a very difficult time. Gracie knew who I was immediately, though she didn't know I was her grandmother. She remembered me from Rachel's store."

"I've even talked to Rachel several times. She never said anything."

"Of course not. You couldn't do anything except give yourself an ulcer. They didn't want that for you and knew I wouldn't have either."

Anabelle was torn between gratefulness that she hadn't known and annoyance that someone else had made the decision for her. Amma was right. She would have worried herself even sicker than she already was over Gracie.

"I talked to Afi as soon as they would let me. He's on his way."

"I know." Tears came from a well Anabelle thought should have dried up long ago. "Oh, Amma, I'm so glad you were with Gracie." She laid her head on her grandmother's shoulder, only to find herself being urged further down until she curled into the embrace that comforted her own mother as a child.

"I am, too, love. If she couldn't have you or either of her mothers, I'm glad I could be there."

Lying there, soaking up her grandmother's strength and love, Anabelle knew what she'd been missing her whole life. Her mother had tried, and done well for the most part, but knowing what she knew now about Grandfather, her mother was under a strain Anabelle couldn't have imagined.

"Don't you have work to do today?" Amma asked softly. "I promise I'll be here when you get back."

"I'm not going anywhere."

It was well after dinner when Kensington made it back to the palace. News of Gracie's rescue still hadn't made the news, though a press conference had been called for first thing in the morning. Rumors were flying that Astrid was back in the hospital or that Gracie had been found, but the outcome wasn't nearly as good as the reality.

In two days, they had tickets for the three of them to see the "'nastics" as Gracie called it. Kensington would have to clear it with security and make sure Gracie was okay with it. Despite having nearly everyone in custody, security would be heavier than normal. Amma had seen the man with the scar. He'd been in the house, but she'd been in another room and didn't get a good look. She'd seen the scar and had seen him again from a distance.

Her description matched Anabelle's, but not enough for an ID. Perhaps enough to put out a call for help, though that hadn't been determined last he heard.

"Kenny!"

Even before he reached the apartment, he heard Gracie calling to him. He turned to see her running down the hall toward him. A few seconds later, he'd swung her up in his arms. "How was your day, sweet girl?"

"My play with Annie an' Amma an' Mimi an' Gigi."

He looked at Anabelle. "Who's Mimi?"

"Your mother." The three of them walked into the apartment together. "She can't say Miriam, and your mother sort of loves it as much as your grandmother loves being Gigi."

Kensington chuckled. "I can see that."

For an hour, he played with Gracie, amazed at how well she seemed to be readapting to her home. Anabelle gave her a bath then together they tucked her into their bed. Anabelle didn't want her anywhere else for a few days. Kensington didn't blame her.

They talked quietly about how the Games were going.

"We still have those tickets for gymnastics in a couple days. Do you still want to go?"

Her face lit up. "Could we?"

"I can talk to security if you want."

"If they say we can, I'd love to go, and I know Gracie would love it, too."

"Then we'll see what we can do." He pulled her into his arms and leaned down to kiss her. "There's a press conference in the morning. We have to be there."

"I know. Gracie will stay with Amma tomorrow. I can't stay home again, unfortunately."

"She'll be well taken care of." Kensington kissed Anabelle again. "But you need to get some sleep. As do I."

With another kiss, they got ready for bed. The next morning, they stood next to his father as he told the country Gracie had been found, and shared the information about Amma. The head of security shared the description of the man with the scar, though no one actually believed he was still in the country.

The head of security and local police chief stayed behind to answer questions while Kensington and Anabelle headed for the Games. He knew she wanted to stay behind, to spend more time with Afi, Rachel, and the others who had arrived late the day before.

Instead, Kensington spoke with Holly to make sure Anabelle would be able to leave in time to spend the evening with all of them and Gracie. Unfortunately, he wouldn't be able to.

He was able to do some PR, though.

This time when he walked through the concourse of the track and field venue, he wouldn't be rushed off. For nearly half an hour, he talked with attendees before the ones he'd been waiting for arrived.

Crouching down, he held out his hand to the little girl. "Hi. I'm Kensington."

She shook it. "I know. I'm sorry you had to leave so fast."

Kensington shook his head. "I'm the one who's sorry. I know you were scared when they dragged me away the other day."

"Mama said it was because they finally found your little girl, but Daddy doesn't think so. He said you didn't find her until the next day."

He leaned closer. "Want me to tell you who's right?"

She nodded quite seriously.

"Your mama is right. My assistant found her near the Athlete's Village, not very far away from here. Because my bodyguards didn't know what had happened yet, they made sure to stick close while they got me to Gracie as fast as they could, but I am sorry you were scared by it."

With a shrug, the girl lifted a small weight off his shoulders. "I'm okay. I'm really glad your little girl is all right."

"She is just fine. In fact, she's coming to see gymnastics in a couple days." He'd just gotten word that security had cleared it. "I would love it if you and your mama and daddy would join us." He glanced up at her mother. "My treat."

She looked up at her mother, too. "Can we, Mama?"

"If Prince Kensington really has enough tickets without any of his other friends not going, then yes."

He grinned. "We actually have a suite, so there's plenty of room. Given everything, we decided it would be easier for all of us to enjoy it rather than in the seats. If you'd rather have seats, though, I have three tickets we aren't going to use now."

"Thank you. We would love to join you in the suite, if that's all right. I think we'd prefer that as well."

Kensington stood. "My wife and I would love to have you join us." He hadn't discussed it with her yet. He meant to, but it slipped his mind the night before with the arrival of Afi and the others. She would, though. "My assistant will contact you with more details."

After another minute or two with the family, he returned to work. He prayed diligently for no emergencies that would keep him from returning to the palace for dinner with his little family and their guests.

But as they finished their dessert, his phone buzzed with something that needed his attention, so he kissed his wife, hugged his little girl, and went back to work.

"Ready?" Butterflies the size of Emperor Penguins had taken

up residence in Anabelle's gut. Their first outing since Gracie's return.

"'Nastics!" Gracie squealed as they took their seats in the car.

The transition home, so far, had been much smoother than Anabelle feared, but this outing could stretch her sanity to the breaking point.

At least Kensington had arranged for a private suite. More likely security had insisted. Regardless, it made her feel a little better.

Amma and Afi would be joining them, along with Rachel, Clari, and Joel. Anabelle had enjoyed getting to know Clari better. After all, they were cousins. Their relationship made her tangentially related to Rachel, which was kind of fun.

The car pulled up to the front of the venue. A small crowd had gathered to wait for them. Their itinerary hadn't officially been announced, but word had gotten out a little bit. Security knew this would happen, which was why everyone else was arriving separately.

Their path was roped off. A member of the enhanced security team opened her door, and Anabelle climbed out after releasing Gracie from her car seat. Holding tight to the little hand, Anabelle and Gracie started for the building, only to find Kensington walking toward them.

Gracie held up her arms for Kensington to pick her up, which he did. The pictures of the two of them would be all over the Internet before long.

They waved at the crowds but didn't stop to talk to any of them. Once inside, in a secure area, surrounded by security, Anabelle started to relax a little bit.

"I don't think I ever had a chance to mention this to you, but the little girl I was talking with when security grabbed me and her family are coming. We tracked them down from social media posts. I met with her the other day and wanted to make sure her last personalized memory of the family with the Games wasn't a scary one."

"That's fine. Another kid for Gracie to play with would be good." She'd wanted to invite Caitlin and Jenny, but though they'd talked by phone a few times, they hadn't seen each other yet. Jenny had strep throat and was still a bit too far under the weather.

But another little girl would also be present.

The still-unidentified child had been released from the hospital earlier in the day. She'd only been kept that long for security reasons. All of her tests came back completely normal, except she refused to talk to anyone as far as Anabelle knew.

But she'd taken to Jacqueline Grace, and Jacqueline Grace had taken to the little girl, going so far as to name her.

Kiara.

She'd indicated that wasn't her name, but when asked if she liked it, the girl nodded so it stuck.

They were being brought in more secretively. No one knew Jacqueline Grace was bringing Kiara to the palace to live for the time being. If Jacqueline Grace had her way, she'd adopt the little girl, but Anabelle wasn't sure if she'd be able to without knowing who the little girl actually was.

"Right here." Kensington set Gracie down and opened the door.

Gracie ran in and pressed her nose against the glass. "'Nastics! Annie, it's 'nastics!"

"Think she'd like to do gymnastics?" Kensington asked, his arms sliding around Anabelle from behind.

She leaned her head back against his chest. "I bet she would."

"Once things calm down, we should see about it."

"Do things ever calm down in this family?" She tried to keep her exhale to a minimum, but failed.

"Good point. It does seem like one thing after another some-times. I meant after the Games are wrapped up."

At least life had been fairly predictable before meeting Kensington, though it would have been much more difficult to get out of marrying Benjamin.

"Annie! Look!" Gracie pointed out the window to something on the floor. "I wanna do that."

Anabelle watched a girl do a tumbling run. "You can learn how if you want." Kensington had nailed it. "There's going to be two new friends with us today."

"'Fia?"

"I don't think Sofia can come, but a girl named Kiara will be here, and so will another girl who's a little older. I don't know what her name is." She glanced at Kensington who winced and shrugged.

The door opened to let in Amma, Afi, Rachel, Clari, and Joel.

"Amma!"

Her appearance was enough to make Gracie forget all about gymnastics. Anabelle had been worried seeing her grandmother would be difficult for Gracie, a reminder of her time in captivity, but instead she adored her newfound *amma*.

With hugs all around, and the arrival of Jacqueline Grace and Kiara followed by several others, including the family Kensington had invited, Anabelle found herself separated from Gracie for an extended time.

But this time, the little girl was within sight at all times. Surrounded by family and friends who were on high alert.

They didn't stay for the whole event, but Gracie got her fill of tumbling and aerobatics and balance. She and Kiara hit it off, as they both did with the other girl who was a little older, but Anabelle never heard her name.

By the time they left for the palace, darkness had fallen.

"It pretty, Kenny." Gracie held his hand from her car seat as she looked at the palace lit up in the darkness.

"It is." He leaned closer. "You know what's prettier?"

Gracie shook her head.

"My two girls are prettier. You and Annie." He glanced at her, but Anabelle couldn't read the look. "Gracie, what would you think if Annie and I adopted you, so we were your mama and daddy? We wouldn't ever want you to forget your first real mama and daddy, but it would mean you belong to us forever."

Gracie didn't answer immediately. "You be my daddy, Kenny?"

Anabelle bit her bottom lip. It wasn't too late to stop the process, but it was already in motion and would likely go through, regardless.

"I would be your daddy," he confirmed. "Annie would be your mama. If we ever have any other kids, they'd be your brothers and sisters."

She hadn't told him about her nearly confirmed suspicion yet either.

Anabelle looked more closely at Gracie. Were her eyes filled with tears?

"No one ever take me away again?"

29

The fear in Gracie's voice tore at Kensington's heart. "Sweet girl, even if you don't want me and Annie to adopt you, we will always, *always*, do our very best to make sure no one ever takes you away again. We love you too much. I can't promise nothing bad will ever happen, but I can promise that I, and Annie, and all the big bodyguards will always do our best to make sure you never go away again."

The tears spilled down Gracie's cheeks as the car slowed to a stop under the portico.

Kensington unbuckled Gracie from her seat. "Let's go upstairs, and we'll talk all about it okay?"

Gracie nodded, but clung tightly to him as they walked up the stairs toward the private quarters.

Once there, Kensington settled on the bed with his back against the headboard, and Gracie curled against him.

"Do you know what kind of house this is, Gracie?"

"A castle."

"That's right. Do you know who my father is?"

"King."

"Right again." Kensington tightened his hold on her as Anabelle sat cross-legged on the other end of the bed and looked worried. "My father is the king. Some day, Sofia's mama will be queen. One day a long time after that when you and Sofia are all grown up, Sofia will be queen. I'm a prince and so is Harrison. Jacqueline Grace and Esther are princesses."

"If you 'dopt me will I be a princess?"

He knew this question would hurt. He didn't know how much. "No, but you are a Lady already and will be a duchess someday. Unfortunately, the way the rules are, you can only be a princess if you're not adopted. You will always be our princess though."

She nodded slightly against him.

"So, here's the thing. Because my father is the king, and I'm a prince, and my whole family is a royal family, sometimes people don't like us very much and every once in a while, someone tries to hurt us. I don't even remember the last time someone really, really tried to hurt my family. But sometimes they do. And this time, they tried to hurt us by taking you away."

"Did it hurt?" Her voice sounded so tiny and broken.

"Oh, Gracie." Tears fell onto the top of her head. "It hurt more than you can imagine. Anabelle didn't stop crying for days and never stopped praying. My heart never stopped aching. Neither of us ever stopped looking for you, even though we had to do other things sometimes. We met with the police every day to see what they found. We prayed constantly. Finally, our prayers were answered when Bertrand found you."

Gracie seemed to curl further into herself.

"What is it, sweetie?" Anabelle asked softly.

"He show me pictures." Kensington could barely hear her words.

"What kind of pictures?" he pressed.

"You an' Annie."

The realization dawned on him and Anabelle at the same time.

"He showed you pictures of us, and it didn't look like we cared that you were gone?"

Gracie nodded.

Kensington shifted. "Let me get my phone out, okay?"

His little girl scrambled over to Anabelle as he dug his phone from his pocket. With just a few taps, he pulled up a picture from the first press conference.

"This is the day after you went missing, before we found Jenny." He turned his phone around. "What do you think?"

Anabelle took the phone and studied the picture. "You an' Annie look sad."

Sad didn't begin to describe it. Anabelle had refused to let a stylist work on her, instead choosing to present to the world just how distraught they were over Gracie's disappearance.

"That's how we looked for days. But we knew we had other things that had to be done because people were depending on us. Like get ready for the Games. Did you know that I'm in charge of absolutely everything about the Games?"

Gracie shook her head.

"So I had to do work. So did Annie. But you know what? Just like people were depending on us for the Games, we depended on the police and security here to look for you and to let us know the *second* there was anything we needed to know." He took the phone from her and pulled up another picture before handing it back. "See this one?"

"Why they pullin' you?"

"That's when Bertrand found you. My security team grabbed me and pulled me away as fast as they could. It was less than five minutes until I found you waiting with Bertrand in my office, and I was far away."

"Oh."

He found another picture, this one from their walk into the ball. "Is this a picture he showed you?"

Gracie nodded.

"Do you know what happened when we got inside and found a spot away from everyone else?"

She shook her head.

"Annie cried. Because she wanted you to be there with us. But we couldn't skip it because sometimes you have to go places and do things when you really don't want to."

"Like brush your teeth." Anabelle poked her in the ribs, making Gracie smile, just a bit. "You know how much you hate brushing your teeth sometimes?"

Gracie wrinkled her nose. "My hate it."

"I hated not being with you a million times more than you hate brushing your teeth." Anabelle hugged her closer.

"My hate not being here."

Kensington stretched out on his stomach so he could prop himself up on his arms and be close to Gracie's eye level. "We want to adopt you, little love. We want to legally be your mama and daddy. But even if we aren't, we will always, always do our best to make sure that never happens again. We can't promise nothing bad will happen, because there are bad guys out there, but we can promise to protect you with everything we have."

Gracie let him hold her hand while she snuggled closer to Anabelle. After a few minutes, she nodded.

"My wan' you to be my mama and daddy."

He watched Anabelle's shoulders slump and a weight lifted off Kensington's shoulders. "Then we'll make it happen."

Anabelle folded the last of the box lids into itself and sat back on her heels. "I think that's it."

"I told you we could finish without you," Holly told her as she picked up the box. "How late were you up with the closing ceremonies last night?"

Stifling a yawn, Anabelle forced herself to stand. "Late, but that's not the point. We're not done until this is done. Reports are turned in?"

"I sent them to the prince and CC'd you in case you wanted to look them over again."

"Thank you."

"Now leave before I make you. The truck won't be here to pick up until tomorrow. Your husband said that was taken care of. Go home and spend some time with Gracie. I'll lock up."

Anabelle hesitated. Wasn't part of being in charge being the last one to leave? "What do we need to finish?"

"Just a final walkthrough."

"I already did that before packing the last couple of boxes."

Holly laughed. "I know, but there's always the final final walk-through."

"Then let's go." Anabelle started for the front of the store.

"It's not just this store. It's all of the stores and stands and kiosks. The stands have all been cleared out and locked up. The kiosks have all been moved to the storage rooms, but we need to do a quick drive around to make sure one wasn't missed."

More than she thought needed to be done, but Holly was right. "The good news is that if I go, we get a driver and security to make sure no one gets in our way." She winked at her new friend. "Let's go."

It took another two hours, but they were finally finished.

They stood next to Anabelle's car. "I'm going to miss working with you, Holly. You were a Godsend the last few weeks. I was a hot mess and didn't have a clue what I was doing, and you really stepped up when we found Gracie."

Holly dropped into a small, and completely unnecessary for many reasons, curtsy. "It was my pleasure, Your Royal Highness. It will also be my privilege to help you with clothes whenever you want. Something exclusive or even maternity, which we normally don't carry, but I know people." She raised a brow.

Anabelle blinked. "What?"

"I know you're keeping it quiet, and I understand why, but part of my job is watching people and understanding what they need even if they don't. I've learned to pick up on subtle clues."

"I'm not even sure," Anabelle confessed. "I mean, I'd be shocked if I'm not given the timing of, well, you know, but I haven't taken a test or gone to a doctor or anything. I haven't even told Kensington yet. I wanted to wait until the Games were over."

She didn't dare confess one of her deepest fears to Holly, even though she'd proven to be a good friend.

"I won't tell anyone," Holly promised. "Even after it's public."

"Thank you." She gave Holly a hug. "I'm sure I'll be asking for clothes advice."

"Your sister-in-law always looks fabulous, since she started wearing bright colors again last year, so whatever the stylists are doing, they're right on point, but I'm happy to help, too."

"I appreciate the offer."

As the car headed for the palace, Anabelle knew she needed to tell Kensington.

But how?

She still didn't even have an engagement ring or wedding band, not that it *really* mattered to her, but she'd overheard comments about it, and it was mentioned in every article about her appearance. Except for the fact that she was married to Kensington, she hadn't actually had any of his titles conferred on her, not legally.

Anabelle had learned during the sojourn on San Mediano that, according to San Majorian law, the titles were only honorary as his spouse unless the king specifically conferred them. He hadn't technically conferred the title of Lady on Gracie yet either. Because she wasn't legally their daughter yet?

That had been commented on repeatedly as well. Was it worth bringing up to Kensington? Could she without seeming like a gold digger and title seeker?

Surely the king's people were aware of the comments.

If they had told the San Majorian people about their marriage sometime besides when Gracie went missing, Anabelle suspected the king would have made an official pronouncement, and Kensington would have presented her with some gorgeous ring.

But Gracie's disappearance had changed everything. Now that they'd found her, maybe that would go forward as originally planned.

Gracie was already sound asleep on a smaller bed brought into the room Anabelle shared with Kensington. As much as she wanted Gracie close, the little girl wasn't a still sleeper. The tossing, turning, and kicking had become too much for both Anabelle and Kensington. It would make moving Gracie back to her own room easier in the long run.

When she found Kensington in the closet pulling a pair of pajama pants on she leaned against the island of drawers in the center. "I need to talk to you."

His head shot up. "Everything all right?"

Was that fear in his voice?

"Yes." That thought caused fear to creep into her own heart. "Isn't it?"

He gave her that grin she loved and walked toward her, making her stomach flip like it had the first time she'd seen him - after she got over her relief that Gracie was all right.

"Of course." His arms slid around her waist until his fingers linked at the small of her back and anchored her to him. "What's going on?"

"I'm glad the Games are over." Start with something simple.

"Me, too. I'll be wrapping up for a few weeks, but the hard part is behind us and most of it can be done from anywhere."

Anabelle rested her hands on the spot where his chest met his abdomen, just at the bottom of his ribs. The warmth of his skin began to relieve some of the fear that came from wondering about his reaction.

Finally she blurted it out. "Gracie's going to be a big sister."

What? Kensington stared down at Anabelle as she finally looked up at him, the emotion in her hazel eyes warring between expectant and fearful.

"Gracie's going to be a big sister?" he confirmed.

She nodded.

Did that mean...? "You're pregnant?"

Another nod.

"We're having a baby?" It was starting to sink in. A little.

"Yes."

But there wasn't the excitement, the joy, he expected in the word. "What is it, love?"

She dropped her arms and tried to pull away, but he didn't let her go so easily.

"Talk to me."

"I don't want people to think we were trying to replace Gracie," she whispered.

His mind scrambled to keep up with her thought processes. "You're afraid that because you got pregnant while Gracie was missing people will think we were trying to replace her?"

Anabelle didn't even nod, but rested her forehead against his chest.

"Anyone who thinks that wasn't paying attention the last couple of months." He wrapped his arms more tightly around her. "If anything, they'll think we turned to each other in our grief and frustration, and when that happens, sometimes babies happen."

"But the naysayers are always louder."

"Usually. But for all anyone knows, we were already trying to get pregnant when Gracie was taken. With all the stress, they'll assume we didn't even consider taking precautions - which we clearly didn't - and things happen. Or with all the stress, whatever precautions we were taking were used inconsistently."

He rested his chin on the top of her head. "But really, it's none of anyone's business with the possible exception of my parents, and technically just my father as the monarch."

"Your father needs to know when we're trying to get pregnant?"

Kensington chuckled. "Not really, but there used to be laws on the books that children of the monarch basically had to always attempt to conceive heirs and couldn't legally do anything to prevent conception without his permission. I don't know if they're still technically the laws or not, but I do know my father leaves our reproductive decisions up to us, and just wants to be among the first to know when another blessing is on the way. I suspect Astrid will care even less about her children as long as there are heirs eventually."

"That's good." She looked up at him and leaned up to brush a light kiss against his lips. "The truth is I'm not even really *sure*. I mean, I am, but I haven't taken any tests or seen a doctor or anything."

"Then we'll talk to Astrid's doctor and get an appointment set up. He comes often to see her, so there shouldn't be any suspicion about him being here. Let him check everything out, and go from there."

"I like that idea."

"If we talk to Astrid, we could even make it coincide with one of her appointments so no one else needs to know anything just yet." As it sunk in, Kensington wanted to tell the world. Immediately.

But he knew that wasn't the right move.

Maybe she'd be okay with telling his family, at least the local ones. As far as he knew, no one had heard from Esther in months. He'd make sure she knew before the public did, but not just yet.

"I'm okay with your family," she said, as though reading his thoughts. "They should be the first to know. Maybe even before Gracie until we know more."

"We have a meeting with my father in the morning. I hadn't had a chance to tell you about it yet." He had no clue what it was about. "We can tell him then. It's possible my mother will be there, as well. I can ask her to be for a few minutes anyway. We can tell my sisters and Harrison later tomorrow."

"I like that plan." She kissed him again, more soundly this time.

He could tell the months of strain were starting to lose their grip on her psyche. Even those couple of times while Gracie had been missing, she hadn't kissed him quite like this.

Kensington held her tighter, then loosened his hold letting his hands slip up her arms until he could grasp her fingers. His thumb slid across her finger where a wedding band should be and the still coherent part of his mind remembered he'd never gotten her an engagement ring.

"As much as I adore kissing you like this, love," he murmured against her lips. "We have a little girl sleeping in our room right now."

Anabelle's eyes sparkled up at him. "And there's nowhere else in this apartment we could go?"

A combo chuckle-groan escaped. "I like the way you think."

Later, when she sat against the headboard of their shared bed, with Gracie snoring nearby, Kensington slid further down until he was eye level with her abdomen, resting his hand just under her belly button. "Our baby," he whispered, awestruck as the realization washed over him again.

She ran her fingers through his hair, hair he wished was as thick and full as his father's had remained. "Our baby."

"A boy or girl?"

"I don't much care."

He placed a soft kiss where his hand had been before moving away. "I know, but what's your gut say?"

Anabelle wrinkled her nose. "I kind of want another girl. I would like a boy, too, but I think I'd like a girl first."

"Me, too."

They rearranged themselves until he curled behind her, his hand once again resting protectively against her stomach.

In the morning, they shared knowing glances as they prepared for the day and left Gracie with Rachel. He wondered if Anabelle's best friend suspected.

"Holly guessed," she told him as they walked toward his father's office. "I didn't tell her, until she called me on it yesterday. I'm sorry you weren't the first one."

He squeezed her hand. "It's okay. I don't blame you for wanting to wait until the Games were over, and Holly has seen you a lot more than I have the last few weeks."

In his father's office, both of his parents waited, their faces serious.

Had they also guessed?

Before he could say anything, his father motioned for them to take a seat. Anabelle glanced up at Kensington, but he knew as little as she did.

His father sat down and folded his hands together. "You have to go back to Eyjania."

30

"**W**hat? Why?"

Anabelle could tell Kensington was keeping tight control of his emotions.

His father waved a hand. "Nothing so dramatic as all that. Because you never did any paperwork to legally move Gracie to San Majoria, her legal residence is still Eyjania. Under Eyjanian law, the adoption has to be finalized there. The biggest concern is that it can also be objected to, though I don't think either your grandfather or Isaiah will do so. That would expose their interest in Gracie, and that wouldn't be good."

He sighed. "I *would* expect another kidnapping attempt while you're there. Security around you will be tight."

"Good." Anabelle had an uneasy feeling in the pit of her stomach. "I have no intention of seeing him, but my grandfather will try something. I don't know what, but something."

"That's our belief as well. You, along with your friends and family, will be leaving on the family plane on Wednesday." The king turned to Kensington. "You asked that your mother be here as well. Is there something you needed to discuss?"

Here went nothing.

Kensington couldn't hide his smile as he reached for Anabelle's hand. She found it endearing. "Actually, there is."

His mother gasped and clasped her hands together. "Can I guess?"

Anabelle laughed. "I think you already have. I'm pregnant. I haven't done the math or talked to the doctor, or even taken a home pregnancy test, yet, but it's been long enough that I can't imagine I'm not."

A smile crossed the king's face. "Marvelous!"

They all moved away from the table and hugs were given all around. The king left his arm around Anabelle's shoulder. "I've been thinking about a few things. The announcement of your marriage, of course, wasn't how we'd hoped it would be. We promised the public more details eventually, and I think that time is almost here. We'll get the doctor over to see you before you leave, just so we know for sure how far along you are."

He squeezed her shoulder. "After you return, we'll announce the adoption, officially confer your titles and Gracie's, and if you're far enough along, announce the pregnancy all in one fell swoop."

"I like that plan." Kensington winked. "One big news story instead of a bunch of smaller ones."

"I can't make Gracie a princess, but I can make her an HRH. She'll be Her Royal Highness Duchess..." He shrugged. "I actually haven't quite figured out what she's going to be duchess of just yet. You aren't likely to get any new titles, Kensington. You're already a prince, duke, count, and something else, aren't you?"

Kensington faked outrage. "You don't remember all of my titles?"

"Sorry, son, but no." The king had a grin on his face. "I do good to remember all of mine."

When the meeting ended shortly thereafter, Kensington headed to his office while Anabelle went to find Gracie. She found all of her out-of-town friends and family together. A quick text to Kensington asked him to join them. This group could be trusted, with the possible exception of Gracie.

In a few minutes, Jacqueline Grace and Harrison had arrived. Gracie and Kiara had run off to play in Gracie's room, and Kensington walked in with his newly-perpetual grin in place.

"What?" Jacqueline Grace asked before either of them could say anything.

Kensington rested his hand on Anabelle's shoulder. "We just talked to our parents, so we wanted to let all of you know, too."

Rachel jumped up, hands in the air. "I knew it! I'm going to be an honorary royal auntie!"

Anabelle laughed as everyone else caught on quickly. Had she ever been hugged so much in her life?

"There's other news, too," Kensington told them as they calmed down. Anabelle stood by his side as he told them the adoption was nearly finalized, and they'd all be heading home on the royal plane in a couple days. They'd all planned to head back to Eyjania on Thursday anyway. Amma and Afi were having a big family get together on Saturday for their sixtieth anniversary. Anabelle was glad they'd get to be there for it. She hadn't planned to go before they found Gracie and hadn't thought about it since.

Less than forty-eight hours later, they were on the plane. Amma and Afi took seats next to each other and started dozing immediately. Anabelle sat next to Clari once they reached cruising altitude.

"Are they all right?" she asked softly.

"Amma being gone was hard on Afi. They were pretty sure she was with Gracie and therefore safe and being taken care of, but it was hard on him. He aged a lot. I would imagine it was hard on her, too. *She* knew she was all right, but she also knew it would be hard on Afi."

Anabelle stared at her hands. "Maybe we shouldn't go on

Saturday, then. I don't want to make anyone uncomfortable by being there when it's our fault she was taken."

"It wasn't your fault." Clari's words were harsh. "You didn't arrange any of it. You are not responsible for your grandfather's actions in anyway. Afi made it very clear to all of us that you were not to blame. Thor agreed."

"Thor?" She knew she'd heard the name mentioned, but Anabelle had a lot to learn about her new family. Amma had told her about many of them, but Anabelle hadn't always been in a frame of mind to remember later.

"My... our uncle. He works in security for the palace. He was quite adamant that none of this had anything to do with you. He gave his 'security team glare' that we all know not to mess with. The only one who ever rolled her eyes at that glare was his wife."

Right. Security guy. Thor. Bald. Not like the movies. "And he has a kid named Thor, too. What's his wife's name?"

"Her name was Tish, but she passed away about a year ago, not long after Joel and I got engaged."

"I do remember Amma telling me one of her daughters-in-law had passed, but didn't realize it was his wife." She covered her face with her hands and groaned. "I'm never going to keep this all straight."

Clari laughed. "Don't worry. We don't expect you, too. Joel still messes up sometimes, and we've been married almost a year."

Anabelle let loose with another groan. "Just promise me there will be name tags."

"Let's see who we have here. Prince Kensington of San Majoria and Anabelle Gregorson of Eyjania?" The judge peered over the top of his spectacles. "Why exactly are the two of you trying to adopt this little girl?"

Kensington stepped forward. "Your Honor, Anabelle and I were married in March. For a variety of reasons, I would be happy to expound on if you wish, my father, King Edward of San Majoria, has not conferred titles on Anabelle at this time. Until then, under San Majorian law, she retains her previous title and residence, and she is only entitled to honorary use of the female versions of mine."

"Does your father intend to confer these titles?"

Kensington pulled an envelope out of his inside jacket pocket. "I have a signed, notarized affidavit from my father stating that he will be doing just that in the near future. The dates have not yet been finalized." He handed the envelope to the judge who opened it and read it to himself.

"Very well. But why should I allow a San Majorian prince and his wife to adopt an Eyjanian citizen?"

"Gracie is my sister, Your Honor." Anabelle stood as she spoke. "My parents adopted her not long after her birth. I know nothing about her biological parents." Not the actual truth, but the official one. All any of them had were suppositions. "Our parents died on the last switchback coming home from Lake Akushla. Their will left full custody to me. My lawyer assured me I didn't actually need to do anything further. When I married Kensington, we began discussing adoption as it better fits our relationship with Gracie, and to ensure that she is legally, irrevocably, part of our family."

"Why here? Why not in San Majoria?"

"My father-in-law, King Edward, told us because we'd never filled out any paperwork making the move official, the adoption would have to take place here."

Kensington pulled out another envelope. "This is a letter from King Benjamin acknowledging your authority in the matter but requesting that we be allowed to adopt Gracie without any delay." His father had surprised him with that one.

The judge took his time reading it.

"Where is Miss Gregorson?"

"Gracie is outside, Your Honor. We were told she should wait there. She's with her grandparents."

"Will you keep this adoption a secret from her? Will she always believe she's a member of the San Majorian royal family only to discover she isn't should the crown somehow land on her head?"

Kensington straightened his back, offended at the accusation, but understanding the reasoning for it. "No, sir. She will always know that she has been twice adopted. When she's old enough, a simple Internet search would show her the truth anyway, so it would be pointless to keep it from her, even if we were so inclined." She would never believe she was a member of the San Majorian royal family, just as she would never know she was likely a biological member of the Eyjanian royal family - a cousin of the king.

"Bring the girl in," the judge called to the guard standing near the door. "While we wait, tell me why I have so many extra security personnel in my courtroom."

Kensington knew Anabelle would let him explain. "Gracie was kidnapped in May. The extra security goes with all of us everywhere since not all of the parties involved have been apprehended at this time." No reason to let on that they actively expected another attempt in the next few days, likely at Lake Akushla. After the attack on Queen Christiana of Ravenzario a few months earlier and the abduction of Princess Yvette of Mevendia and Ravenzario, along with one of her friends, a few days earlier, no one was taking any chances.

The door opened and Gracie walked in holding the hand of the bailiff.

"Are you Grace Gregorson?" the judge asked.

Gracie's eyes were wide, but she nodded.

"Do you know the difference between the truth and a lie?"

She nodded again.

The judge's eyes narrowed. "Can you talk?"

"Uh huh."

Several people in the courtroom had to smother giggles. Kensington managed to maintain his straight face.

"All right." The judge glared at all of them. "Can you tell me your name?"

"G'acie."

"Grace Gregorson?" the judge prompted.

"Uh huh."

"Who do you live with?"

"Annie an' Kenny, 'cept when the bad guys had me."

"Do you want to live with Anabelle and Prince Kensington?"

Kensington was surprised by the use of his title, but appreciated it anyway.

"Uh huh. My love Kenny an' Annie."

The judge shuffled through the paperwork on his desk. "Very well. Is there any objection to this adoption?"

Kensington felt Anabelle tense up next to him as he held his breath, but no objections were forthcoming. Neither Anabelle's grandfather nor Isaiah would be so public in their attempts to gain control of the little girl.

"Very well. Grace Gregorson is now the legal daughter of Prince Kensington of San Majoria and Anabelle Gregorson. Should they desire to change her name, it will be done in accordance with the laws in San Majoria as they govern name changes for children who are adopted by a step-parent."

Kensington knew that part of the ruling would never hold up but it wouldn't matter.

The judge banged the gavel. "It is so ordered."

The room erupted in cheers, mostly from Anabelle's extended family.

"Are you my mama and daddy now?" Gracie asked above the din.

Kensington snatched her up, throwing her in the air, just a bit. Gracie giggled. "You bet we are. I'm your daddy, and Anabelle is your mama." His heart swelled as he realized she was his child, just as surely as if she'd been his from birth.

They would need to be careful to make sure Gracie never felt he or Anabelle loved their biological children more, though at the moment, he didn't believe that to be possible.

With Gracie situated on one side, Kensington put his arm around Anabelle as they walked out of the courtroom surrounded by family and friends.

They would head to Lake Akushla for a luncheon celebration then remain with a few of the family members until they all arrived for the anniversary celebration.

As happy as he was, a sense of foreboding settled over Kensington.

This wasn't over.

The trip to Lake Akushla nearly flew by. Kensington's security team made sure to go the other way and didn't pass the switch-back where Anabelle and Gracie's parents had died.

They reached the cabin about lunchtime, though cabin appeared to be a bit of a misnomer. The place was huge.

Inside, Amma sent her to one of two rooms that actually opened into the main living/dining/kitchen area.

"This is usually Clari and Joel's room," Amma explained. "But they won't be staying the night anyway, so she insisted that you and Gracie use it." Once inside, she closed the door behind them. "Besides, this was always your mother's room, and it has a secret passage. It doesn't really go anywhere special, but if you need to leave in a hurry, this is the way to do it." She showed them how it worked and had them try it out so they would be able to use it in an emergency.

Lunch had been prepared by another cousin who had come up

early. They all sat around the large table, laughing and joking in a way Anabelle hoped to join someday.

Despite the warm welcome from Kensington's family, this was something she'd never really known, something she'd always missed, even though she couldn't really define it, even to herself.

Her large, half-Icelandic, family had been out there with undefined holes in the shape of Anabelle, her parents, and eventually Gracie. Anabelle had always wanted a large family, and this certainly delivered.

The adults spent an hour at the table, eating, talking, eating some more. Gracie and the few other kids went to play in the living area.

Back in their room after lunch, Kensington tucked Gracie into the cot.

"Do I hafta nap, Annie?" Gracie whined.

"No." Anabelle gave her the same answer she always did. "But you do have to rest for a little bit." Gracie would be asleep in less than ten minutes.

The little girl seemed to be thinking something over.

"What is it?" Kensington asked.

Gracie shrugged.

"Are you wondering about this morning?"

She nodded.

Had they not explained what was happening well enough?

"Remember the man in the black robe with the funny hair?"

Gracie gave another nod.

"He's a judge. He was the one who would decide if you should be our daughter forever. He said you should."

She thought about that. "You my daddy?" She'd asked the same question earlier but asked again.

"Yep."

Gracie looked at Anabelle. "You my mama now?"

"For always."

Her brows pulled together. "My call you Mama an' Daddy?"

"If you want." Anabelle wasn't about to make her, but loved the idea, and knew Kensington did, too.

"'Kay." She snuggled deeper under the covers, and her eyes started to drift closed.

Commotion in the other room caught their attention.

"Wait here." Kensington started for the door.

Anabelle followed him anyway until he glared back at her.

"Stay with Gracie."

That stopped her in her tracks, as he must have known it would.

Kensington peeked out the door. "It's Isaiah."

"Why is he here?"

"I'll find out." He gave her that look again. "Wait here."

She kept the door from closing behind him and stayed as close as she could while still remaining out of sight but still hear what was going on.

"I saiah!" Kensington pasted on a smile and faked enthusiasm. "To what do we owe this pleasure?"

The rest of Amma and Afi's family looked uncertain.

Security had come in with Isaiah - both his own and San Majorian. Kensington found himself wishing Thor was there. He wouldn't be afraid to stop Isaiah from doing something moronic.

Kensington had to believe that Isaiah wouldn't do something stupid in front of witnesses.

"I heard you were in the area, and your adoption was finalized. I wanted to add my congratulations."

Their suspicions were correct. Isaiah was Gracie's biological father or at least believed he was. From a political/international relations standpoint that was far preferable to Benjamin being her father. If Gracie could even legally be on the line of succession to the Eyjanian crown, she was so far down it that it wouldn't matter. Benjamin's eldest child was a far, far different matter than Isaiah's.

"We appreciate your visit." He took a seat and motioned for

Isaiah to do the same. "My wife and I are thrilled that Gracie is legally our child."

"And her biological parents didn't protest?"

"She was originally adopted by Anabelle's parents before their deaths. Her birth mother is deceased, and her biological father never protested their adoption so he doesn't count anymore. Since both of their parents were killed in that car accident, there isn't anyone left to protest, is there?" Kensington raised an eyebrow at Isaiah. He would never admit they knew the truth, but what would Isaiah read into the statements?

"You wouldn't want her to get to know her biological father if he did come forward?" Isaiah sounded shocked.

Kensington barely lifted one shoulder. "If it turned out he was someone worth knowing, I suppose we'd consider it. Can't say I'm disappointed that I'm the only real father she'll ever know." Did he dare mention they had suspected Benjamin was the father but that he'd denied it?

No.

Best continue keeping that tidbit close to the vest. Kensington thought it unlikely Benjamin had mentioned it.

"And I'm certain you'll be a wonderful father. Possibly as good a father as I would have been had I ever been given the opportunity to raise children." Isaiah leaned back against the sofa and crossed one leg over the other, looking completely at ease.

Settling in, Kensington tried to project the same confidence. "It's not too late, I suppose, though you'd have to find a woman to settle down with. That might put a crimp in your bachelor lifestyle. Rumor has it you love your freedom."

"I do," Isaiah conceded, "but for the right woman, or at least the right child, I would give it up. Like you did."

Kensington didn't take the bait. "I do love my life, now that Gracie is back home with us. I don't know how I maintained my composure in public. I don't know what I'd do if left alone with the man responsible this time, or should they or anyone else ever try again."

Isaiah didn't rise to his bait either. "How long will you be in Eyjania?"

"At least Sunday." He nodded toward the rest of the family. "We're attending an anniversary party and family reunion this weekend."

"You're part of the Sørensen clan? I believe a couple of them work for the palace. I hope they have clearance for this weekend."

The veiled threat wasn't lost on Kensington. He chose not to respond. "Now that you've given us your congratulations and discussed parenthood with me, is there anything else on your agenda?"

"Agenda? Who says I have an agenda?"

Kensington chuckled. "Doesn't everyone?" Isaiah more than most.

"I suppose, but I don't have an official one."

"Then would you care to join us in a card game?" He didn't know for sure that was their plan, though it had been mentioned during lunch.

Isaiah stood and buttoned his suit jacket. "Thank you for the invitation, but I must be returning to the palace. I do hope nothing detains you, or sends you packing for home earlier than planned like it did last time."

"I'm sure everything will go according to plan this time." Kensington didn't bother standing. "Have a safe trip back to Akushla. I'm told there's a switchback that's absolutely murder if you're not careful." He grinned to take any innuendo out of his words.

"My driver wouldn't dare take anything but the utmost care."

"I'm sure he wouldn't."

Isaiah gave an offhanded wave in the general direction of the rest of the group as he walked to the door. He waited for it to be opened by someone else before exiting.

A virtual exhale sounded around the room as the door closed.

"Thank you for handling him." Clari stood from her seat at the table. "You can get away with far more than any of us can. I work for the Queen Mother, but his influence is felt all over the palace. I doubt even Thor would be safe if Prince Isaiah wanted him gone."

Kensington finally stood. "Be sure to let me know if there's any undeserved consequences with his fingerprints on it. I do know his nephew, and so does my father. His nephew has far more influence than he does."

"I will."

The rest of the family left the table as Kensington started for the bedroom to make sure Anabelle knew it was safe to come out. She opened the door before he reached it.

"I heard." She rested a hand on her chest. "Thank you for not letting him get to you."

He smiled at her. "Oh, it's easy not to let him get to me. He's like that roaring lion. He's big and scary and likes to act tough, but especially when it comes to a member of another royal family, he has absolutely no bite."

"I'm glad you can stand up to him. I don't think I could."

"But you can." He kissed her softly. "You're part of the San Majorian royal family now. He has no power over you, especially after the proclamation from my father next week."

She patted his chest. "I'll remember that, but if it's all the same to you, I'll let my knight in shining armor continue to fight the battles for me."

Kensington gave her another kiss. "It would be my honor."

Anabelle laughed and played games with her extended family. Some of the tension had finally left since Isaiah's visit with no incident or real threat during the conversation.

The specter of her grandfather still hovered, but even that couldn't dampen her spirits. She was legally Gracie's mother, and she had so much to look forward to with her new family.

Before she knew it, the family reunion and anniversary party had arrived. The entire Sørensen family arrived at the cabin. A big pile of nametags had appeared on the kitchen counter along with a marker and a paper instructing everyone to write their name along with their relationship to Amma and Afi.

Whoever had done it earned Anabelle's undying gratitude. It made it so much easier to hold an intelligent conversation when she didn't spend the whole time trying to remember who this person was and how they were connected.

She, Kensington, Clari, Joel and a couple of other cousins about the same age played card games. Gracie ran around with her cousins, playing tag and blocks and other games. One of the tween girls took a special interest in Gracie and refused to leave her side.

By the time bedtime rolled around, Anabelle tried to convince Clari and Joel to take their room back, but they refused, saying it was better for Gracie.

Gracie was tucked back into the cot while Kensington and Anabelle both got ready for bed.

"Mama!"

Anabelle met Kensington's widened eyes in the mirror as a thump sounded in the other room as Gracie's panicked voice called out.

"Daddy!"

By the time the second call finished ringing out, Kensington was out the bathroom door with Anabelle following closely behind.

Anabelle almost couldn't see around Kensington, but a man in black held Gracie with one arm around her middle and another clamped over her mouth.

Gracie kicked and squirmed and finally one foot connected

enough that his grip loosened. Gracie managed to wiggle enough that he lost his hold all together.

Kensington tackled him as Anabelle snatched Gracie up off the ground and headed for the secret passage. At least they could hide there.

"Get Thor!" Kensington called as he rolled on the ground with the masked man.

Anabelle changed direction, clinging to Gracie. She threw open the door to the main portion of the cabin. "Thor! Help!"

She hadn't realized there were still several people in the living area. One was the security officer.

He had already started for the stairs leading to her room when she screamed.

As she flattened herself to the side, Thor bounded past her.

Crashing noises came from the room, but Anabelle couldn't bring herself to look. The other men and one of the women in the living area followed Thor, while the others formed a protective circle around Anabelle and Gracie.

Thor rushed back out, his phone in his hand. "...out the window," he said into it as he skirted the furniture and headed for the front door. He described the build of the man in question, but didn't stop to talk to them.

Security had been tight. How did the man get in? Would he get away without being caught?

Anabelle forced herself to ignore what was going on outside of her small sphere. Gracie's cries were beginning to border on hysterical.

Holding her close, Anabelle spoke words of comfort to her little girl. A minute later, Kensington emerged from the room. She breathed a sigh of relief as he seemed relatively unscathed.

"Are you all right?" he asked. "Gracie?"

"We're okay," Anabelle reassured him. "You?"

He touched the corner of his mouth and the bit of blood there.

"A bit banged up, but I'll be okay. Maybe a black eye and definitely sore tomorrow."

"Thor went outside."

"He was talking to the on-site head of security. They're chasing him through the woods. I hope." The last word was barely audible as he sat next to her on the couch and wrapped his arms around both of them. "We've got you, Gracie girl. You're okay."

Gracie's wails grew louder as Anabelle held her tighter.

Amma and Afi appeared in front of them. Amma laid her hands on Gracie's head, and began to pray in her native Icelandic. Slowly, Gracie's cries calmed until they were whimpers and then stopped all together.

Her even breathing told Anabelle the girl had fallen asleep.

"Good girl," Amma whispered. "Rest." She looked between Anabelle and Kensington. "Now, someone tell me why my great-granddaughter is hysterical."

"Someone was in our room. Gracie managed to get loose then Kensington fought him, but he got out the window. Thor and the others are chasing him," Anabelle told her grandmother.

The front door opened and Thor walked in. From the droop in his shoulders, Anabelle knew what he was going to say.

"He got away, didn't he, *Föðurbróðir* Thor?" Anabelle tried to get it right, but knew she butchered the pronunciation she'd heard from the others.

Thor gave her a weak smile. "Technically, I'm your *móðurbróðir* - your mother's brother. To everyone else, I'm their father's brother, which is why you're really the only who could use that. Just call me Thor. It's easier that way."

Sure. Whatever. She'd figure it out later. "But you still didn't find him."

"No. There was a boat waiting at the dock. Two guards were knocked out, but otherwise seem to be okay. We got our boat started and followed them, but a car was waiting near another dock. They took off down an abandoned logging road not too far away. None of us even knew it existed. I didn't, and I grew up traipsing through these woods."

"Thank you for trying, Thor." Kensington sounded as weary as Anabelle felt. "I think we need to get back to Aberswythe Hall. It's more easily defensible, and a trip back to San Majoria is likely in order as soon as possible. We don't want any of you accidentally caught in the crossfire."

Thor crossed his arms over his chest. "You're family. We stand together."

Anabelle looked around to see nearly two dozen family members with the exact same look on their face.

She and Gracie, once alone, now had two sets of formidable allies. As they joined forces, there was nothing that could hurt them. Between the Sørensens and the Majorian Dynasty, she and Gracie couldn't be safer.

Kensington wanted to curse. To hit something or someone. Specifically, two men. The two, or possibly three if there was a separate getaway driver, responsible for nearly taking Gracie away from them again.

He even wanted to pummel, a little bit, the men who let themselves be caught off guard, though he knew they would already pay a stiff price.

Instead, he kept his calm as they loaded a sleeping Gracie into the heavily armored vehicle they'd been using in Eyjania. Amma and Afi lead the family in a prayer over them, then promised to come visit soon.

The driver, once again, avoided the switchbacks that took the lives of Anabelle and Gracie's parents, choosing to go the other direction back to Akushla, despite coming out on the wrong side of town.

Back at Aberswythe Hall, Gracie was tucked into bed in the same room he and Anabelle would sleep in - if they slept at all. A member of the security team was stationed inside the room for the moment.

Thor had followed them in his own vehicle, his sons staying behind with the rest of the family.

"We think they went out the other way," he told them, pouring himself a cup of coffee in the kitchen. "We had teams stationed at the other end of the road, but no suspicious vehicles have passed. It's possible they stopped in one of the towns near Lake Akushla, or took one of the other routes north, but those roads are little more than dirt tracks. It's possible, but it doesn't make sense."

"Could they have changed cars somewhere? To something more innocuous?" Anabelle asked.

"It's possible," Thor conceded. "We don't think it's likely. Inconspicuous is good, but so is power if they feel threatened and need to get away from pursuers. It doesn't seem like a trade-off they'd be willing to make."

Kensington nodded. "That rationale makes sense to me. Where else could they be? Holed up in a house in town or on the lake with the car in the garage while they regroup? Possibly plan another attempt?"

"We believe another attempt is just a matter of time. Of course, we already believed that, and they still got the drop on us."

It was a small comfort to Kensington that the men found unconscious were Eyjanian and not San Majorian.

Thor's phone rang. He walked off to take the call then came back a minute later, his face grim. "We think we found them. Not quite how we wanted, but likely for the best."

"How?" Anabelle's hand slipped into Kensington's.

"Dead. They appear to have driven off at the exact same place, more or less, that your parents did. There's accidents there all the time, but it still seems a bit coincidental. We'll be looking to see how it happened. It's light most of the day right now, but it was at the darkest when it happened. Was someone coming toward them and the driver was blinded by their lights or what?"

Thor looked at Kensington, trying to communicate something with his eyes that Kensington didn't quite understand. Finally, his gaze shifted to Anabelle. "That's not all."

"What?" Her grip had begun to loosen but it tightened again.

"None of this is official or even necessarily definitive yet, though our confidence is high. There was one man in the car dressed in all black with wounds consistent with the fight with Kensington. The driver was also dressed in black, and his clothes were wet like the driver of the boat likely would have been. He has a scar on his hand. But in the passenger seat was another man."

Kensington watched Anabelle and knew the second she realized what Thor was trying to tell her. "My grandfather."

"Yes."

"And they're all dead?" she confirmed.

"Yes."

Her head dropped for a moment. "Then good riddance. And I can finally get access to the money my parents' left me."

"You'll likely also inherit everything he has. You, and Gracie legally by adoption, are his only living heirs as far as we know."

Anabelle shook her head. "I don't want any of it. But, if that's the case, the security teams or police have my permission to go through everything and use whatever's there to bring down any criminal enterprises that might still exist. Just make sure I hear anything I might be interested in."

"I'll see about getting everything closed off so others can't come in and destroy evidence, and we'll go from there." He took a long sip of his coffee. "It's also a good thing you didn't go out the secret passage. The light bulbs weren't working and the path that leads to the woods has caved in sometime in the last few months. We'll get it dug out and reinforced before long."

"I almost went that way," Anabelle told him. "But Kensington told me to get you."

"I was already on my way, but I was on the far side of the room and didn't hear it right away." He pointed his coffee cup at Kensington. "You did all right for yourself. You've had training?"

"We all have. I need to talk to our head of security about training for Anabelle. I know Jordan's had some since he married Astrid, but he was a hockey player growing up, so he already knew how to take a hit and keep going and how to give one, too."

"You're sure my grandfather is dead?" Anabelle blurted out.

Thor nodded. "Not officially, but yes. The car is registered to one of your grandfather's companies."

On one level, it bothered Anabelle how relieved she was, but mostly she was just relieved. One of the threats against Gracie was over.

Thor rested his elbows on the kitchen counter and looked at her over the top of his coffee mug. "You know, you remind me a lot of your mother. It shouldn't surprise me, but it does. Some of your mannerisms, the way you bite your bottom lip sometimes, those are all things I remember from Clarice." He walked around the counter to give her a hug. "I wish she had come to us rather than faking their deaths, though I understand why she did. I miss her, but I'm glad to get to know you in the here and now."

Anabelle hugged her uncle, hard. "I'm glad I have all of you."

As the wheels left the ground, Kensington let loose the breath he'd been holding. Gracie seemed no worse for the wear after the attempted abduction. One of the threats had been permanently neutralized without any action on their parts. A nationwide celebration of the changes in their lives was being planned back home.

Not only would his father finally confer the titles on both Anabelle and Gracie, making them officially members of the family, but Amma would be recognized and rewarded for her role in taking care of Gracie, as would Bertrand for the rescue. There would be a small commitment ceremony with Anabelle, a repeating of their wedding vows for the country to hear, and he'd finally give her the ring his mother helped him pick out the week before.

"Feel better?" Thor sat across from him, having been tasked by King Benjamin to coordinate with security forces in San Majoria to make sure the threats had been neutralized.

"Much. I do love Eyjania and wouldn't mind being based out of there someday to let Anabelle spend more time with her family, where she grew up, but despite the good that came out of it, I'm ready for this trip to be over."

"I don't blame you."

Kensington had spent a few hours here and there working on the aftermath of the Games, but needed to work in earnest on the flight home. Anabelle sat with Gracie the whole time and colored or read books and watched Gracie's favorite Disney movie.

By the time they landed, Kensington had made a dent in what should have already been done. At the palace, they were greeted by his entire family, except Esther, who was still missing in action, and Astrid, who was resting. There had been no relapses just yet, but she was still under doctor's orders to take it easy.

Her regular doctor had been out of the country on vacation before Kensington and Anabelle left for Eyjania. Though the replacement was well-trusted, they all decided to wait for the one who would care for Anabelle and the baby to return. He would be arriving at the palace later in the afternoon to check on Astrid and conduct Anabelle's first exam.

After hugs were exchanged, Gracie took Kiara by the hand and started up the stairs.

"We go play!" she yelled to anyone who would listen.

Jacqueline Grace rolled her eyes and started after them. "I got it."

"Thank you!" Anabelle hollered.

His sister would make sure the girls didn't accidentally wander somewhere they weren't supposed to. Sofia screamed for them to wait as she struggled to climb the stairs as fast as she could. She was doing better, but she was only two-and-a-half. It took time.

Jordan swooped in behind her, snatching her into the air. Sofia squealed as Jordan took the stairs two at a time.

Kensington rested his hand on Anabelle's lower back as they followed at a more sedate pace.

"How is Gracie really doing?" his mother asked. "That had to be almost as scary as when she was actually taken."

"She seems to be fine." Anabelle's relief could be heard in her voice. "She's slept in our room the last couple of nights, but she hasn't had any nightmares. That's something."

"We've been praying." His mother laid her hand on Anabelle's shoulder as they reached a landing. "I know there's no love lost between you and your grandfather, but it's still not easy to lose someone. For years, he was the only grandparent you knew. I'm sure you loved him at one time."

"I'm relieved more than anything, but it does bother me that I'm not more upset." The weight settled back around her shoulders. Kensington could feel it all the way into her lower back. "I think I'm more upset by what could have been but wasn't because of who he was, even if I didn't understand that until recently."

"That's perfectly understandable." They continued up the stairs.

"It means I'll never take your family or my new family for granted." Anabelle looked around. "Where's my uncle?"

"He already went to security," Kensington's father told them. "They want to get this sorted out as quickly as possible."

"With the scar guy dead, doesn't that mean everyone who was part of the kidnapping are either in custody or dead?" Kensington asked his father.

"As far as we know." He seemed to think about his next words. "The two men Bertrand subdued were found dead yesterday. Suicide. Your grandmother tentatively identified the woman who brought Kiara to the hospital as the woman who had been taking care of Gracie before her. She turned up dead yesterday after an altercation with another inmate. The woman she shared a cell with was undercover. The woman did admit to having Gracie and that Gracie wouldn't stop talking about the Games. The theory that Gracie threw a fit long enough that they finally took her seems valid. It's possible there's someone else we're not aware of, but we don't think so. We hope not, of course, but we have to be sure."

"Thank you." The relief had found its way back into Anabelle's voice.

"And the ceremony?" Kensington asked. "It's next weekend, right?"

"Saturday," his father confirmed. "You'll both need to be part of finalizing details. Anabelle, Holly has provided several dresses for you to choose from."

"This is the ceremony with the titles?" she asked. "Does it have to be a big deal?" Hints of whine echoed Kensington's thoughts.

"We didn't have a wedding, love. This is an alternative to that." He'd explained it all once and knew she understood. That didn't mean she liked it.

"My family will be here?"

"As many as are able," he promised. "I have a feeling Isaiah will try to stop Clari and Thor, if he can."

They reached their apartment and separated from his parents. Inside was eerily quiet.

"The girls must have gone to Jacqueline Grace or Astrid's apartment." Kensington grinned. "That means we have a few minutes alone."

He wrapped his arms around his wife and kissed her soundly. By the time they broke the kiss, he'd gone a little weak in the knees and knew she had, too.

Before he could kiss her again, a knock sounded on the door. Kensington gave her a quick peck then turned to open it.

"Dr. Grady!" He grinned at the sight of the gentleman. "Won't you come in?" Kensington stepped to the side. "Anabelle, this is Dr. Grady. He helped deliver all of us when he was younger and is now the doctor for the whole family."

Anabelle shook his hand. "It's a pleasure to meet you. I'm sure you know why you're here?"

Dr. Grady chuckled. "Of course I do. Now, why don't we go down to the hospital section of the palace. We can get a good look at your insides and see when we're going to welcome another blessing into the family."

Anabelle gasped as cold goo from the tube hit her skin.

Kensington sat on one side of her, his hand holding tightly to hers as the doctor applied the ultrasound wand.

"You're not far enough along that we definitely could hear the baby's heartbeat," he explained. "Because you're not certain of your dates, which is completely understandable given the upheaval in your life, I'd like to see what we've got."

Anabelle knew her last cycle had been after Gracie went missing, but couldn't be more definitive than that. One of her aides, or the maids who cleaned their apartment might remember better, but she wasn't about to ask.

That said, she knew the date of conception and had told him so. Dr. Grady said he wanted to do the ultrasound anyway.

He pressed and moved and pressed again until the sound of a rapid heartbeat filled the room. "There we are." Pointing to the screen, he showed them the heart, arms and legs, spine, and even the beginnings of fingers and toes.

Tears streamed down Anabelle's cheeks. She finally glanced up at Kensington to see tear tracks on his face as well.

"This is incredible," he whispered. "Our baby."

"Our baby," she repeated.

A minute later, the doctor removed the wand. "I've printed a couple of pictures for you. You're just over nine weeks along. That puts your due date right around February 28, 2018."

"Thank you." She took the washcloth he offered to finish wiping the goo off her stomach, though he'd gotten most of it.

For several minutes, they talked through things she should be doing or not doing. It relieved Anabelle to hear she was already on the right track, except for the avoiding stress part, but there wasn't much she could have done about that.

"And everything looks good?" she asked again, just to confirm for herself.

"Everything looks perfect. I promise."

"And there's really only one in there?" Kensington asked.

Dr. Grady laughed. "Yes. There's only one. I looked."

"Good." Kensington's relief might have been a little exaggerated, but Anabelle was right there with him.

After a few more instructions, Dr. Grady packed up his things. Anabelle met with Brittany who took her to a part of the palace Anabelle hadn't explored yet. Holly waited with the dresses she'd picked for Anabelle to try.

As soon as she saw it, Anabelle knew which dress was the one. Her wedding dress had been based on what was available to her at the time.

This was what she would have picked given all the choices in the world, though it wasn't an actual wedding dress since this wasn't a wedding.

"Pretty sure you need to coordinate with the stylist forever," she told Holly as she stared at herself in the mirror. "This is absolutely perfect."

"I knew that was the one you'd want." She could see Holly grin as she fussed with the skirt. "I'm happy to help whenever I can."

That this woman had been told her services wouldn't be needed for the Games was all Anabelle really needed to know about the operation in place prior to her taking over. She was a Godsend in many ways and over-qualified for the job she'd done.

As she stood there, Esther's stylist helped Anabelle chose a hairstyle to go with the tiara she'd be wearing.

A tiara!

A real, likely irreplaceable, tiara!

She found it very cool - and a bit intimidating.

"You'll be here, won't you, Holly?"

Her new friend smiled. "Of course. I'll be with you while you're getting ready, and I've been invited to the dinner."

That relieved Anabelle. "I'm so glad." She looked around. Brittany hadn't officially been told the news, but Anabelle thought she suspected. "And I saw the doctor a little while ago." She reached for her iPad folder and pulled out the picture. "There's our peanut."

Holly gasped. "I knew I was right! I mean, I know you said you suspected, but now we *know* I was right!"

Anabelle laughed at her excitement. "Yes, you were. We're still not going public for a while. I'm not sure when yet."

"No one will hear anything from me. But we need to get you changed back. I'm sure you'd like to check in with Gracie before whatever else you've got going on later."

Anabelle stepped off the platform to let Holly help her take the dress off. As she changed, she asked Brittany to find out where Gracie had been taken.

Ever efficient, Brittany already knew. "She's been taken back to your quarters for a nap, ma'am. I've also been told you'll have special guests in a couple of hours. Caitlin and Jenny are on their way from San Mediano."

Anabelle clapped her hands together. "Oh, good! I've talked to her several times, but haven't seen her since we found Gracie."

Fifteen minutes after Gracie awakened from her nap, Anabelle held her hand as they walked into the Reception Room.

Gracie wrenched away as soon as she saw her friend. "Jenny!"

The two girls hugged as Anabelle walked toward Caitlin. Caitlin tried to hold herself apart, but Anabelle wouldn't let her. She hugged Caitlin who hugged her back.

"I was so glad to hear she's safe," Caitlin told her as they clung together. "They took care of her?"

"As best as they could take care of a little girl they didn't know. They didn't hurt her and, except for being confined, treated her well."

They let go of each other. Anabelle led the way to the gardens. Despite everything, Caitlin and Jenny weren't cleared for most parts of the palace.

"The Mommy and Me group asked when you're coming back," Caitlin told her. "Everyone misses you, and it doesn't have anything to do with being married to Prince Kensington, at least not for most of them."

The thought made Anabelle smile. "I think I know who you mean. I'd love to come back, but we'll have to see what our plans are. I'm not sure if we're moving back to San Mediano or not. Even if we don't, I may ask about stopping by when we are there."

"You're always welcome, Anabelle. You, Gracie, and any other kids you might have."

Anabelle tried to keep the look off her face, but Caitlin just laughed. "I didn't actually suspect anything, but I'm pretty sure you just told me anyway."

With a shake of her head at her friend's perceptions, Anabelle confirmed Caitlin's suspicions then watched their girls play.

Thank God Gracie was finally happy and acting like a normal little girl.

Anabelle would never take that for granted ever again.

EPILOGUE

T his wasn't a wedding.

But it still felt like it, at least a little bit. The family photographer did a first look series of shots. Kensington nearly cried when he saw Anabelle for the first time. He wouldn't wait at the front of the room. There were no maids of honor or groomsmen. They would walk down the aisle together in front of the small crowd.

Of course, "small" in royal terms, wasn't really all that small for everyone else. Nearly two hundred people filled the room.

"You look beautiful," he told her as they waited for the signal. He'd already told her that several times.

"Thanks. I feel nauseated. I'm not ready for this. Yesterday was better."

The day before Bertrand had received his medal and award for bravery above and beyond in a private ceremony with just the family and staff. Though well outside the scope of his job description, because he was an employee, things were handled a little different.

"You'll be fine. I'll be with you the whole time."

"I'm very glad for that."

The doors opened, and he took a step, having to tug just a little on Anabelle's arm to get her to walk next to him.

Everyone stood, watching them as they walked forward. Music played softly in the background, though it wasn't a wedding march.

A minister didn't wait at the front either. Rather, the king stood there, regal in a suit and his robes, complete with the official crown on his head.

Kensington's mother stood off to the side, wearing a formal dress and tiara. Jacqueline Grace and Harrison stood to one side. Grandmother, Astrid, and Jordan stood on the other. Esther was still missing. There would be press reports about that for days to come.

His father motioned for everyone to be seated then began reading off the tablet in front of him. "Insomuch as Prince Kensington and Anabelle Gregorson have proclaimed their vows before God and each other, this assembly has gathered to witness the declaration of their commitment before the people of San Majoria."

He read statements similar to wedding vows. First Kensington then Anabelle said "I do" to the commitments they already made.

"At this time, Kensington would like to say a few words."

They turned to look at each other. Kensington took her left hand in his. "Anabelle, circumstances conspired against giving me the opportunity to present you with a token of my devotion before our wedding. I'm almost glad I didn't, because this isn't what I would have chosen then."

He reached into his pocket and pulled out the ring, positioning it on his pointer finger so she could see it. "When my mother showed me some of the rings I could choose from, I knew immediately this was the one. I remember my great-aunt wearing it when I was a child. My great-uncle, my grandfather's younger brother, commissioned it for their fiftieth wedding anniversary.

She was from Iceland, and this ring is Icelandic obsidian paired with Eyjanian rubies. I knew it was meant to be yours."

"It's beautiful," she whispered. "Perfect."

He slid it onto her finger. "With this ring, I signify that I choose you, Anabelle Gregorson, to be my wife, to be at your side for as long as we live."

Kensington's father took over again. "With that declaration, I decree you are no longer Anabelle Gregorson, but Princess Anabelle of the Majorian dynasty, Duchess of Pennington, Countess of Caromache, and Baroness of Navarricia. Your daughter, formerly Grace Gregorson, shall henceforth be known as Duchess Grace of Runcimache. For now and eternity, let it be so!"

The crowd replied. "Let it be so!"

Kensington tucked Anabelle's hand back in his elbow and led her off to the side in front of Jacqueline Grace and Harrison for the next portion of the ceremony.

"Annabella Thorbjørnsdóttir, please present yourself to the crown!" his father called.

Amma rose as his father pulled his sword from the scabbard and used it to point to a kneeling bench that had been placed in front of him.

Kensington dropped Anabelle's hand as he and Jordan moved to Amma's side to help her. Though not as frail as many women her age, kneeling and rising could be a little bit of an issue.

When she didn't seem to need their help, they waited a couple steps back.

"For service to the crown, far above and beyond the call of duty, for caring for Duchess Grace of Runcimache in the face of great adversity, it is my honor to award you the Order of Michael. The Archangel Michael is believed by some to be the protector of those who work in emergency services - police, firefighters, paramedics - as well as military personnel."

Kensington picked up the ribbon with the order affixed to it and fastened it around Amma's neck as his father went on.

"Their training prepares them to protect others as Michael is believed to protect them. You were not trained as they are, yet you took that role willingly, protecting Duchess Grace even when you had the chance to leave."

He lifted the sword and rested it on her right shoulder. "For your service to the crown, I create thee Dame Annabella of the Order of Michael." The king switched the sword to the others side. "For now and eternity, let it be so!"

"Let it be so!" Kensington and the others gathered in the room replied.

He and Jordan stepped forward to take Amma by the elbows and help her to her feet. Jordan wore the same Order of Michael on his left chest after rescuing Sofia from drowning the fall before. Jordan's best friend and brother-in-law had received it at the same time.

The room filled with applause as Amma stood, then curtsied to the king. He inclined his head, and she returned to her seat.

Kensington offered Anabelle his arm then held out a hand to Gracie, and the three of them walked back up the aisle first, followed by Amma and Afi.

He led them off to the side, a small room where no one would see them. With Gracie in one arm, he pulled Anabelle closer with the other and kissed her softly.

"I have a surprise for you."

She smiled up at him. "What's that?"

"A week in Athmetis. Gracie and Elise are going with us so she's not here alone, but mostly, it will be just you and me whenever we want."

Her grin widened. "I love that idea. Thank you."

That was the segue Kensington needed. "I love you."

It was the first time he'd said it, though he hoped he'd shown it in more ways than she could count.

"I love you, too, Kenny." She leaned up to kiss him.

She had shown him day after day, time after time, that she

loved him. He'd never doubted it, but he did enjoy hearing the words.

In a minute, they'd have to leave this shelter, a space with just his little family, but for now, this was perfect.

"It's official." He stared down into her shimmering eyes. "It might have been inadvertent at first, but now it's official. For now, and all eternity, you are my princess, love."

Anabelle smiled back up at him. "I wouldn't have it any other way."

LETTER TO READERS

Dear Reader,

Thank you for joining Prince Kensington, Anabelle, and Gracie in *The Inadvertent Princess*! I appreciate you and hope you enjoyed it! This is the second book in the *Crowns & Courtships* series!

There's a whole back end, behind-the-scenes, thing with the numbering. Some of you may have noticed *The Inadvertent Princess* was labeled book 3 at one point. Yeah. It's a whole thing ;).

This series title will accommodate the royal families of Eyjania and San Majoria (and beyond?) through the use of subtitles - *Heart of a Prince* is *Crowns & Courtships, Book 1: Royals of San Majoria*. Just replace the country name when necessary ;).

The *Crowns & Courtships* stories have been divided into two separate series - the main one with the novels, and the novellas. As currently envisioned, the novellas will be shorter (clearly ;)) and come in between or around the novels and won't NEED to be read. Rather, they'll enhance your understanding of the stories. For instance, if you read *A Kærasti for Clari*, you'd already met

Mrs. T and Rachel (and Anabelle and Gracie). However, if you didn't, it shouldn't have limited your understanding of *The Inadvertent Princess*. The blurb section of Amazon's product page will have a list of the combined order in case you'd like to make sure you've read them all :).

Next up is Princess Esther! Clearly something has been going on with her, and you'll find out what soon! In a couple of pages, you'll get a preview of *A Royally Beautiful Mess*! YAY!

That will catch the timeline up to the end of *Reclaiming Hearts* and then...

THEN!!!! AH! King Benjamin finally gets his story! I've already written most of it (last November for National Novel Writing Month), and I absolutely love his story - and his heroine! I can't wait to finish Esther's so I can get back to it! It should be out by summer at the latest!

HEA-TV

I've mentioned this before but it's getting better! It's still VERY MUCH a work in progress, but it's being worked on (and hopefully, by the time this releases, all of the Crowns & Courtships books will be done, along with a couple more Belles Montagnes).

It's found at www.hea-tv.com (that's the name of the Hallmark type channel in this universe, remember?) you'll find "Everything You Ever Wanted To Know About Carol Moncado's Fictional Universe... & More"! There's a "universe" timeline where you can see how everything fits together. Each book will have (or already has) it's own timeline. There's book wikis with character and location/business lists (what was that restaurant again?! ;)) with each entry as a glossary term so you can hover over it to find out more about that character/place, along with summaries of what that book was about. Hello, SPOILERS! :D

There aren't any character or location/business wikis - yet. But eventually. Once we (and by we, I mean the AMAZING Tory with a little bit of help and direction from me ;)) get the book wikis caught up, we'll work on the others.

Previews

Next up you'll find that preview for *A Royally Beautiful Mess*, Book 3 in Crowns & Courtships along with more information about it.

After that, you'll find chapter 1 of *Good Enough for a Princess*, book 1 in the Montevaro Monarchy series which is FREE on all retailers! Though it was two series ago, that book is the beginning of the events that lead to *Reclaiming Hearts*. The two timelines will merge in King Benjamin's story here in a few months, with his book picking up just a few hours after Benjamin's last appearance in Prince William and Maggie's story.

Many of you have likely already read *Finding Mr. Write*, but if not, it too is FREE on all retailers!

Serenity Landing Book Club

What is that?! It's the Facebook reader group that started last summer! I'd love to have you there! It's easier for you to see what's posted than on a Facebook page and we do fun stuff! There will be discussion questions after the release of a book, sneak peeks of the next one, general discussion, and chances to win copies of books and other goodies! I'd love to have you there!

Other Stuff

I see a meme floating around Facebook from time to time that tells readers what they can do to help their favorite authors. Buying their next book or giving a copy away is kind of a no-brainer, but the biggest thing you can do is write a review. If you enjoyed *The Inadvertent Princess* would you consider doing just that?

I would LOVE to hear from you! My email address is books@candidpublications.com. To stay up-to-date on releases, you can sign up for my newsletter (there's fun stuff - like a chance to get *Dare You* free for a VERY limited time! You'll also get notices of sales, including special preorder pricing! And I won't spam!) or there's always my website :). You can find my website and blog at www.carolmoncado.com. I blog about once a month at www.InspyRomance.com. And, of course, there's Facebook and my Facebook page, Carol Moncado Books. But... the way pages work, sometimes very few people (often 1-5% of "likes") will see anything posted. I keep trying to find the best way to get to know y'all and "spend time" together outside of your Kindle - at least for those of you who want to!

Thanks again!

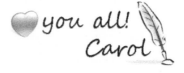

you all!
Carol

ACKNOWLEDGMENTS

They say writing is a solitary endeavor, and it absolutely can be. Sitting in front of the computer for hours on end, talking to imaginary people.

And having them talk back ;).

But the reality is no one walks alone. Since I began this writing journey over six years ago, I can't begin to name all of those who've helped me along the way. My husband, Matt, who has always, *always* believed in me. All of the rest of my family and in-loves who never once looked at me like I was nuts for wanting to be a writer. Jan Christiansen (my "other mother") has always believed in me and Stacy Christiansen Spangler who has been my dearest friend for longer than I can remember.

Ginger Solomon, author of *One Choice* and a bunch of other fantastic books (but *One Choice* is still my favorite!), has been invaluable with her proofreading services. Check her books out!

Then there's my writer friends. Bethany Turner (have you read *The Secret Life of Sarah Hollenbeck* yet?!) and Mikal Dawn (AH! *Count Me In!*) have both been so wonderful the last few months keeping me laughing and my spirits up. Then Jennifer Major, a

Canadian no less ;), who does life with me and loves me anyway! There's Jessica Keller Koschnitzky, Joanna Davidson Politano (*Lady Jayne Disappears* is amazing!), Jen Cvelbar (writing as Jennifer A. Davids and the best case of misidentification *ever*, not to mention best conference roomie - and has a new book coming next summer! YAY!), Kristy Cambron, and Stacey Zink are Brit-Critters, too. We do a lot more living than we do critting, and I wouldn't have it any other way. All five of them are beyond gifted as writers, and I thank God they're in my life. There's my MozArks ACFW peeps who laugh with me, critique, and encourage to no end. Then there's the InspyRomance crew, the CIA, my Spicy peeps (you know who you are!), and all of the others who've helped me along on this journey.

And Emily N. and Tory U. who are both INVALUABLE to my writing process! I have NO IDEA what I'd do without the two of you!

I said I could go on for days, and I could keep going. On and on. I know I've forgotten many people and I hate that. But you, dear reader, would quickly get bored.

So THANK YOU to all of those who have helped me along the way. I couldn't have done this without you and you have my eternal gratitude. To the HUNDREDS of you (I'm gobsmacked!) who pre-ordered and encouraged me without knowing it as that little number continued to climb, you have my eternal gratitude. I hope you stick around for the next one!

And, of course, last but never, *ever*, least, to Jesus Christ, without whom none of this would be possible - or worth it.

Until next time,
Carol

A
Royally
Beautiful Mess

Crowns & Courtships
Book 3: Royals of San Majoria & Eyyania

Previews subject to change and may contain errors.

"I'm pregnant."

Esther, Princess of San Majoria, stared at herself in the mirror, specifically at her hands splayed against her lower abdomen. Somewhere beneath them a small life had already begun.

She had to deal with the consequences of her choices. The choices that began with her desire to remain anonymous at a private resort in Islas del Sargasso a month earlier.

Innocent flirtation with a handsome foreigner about her age led to heated kisses and four days when she ignored the niggling voices in the back of her head that her actions would cause reactions.

This one had come a bit out of the blue, though.

When ignoring potential outcomes those days holed up in a secluded hut, *pregnant* had never crossed Esther's mind.

What was done was done, and now she had to deal with the fall out.

She hadn't even known who he really was. He'd used the nickname Dare, which she'd found amusing given it was also the nickname of her brother-in-law's best friend. Canadian Dare was handsome in that older brother, crazy hair, hockey player sort of way.

This Dare, the one she'd thrown her future out the window for, defined cute in a way she found far, far more desirable.

If only she'd realized why he looked familiar before she found a business card he'd dropped.

The morning after he left.

When she woke up alone, rejected, and loathing herself for everything that had happened in the days prior.

Upon seeing his name, in black script on a white card laying halfway under the side table, Esther had bolted to the bathroom and heaved for ten minutes straight.

A quick knock sounded on her door seconds before it opened. "Your father will see you now, miss."

"Thank you."

A month in Eyjania, avoiding everyone and everything, even her older brother Kensington who was also staying at Aberswythe Hall, and it boiled down to this.

Her father had come to visit for some reason she didn't understand, but she couldn't wait any longer to tell him the truth.

Footsteps echoed through the empty halls as she approached her father's office. No one waited in the outer area. His door was cracked open, so she went in.

He was on the phone, jabbering away in Italian as he waved for her to have a seat. She perched on the edge of one of the armchairs and waited. A minute later, he hung up and turned.

Tears filled her eyes at the thought of his impending disappointment in her.

"Do I need to have a seat for this conversation?"

All she could manage was a curt nod.

He sat in the chair behind his desk and waited for her to speak, but his patience wouldn't last forever.

"I met someone," she finally blurted out.

Her father just rocked a bit in his chair and stared at her.

Anything but the disappointed stare that was only going to deepen.

She had to just say it. "I'm pregnant." She forced the words past the lump in her throat, the whisper ripping from her.

His face remained impassive, though his rocking faltered for just a second. He was a king. Presenting the face he wanted to the world was part of his nature.

After nearly two minutes of disappointed silence, he spoke. "Who is he?"

Tears had streaked down her face, and Esther swiped at them with the back of her hand. "He went by Dare."

His face shot up at that. "Not Jordan's friend?"

She shook her head. "No. He would never cheat on Betsy, you know that."

"I know a lot of things, some of which I didn't know as well as I thought."

The now well worn card went on his desk. "I found that after he left. I looked him up, and the picture matched."

Her father picked it up and stared at the words on the card stock. "You didn't recognize him beforehand?"

She shook her head. "I hadn't seen him since we were children. Probably before his father died."

"Did he know who you were?" He held out a box of Kleenex to her.

"Thank you," she whispered, taking one. "I don't think he did. I told him my name was Star."

"So you want me to march in there and inform them that he's the father of your child when he doesn't even know he slept with a princess, much less the daughter of his father's best friend?"

"I didn't ask you to do anything." She wanted him to, needed him to, but she hadn't actually asked him to do it.

He let out a deep sigh and stood, walking around the desk until he stood in front of her. "Oh, Esther. My little star. Come here." He held open his arms and she stood, collapsing against her father and his strength.

Deep, gut wrenching sobs, tore from her as he held her in his arms until they slowed.

"How far along are you?"

She managed a shrug. "I haven't seen a doctor."

"Then when did you meet him?"

"A couple of months ago when I went to that resort on Islas del Sargasso." Jacqueline Grace was supposed to go with her but had taken sick and decided to stay home. Given the security already inherent at the private resort, she'd only taken minimal security of her own and was left basically to her own devices - especially when she essentially didn't leave her hut for several days in a row. Either her small security team didn't know Dare stayed with her those days, or chose to keep their mouths shut since there was no actual danger to her.

"Six weeks ago?"

"Something like that."

He moved away from her and her father disappeared to be replaced by his king persona. "I have to go see them in ninety minutes or so anyway. Get cleaned up. You're coming with me, and we'll deal with this together."

Esther nodded. She had no real choice, and no stylist to help her. She'd have to do her best and pray she didn't look like an absolute mess when she came face-to-face with Dare again.

No.

Not Dare.

Prince Darius.

Younger brother of King Benjamin and first in line for the throne of Eyjania.

You can find *A Royally Beautiful Mess* on Amazon now!
Release date (subject to change): April 27, 2018
Life is messy.

Even more so when you have to deal with two royal families and the expectations of two countries.

And a 200-year-old treaty

Add a scheming royal uncle and one really big surprise, and things just might get a little out of hand.

Princess Esther of San Majoria has always done what's expected of her. Until she met a handsome stranger at an exclusive resort. Weeks later, she's discovered his true identity and is dealing with the fallout of their time together. With her father's help, she's going to make things right, then head straight to Serenity Landing University to finish her schooling.

Prince Darius of Eyjania isn't sure what being called into a meeting with his older brother, King Benjamin, and his uncle could mean, but he's sure it's nothing good. His suspicion proves correct when the King of San Majoria confronts him about his secret vacation a few weeks earlier. When his uncle tries to threaten King Edward, the other king threatens to invoke the Treaty of 1702 - whatever that is.

To appease their most important trading partner, and because it's the right thing to do, Darius finds himself living in the States and married to the most beautiful girl he's ever known - and she wants absolutely nothing to do with him.

With secrets, international treaties, an uncle who will stop at almost nothing to get his way, and a potential exile, Darius and Esther have to learn that even in the mess, it can be beautiful. It can be *A Royally Beautiful Mess*.

Good Enough for a Princess

C harlie Brewer pushed the hood of his heavy winter coat back with one gloved hand. A fender bender? Really? Like he didn't have anything else to do? Like get home to... Screaming interrupted his thoughts. He rapped on the window and prayed for it to stop. "Ma'am. Are you okay?" Stinging bits of ice pelted his face and peppered the car as he prayed she wasn't hurt.

Abruptly, her mouth clamped shut.

Bits of sleet pelted his face as he knocked again. "Are you okay?"

The girl looked up and the first thing he noticed was her big hazel eyes, filled to overflowing with tears.

"Are you okay?" Broken records had nothing on him. He cupped his hands and peered in the window. She didn't look hurt. He flinched. Except maybe for the gash on her forehead.

She nodded but didn't say anything and didn't roll down the window.

"I need to give you my contact information."

The window creaked down half an inch or so.

"No. I do not need your information. I will take care of my own vehicle, thank you." Even with the frantic note in her voice, he knew it would be almost melodic in a calmer situation. The window scratched its way back up and slid into the rubber casing.

He tried to take a deep breath but the frigid air pierced his lungs. "Let me buy you a cup of coffee. You'll need a tow. Your wheel well is all messed up and you've got two flat tires."

She bit her bottom lip as her eyes flickered to the café across the parking lot. The look in her eyes suddenly reminded him of a scared little girl.

With both hands held up, Charlie tried to look less threatening than he must have when she first saw him with his hood up and face shadowed. He gave the best smile he could with frozen cheeks. "I promise I'm a good guy."

Finally, with a nod, she grabbed her purse from the front seat of the SUV, and turned the engine off. She reached for the handle on the inside of the driver's door. It didn't budge.

Bright lights caught him in the eye. A semi-truck passed a little too close for Charlie's comfort. If she had that door open and slipped...

"This side," he hollered at her and pulled on the handle.

She nodded and climbed across the center console while he pulled again.

Frozen shut.

Ice continued to fall, sliding down the back of his neck and into his shirt. If he wasn't already frozen through, that would have done it.

"You push from that side," Charlie yelled. "I'll pull."

Another nod and she pushed with one hand but it didn't move. He closed his eyes and breathed a quick prayer. "Put your shoulder into it."

Tears flowed, but she pushed against the door with her shoulder as he pulled. The door popped free and she tumbled out.

He caught her by the elbow to steady her on her feet, caught off-guard by the whiff of sunshine in her hair. "Are you okay?"

She nodded, her chin quivered just a little and Charlie gentled his hold on her. "I am. Thank you, sir."

There was something in her voice, or maybe her perfect

posture, that brought visions of Mary Poppins to mind. He shrugged them off and closed her car door behind her. With a slow steady pace, he continued to hold her arm as started toward the inviting warmth of the café.

Warmth? Yes. He couldn't feel his nose anymore.

"You do not need to help me." The dismissive note in her voice bothered him until she jerked her arm away.

And slipped, wobbled, then righted herself. But she didn't fall.

Charlie contained his smirk and a dutiful bow. "I'm sure I don't, miss, but I'd feel much better if you'd allow me. I already crashed into your car. If I let you get hurt in the parking lot, I'd never forgive myself."

She sighed. A puff of white air blew out in front of her but she didn't pull away again. The thirty-second walk took nearly five minutes. Slow, half-steps, muscles tensed, toes bunched inside his boots trying to grip the slippery surface on top of the asphalt. They finally made it to the door. Hot air and the smell of sizzling bacon blasted him.

"Have a seat anywhere, kids!" a woman's voice called.

Charlie turned toward a row of booths along the front window. "After you?"

The woman pulled the knit cap off her head. Golden brown curls tumbled around her shoulders. She looked around carefully before walking all the way to the far end and sliding in the seat against the wall.

He sat across from her and held out a hand. "I'm Charlie."

One corner of her mouth twitched up before she shook his hand. "Adeline."

"A pleasure to meet you, Adeline. I just wish it was under other circumstances."

"Agreed. A car accident..." A flash of awareness crossed her face and she set her large black bag on the table. She flipped open one flap and dug around. "Where is it?" she muttered as she searched. Somehow, even that action seemed delicate. She wasn't from here.

"What are you looking for?"

"My phone. I need to call..." She stopped abruptly, gaze traveling to the café window. "Do we need to move the vehicles?"

Charlie shook his head. "We're far enough out of the main lane and the cars are stuck together. We'll have to wait for a tow. It could be a while." He pulled out his own phone to call roadside assistance.

"Should we call 911?" Adeline asked as she took a sleek black phone out of her purse. He tried to control an eyebrow quirk but failed. There were cell phones. There were nice smart phones. There were really nice smart phones. Then there was this one.

"No. They're on emergency status only. As long as no one's hurt, you deal with it yourself."

"Of course," She whispered and stared at her phone for a long moment. "I do not have a card for roadside assistance. Perhaps you could ask your service to send an extra tow truck for my vehicle?"

Something in the way she asked made him wonder if she'd ever called for auto help. The tilt of her chin and honest curiosity in her eyes reminded him of the children's fairytales he used to read. Did fairies come into the real world during ice storms? "I'll take care of it." It made him feel protective. Almost manly. When was the last time he'd felt the need to protect a woman? Ever? He found the right entry and pressed the screen. After listening and going through the process, he finally got a real person. Holding up one finger to Adeline, he stood and walked toward the front door to explain the situation.

Crown Princess Adeline Julianne Elizabeth of Montevaro relived the sickening crunch of metal as her car slid to a stop in the ditch outside. She could still feel the steering wheel as she'd gripped it, trying to keep the tears, and the panic, at bay. Her unsuccessful attempts now showed on her face, she was certain. Red, blotchy eyes. Tear-stained cheeks. Moisture still leaking out from time to time. Her mother would be mortified.

She knew when she left the house an accident could happen. No one ever dreamed of letting the Crown Princess learn to drive on ice, of all things. But she had taken matters into her own hands. Adeline, the girl who never did anything wrong, who always did what was expected of her, had slipped away from her security detail, taken the safer of the two vehicles at her disposal, and left. All because she wanted a few moments of freedom before the ice storm settled in.

A shaking hand had pushed the hair back from one side of her face as she ran through her mental checklist.

No airbag deployment. Good.

Pain in her head meant she likely hit the steering wheel. Bad.

Slow speed at time of impact. Good.

Impact. Bad.

As long as she did not have a concussion or bruising from the steering wheel or seat belt, she would be able to convince Mark and Todd she was fine. They would read her the riot act. Debate long and hard about calling her father. Eventually, they would call their superiors, debate some more and, sooner or later, her father would find out. She had rested her head on the steering wheel. He did not need the additional stress. The last two times she visited Montevaro, her father had seemed off. She feared what he would tell her when she returned home for good in a few months.

She had contemplated digging her cell phone out and giving a preemptive call. Cut them off at the pass. Reassure Mark she was rattled but fine and his relief would overwhelm his anger and concern.

She took a deep, shuddering breath and dug her phone back out of her purse. Addie closed her eyes and finally turned her phone back on. Three times, her finger slipped off the "on" button. It went through its start-up procedure and buzzed with missed calls and text messages. Every one of them came from Mark, Todd, or the house. Before she could listen to any of the twenty voice mails, the phone rang again.

With a deep breath and a whispered prayer, she pressed "answer." "Hello?"

Mark's bellow did not help her headache. "Where are you?"

She sighed. "At the Serenity Landing diner on Highway 60 about two miles from town."

"What are you doing there?" His voice softened slightly as she heard the garage door open in the background.

Just saying the words made her wince. "I was in an accident."

His bellow returned. "What?"

"I am fine, Mark. A gentleman ran into the back of the SUV. He helped me out of the vehicle and to the restaurant. He is calling tow trucks right now."

"We're on our way." His words were clipped and nearly cut off by the sound of a slamming car door.

Once the connection severed, Addie set the phone on the table and rested her face in her hands, biting back the groan threatening to escape her throat.

"Tow trucks will be here when they get here." Charlie scooted into the seat across from her. "We're way down on the list since we're not on a major highway. We're somewhere safe and warm, we're not blocking traffic, and no one's hurt."

"I will likely be gone long before they get here." She put her phone in the side pocket of her purse and snapped the flap closed.

"At least let me buy you that cup of coffee." He turned to look for a waitress.

Addie looked at Charlie for a moment before deciding she could trust him. Something about his curly, dirty blond hair and mocha eyes convinced her to give a curt not. "Very well."

The waitress, stereotypical for a restaurant of this kind,

bustled up. "Sorry, kids." She handed them each a menu. "What can I get ya?"

With a smile, Addie looked at her. "Hello, Melony."

A wide grin split Melony's face. "Well, hey there! How are ya, sugar? Where's Mark and Todd? What're they thinkin' lettin' ya out here in this weather?"

Addie nodded toward the street. "Mr. Brewer and I had a bit of an accident. We are fine. Mark and Todd will be here short-ly." She tucked her hair behind her ear. "Could I get a cup of tea?"

Melony gasped. "You're bleeding." She grabbed a napkin, sending a fork and spoon clattering to the floor.

"I am fine, Melony. I promise."

"Nonsense." Charlie watched as Melony pressed the napkin against Adeline's forehead. "You need to go to the hospital."

"No. Mark and Todd will be here soon. Mark has medic train-ing. If I need stitches, he can do it." The girl took over holding the napkin to her own head, leaving Charlie wondering who Mark and Todd were and why she seemed both annoyed and comforted by the idea of the two men.

Her brothers maybe?

But if they were on their way, he needed to get to know her and fast. Because he'd never met a woman who intrigued him so much from the first moment he heard her speak. Was it the accent? The lilting tone? He didn't know but he wanted to find out. Charlie turned his best smile up to the waitress. "Melony, is it?"

The dark curls bounced up and down as she nodded. "Sure is."

"Melony, would you get Adeline that cup of tea? I'd love some coffee if you've got it. Do you still have breakfast?" He'd driven by the diner many times but had never stopped. Most of these places had breakfast all day, didn't they?

"Sure do, hon. Twenty-four seven. Why don't you two decide what you want and I'll get those drinks?" She looked pointedly at Adeline. "Keep pressure on that."

More than anything Charlie wanted to reach out and brush the hair back, away from the cut in the otherwise smooth skin. He tilted sideways and pulled a handkerchief out of the pocket of his pants. He dipped it in the water glass Melony had set there. Half-standing, he leaned over the table. "Let me see?"

Adeline nodded and pulled the napkin away. "It feels as though the bleeding has stopped."

The cut didn't look good, but it didn't look too bad either. "Here." With slow movements, he did his best to wipe off the dried blood. "I think you'll be okay."

"Thank you, Charlie." Her eyelashes lifted enough for him to see the gold-flecked hazel of her eyes then moved downward again.

He finished cleaning around the wound, refolded his handkerchief, and held it to her head. "You might still want to hold that, though."

Her fingertips brushed his hand as she reached up, sending chills, the good kind, down his spine. "Thank you, again."

He settled back in his seat. "You're not from around here, are you?"

The silky brown hair shifted as she shook her head. "No. I am not."

"Where are you from?"

Melony set two steaming cups in front of them. "Just like you like it."

"You are a queen among women, Melony." Her voice drew Charlie further in.

"Don't you know it?" Melony winked, covering one of her pale green eyes. Charlie couldn't help but compare them to Adeline's.

Though they were both primarily green, they were as different as the Amazon rain forest and split-pea soup. "Now, what can I get you to eat?"

Charlie ordered pancakes and bacon. Adeline decided on her "usual," whatever that was.

Once Melony headed for the kitchen, Adeline resumed their conversation. "Have you ever heard of a country called Montevaro?"

With his brow furrowed, Charlie tried to think, but came up mostly blank. "I think I have but that's all I can say."

One corner of her mouth tipped upward. "It is a small nation, sandwiched between Mevendia, Switzerland, and Italy."

"Mevendia?"

"Yes. It is even smaller than we are, on the southeastern border of Switzerland. We have cultural and historical ties with Mevendia and Ravenzario. Ravenzario is..."

"Two islands off the coast of Italy and France in the Mediterranean. I think I visited there as a kid."

Adeline nodded. "Yes."

"And you're from Montevaro, is it?"

She nodded. "Yes. Three of us were chosen to come here and study International Relations at Serenity Landing University."

"Chosen?" He quirked an eyebrow at her. "Did you do the best on some sort of test?"

This time the smile was a bit more full-fledged but still didn't reach her eyes. "Something along those lines, yes."

"I'm sorry I hit you, but I'm glad you're here so I could meet you." Deep inside, he cringed. That sounded like such a line.

"You did not hit me, Charlie. You hit my vehicle. And given the weather conditions, it could hardly be considered your fault."

"Still. I'm glad we've met. But what exactly does one study in international relations?"

"The relationship between countries. The relationship between countries and all kinds of different organizations: intergovernmental organizations, nongovernmental organizations, multinational corporations. Things like that."

"So will you work for the State Department of your country?" Charlie wrapped his hands around the mug to warm his fingers and sipped his coffee.

"We do not have a state department like America's, so no. But yes, I will be involved in foreign relations between Montevaro and any number of other entities."

"Is it interesting?" He didn't see how it could be, but different strokes for different folks and all.

She gave a bit of a half shrug. "It is not uninteresting. International relations is the family business."

Family business? Like the Kennedys? Or what was the local family he saw in the tabloids while stuck in the checkout lane? The last name was Langley, he thought, because it always made him think of the CIA.

"So it's expected of you."

"Something like that."

Melony chose that moment to come back and set their food in front of them. "Here ya go. If you need anything else, just holler."

They ate in silence for a few minutes until lights flashed across them. Charlie looked outside. A dark sedan with tinted windows pulled up.

Adeline set the rest of her sandwich on her plate and picked her napkin up from her lap. "That is my ride. Thank you again for your assistance."

Charlie chuckled. "I hit you. It's the least I could do to offer to help."

She reached for her gloves and hat before setting them back down and reaching into her purse. "Here is my card if you need to reach me." She left it on the table.

The door jangled open behind him and he heard boots stomping.

"Adeline, let's go."

Turning his head, he saw a giant hulk of a man standing near them.

"Of course." She slid out of the booth and stood.

Charlie followed suit.

"Thank you again, Mr. Brewer."

He took a deep breath, ignored the man towering over him, and plunged in. "Can I call you? Once this storm blows over?"

Adeline smiled, this time showing perfect rows of pearly white teeth. "I suppose that would be all right."

Charlie watched as she and the man walked toward the front door. He wondered if he'd see her again. The thunderous expression on the face of the man in front of him said, "no."

Good Enough for a Princess is available FREE on all ebook retailers!

The Monarchies of Belles Montagnes

Book 1: Montevaro

Crown Princess Adeline of Montevaro has her life planned out for her: get her Master's in international relations, marry nobility, produce an heir, inherit the throne. There's no room for romance with the single father she meets when their cars collide on an icy winter night. Parliament - and her father - would never approve.

Charlie Brewer grew up without roots. The son of an archaeologist father and anthropologist mother, he either traveled along or lived with his aunt and uncle in the States. He's determined to give his daughter the stability he never had. He also wants to give her a mom, but the beautiful European he's falling for refuses to move to Serenity Landing, Missouri permanently.

He won't move. She can't stay. What will happen when they try to forget each other by dating someone "acceptable"? They find themselves drawn together by one of the girls in the after school program Addie supports - a girl who happens to be Charlie's daughter. How will Charlie, and his daughter, feel when they find out the woman they've both fallen for is a... princess?

A trip halfway around the world shows Charlie and Addie how much they long to be together - and how impossible it is. Is there any way he can prove he is *Good Enough for a Princess*?

ABOUT THE AUTHOR

When she's not writing about her imaginary friends, USA Today Bestselling Author Carol Moncado prefers binge watching pretty much anything to working out. She believes peanut butter M&Ms are the perfect food and Dr. Pepper should come in an IV. When not hanging out with her hubby, four kids, and two dogs who weigh less than most hard cover books, she's probably reading in her Southwest Missouri home.

Summers find her at the local aquatic center with her four fish, er, kids. Fall finds her doing the band mom thing. Winters find her snuggled into a blanket in front of a fire with the dogs. Spring finds her sneezing and recovering from the rest of the year.

She used to teach American Government at a community college, but her indie career, with over twenty titles released, has allowed her to write full time. She's a founding member and former President of MozArks ACFW, blogger at InspyRomance, and is represented by Tamela Hancock Murray of the Steve Laube Agency.

www.carolmoncado.com
books@candidpublications.com

OTHER BOOKS BY CAROL MONCADO

The CANDID Romance Series

Finding Mr. Write
Finally Mr. Write
Falling for Mr. Write

The Monarchies of Belles Montagnes Series
(Previously titled The Montevaro Monarchy
and The Brides of Belles Montagnes series)

Good Enough for a Princess
Along Came a Prince
More than a Princess
Hand-Me-Down Princess
Winning the Queen's Heart
Protecting the Prince (Novella)
Prince from her Past

Serenity Landing Second Chances

Discovering Home
Glimpsing Hope
Reclaiming Hearts

Crowns & Courtships

Heart of a Prince
The Inadvertent Princess
A Royally Beautiful Mess

Crowns & Courtships Novellas

Dare You
A Kaerasti for Clari

Serenity Landing Tuesdays of Grace
9/11 Tribute Series

Grace to Save

Serenity Landing Lifeguards
Summer Novellas

The Lifeguard, the New Guy, & Frozen Custard
(previously titled: The Lifeguards, the Swim Team, & Frozen Custard)
The Lifeguard, the Abandoned Heiress, & Frozen Custard

Serenity Landing Teachers
Christmas Novellas

Gifts of Love
Manuscripts & Mistletoe
Premieres & Paparazzi

Mallard Lake Township

Ballots, Bargains, & the Bakery (novella)

Timeline/Order for Crowns & Courtships and Novellas
1. *A Kaerasti for Clari*
2. *Dare You*
(the first two can be read in either order, but technically this is the timeline)
3. *Heart of a Prince*
4. *The Inadvertent Princess*
5. *A Royally Beautiful Mess*

Made in the USA
Las Vegas, NV
05 March 2022

45067844R00194